"Gabriel," she said in a whisper. "You are in my brother's house, and as such—"

"I love your hair loose," he said quietly. "I never dreamt it was that long and lustrous. Why don't you wear it down more often? You look like one of those Italian princesses in a painting."

"A lady of our time observes certain rules," she managed to get out, "and a gentleman today does not—"

"—take advantage?"

Which he did, rubbing his closely shaven cheek against hers before he claimed her mouth in a hard, unapologetic kiss. And then another until her mouth softened under his gentle aggression. His hand locked around her waist, pulling her against his body until she felt herself yield to his strength.

Dangerous? Without a doubt.

But like a fire in the midst of winter, the heat he offered beckoned. And if she burned herself, would that not be better than the cold isolation of the past year?

Wicked As Sin

A Novel

Jillian Hunter

BALLANTINE BOOKS • NEW YORK

A Ballantine Books Mass Market Original

Copyright © 2008 by Maria Hoag
Excerpt from *Wicked at the Wedding* by Jillian Hunter © 2009 by Maria Hoag

Published in the United States by Ballantine Books, an imprint of The Random House Publishing Group, a division of Random House, Inc., New York.

BALLANTINE and colophon are registered trademarks of Random House, Inc.

This book contains an excerpt from the forthcoming edition of *Wicked at the Wedding*. This excerpt has been set for this edition only and may not reflect the final content of the forthcoming edition.

ISBN 978-0-345-50393-0

Cover illustration: Craig White, based on a photograph by Shirley Green
Step-back illustration: Aleta Rafton

Printed in the United States of America

www.ballantinebooks.com

OPM 9 8 7 6 5 4 3 2 1

For Paul

Chapter One

ENFIELD, ENGLAND
1816

The devil had come to take possession of Helbourne Hall. It was an event not entirely surprising considering the manor house's recent history of wicked deed-holders. Lady Alethea Claridge could not properly discern the details of her neighbor's undignified arrival through the cracked spyglass she held to the window. What she managed to perceive, however, brought scant comfort to one who had sought seclusion from Society's ill-behaved gentlemen. She and the two servants who stood beside her in the long gallery of her brother's house watched the horseman in spellbound silence.

As she reconsidered her dramatic comparison of this person to Mephistopheles, she realized it could more kindly be said that he resembled a dark knight from the misty ages on a mission of rampage. This image might have brought more reassurance had she understood the nature of his quest.

The tall, darkly cloaked usurper sat his beautiful

black Andalusian as if leading a cavalry brigade. He thundered down the moonlit hill with an apocalyptic disregard for safety or decorum.

Was he on the attack or on the run? She did not see anyone chasing after him.

"The innkeeper's wife said he'd been half-killed at Waterloo," Mrs. Sudley, the housekeeper, said under her breath, crowding in for a closer look. "Hideous scars on his neck from an injury that would have done in a normal man."

"I thought you'd stopped listening to gossip," Alethea murmured. "Furthermore, unless he is a ghost, that foolhardy display of horsemanship could not have been accomplished by a man not in the prime of his physical abilities."

Mrs. Sudley's loud sniff indicated that she had taken offense. "I only listened to the village talk to learn about him for *your* sake, Lady Alethea."

"For my sake?" Alethea glanced at her askance. "What do I have to do with him?"

Mrs. Sudley frowned. "It is vital to your welfare to know whether he will prove a kind guardian to his estate."

Alethea sighed at this unlikely possibility. "How many 'kind' guardians rob a man of his home in a card game, may I ask?"

"He's from London, apparently," Mrs. Sudley added in a tone of voice that said he might as well have sprung up from the underworld.

She smiled. "Not everyone from London—"

A spine-tingling ululation rose into the tranquillity of the country night. Alethea glimpsed a flash of steel in the horseman's upraised hand—not the medieval shield she would have preferred a neighbor to brandish but rather a sword. Her scalp pricked in foreboding.

"Dear heaven," she said, her brown eyes wide with astonishment. "It sounds as if he has given a battle cry. Is he planning to attack his own home?"

"He's woke up every child and dog in the village," her stoop-shouldered footman muttered with an ominous shake of his head. "Just listen to that bedeviled howlin'. He'll be raisin' the dead next with his carry-on. 'Tisn't decent. I say we lock all the doors and arm ourselves until his lordship comes home."

"He'll be dead himself if he doesn't heed where he's going," Alethea said in alarm. "He's approaching the old bridge. He'll never make it going—"

"—like a bat out of hell," the footman muttered with relish. "Good riddance is what I think."

She shot him a stern look. "Then keep those thoughts to yourself, Kemble."

The housekeeper lifted her blue-veined hand to her eyes. "I cannot bear to stand witness. Tell me when it's over, and if the news is bad, be gentle in describing the manner of his death. I've a weak stomach for gore and such."

"Here," the footman said impatiently. "There's a warning sign standin' right in front of that bridge unless them little ruffians from the parish orphanage took it down again. The fool can only blame himself if he breaks his neck."

Alethea shook her head of sable-brown curls in exasperation. "One cannot argue that. However, it will not be the horse's fault if his rider doesn't bother to read it. It's beyond irresponsible."

She banged her fist helplessly upon the window as the reckless horseman wheeled and guided his horse into the woods that led to the bridge, the most direct route to Helbourne Hall.

"No," she said aloud, her oval face paling. "Stop. Stop before—"

Of course he could not hear; how absurd to even attempt a warning. The rider had vanished from her sight into the thin stretch of trees that divided the lower lands of the two estates. She backed away from the window. She would not forgive herself if the horse took a fatal fall through the rotten bridge onto the sharp-toothed rocks below. The fact that it was not her brother's bridge to maintain, but that of whoever happened to own Helbourne Hall, did not matter at the moment.

"Let the dogs loose, Cooper," she instructed the second footman, who had come running to the top of the staircase upon hearing all the commotion. "Mrs. Sudley, bring me my boots and—"

"Shall I boil some water, my lady? And fetch a warm, clean blanket?"

"I doubt he's going to give birth," Alethea said in amusement. "However, a flask of brandy would not hurt. Even if I only use it to restore my nerves." She cast one last worried look out the window. "Perhaps he's hoping to kill himself. I might be so inclined if I had to take responsibility for that place."

Helbourne Hall, the estate whose arable lands neighbored the well-tended acreage that belonged to Alethea's brother, had been surrendered a month ago in a London gaming hall by its frivolous owner to an unidentified master. The once-grand Georgian manor seemed to have fallen under a curse. This was the fourth time in so many years that the mortgage had changed hands.

Each successive landlord had proven more neglectful than the previous until it was a wonder the hall still existed. Alethea supposed one could not expect finer aspirations from a seasoned gamester, although she could not remember a prior master seizing his assets in so unsettling a manner.

Her footman Kemble might be right. This nocturnal besiegement did not bode well for a slumberous village that held only one assembly a year.

Nor did it foreshadow a safe future for a young lady like Alethea who wished to withdraw from the world and to heal from the invisible wounds that another man had inflicted upon her.

Chapter Two

❧ ❧

Colonel Sir Gabriel Boscastle uttered a hoarse war cry for the sheer hell of it and unsheathed his sword to swipe at the bats he had disturbed in his pounding ride down the embankment. To his left rose a large Elizabethan mansion whose leaded windows shone with gilded warmth. To his far right loomed an unmajestic monster of a Georgian farmhouse with nary a candle lit to dispel its gaze of haunted gloom.

And in his immediate path, at the bottom of the grassy hill, stood a bridge that absolutely would not bear the weight of a half-drunk knight and his sturdy Spanish horse. He tightened his knees, his arse, his spine.

"Fine. Then we shall take it. Or not. I am not of a mind to argue. It's your decision."

His mount slowed to a canter.

The brandy Gabriel had drunk at the last inn had begun to wear off. The voice of reason he so frequently managed to subdue reared up to remind him he was no longer the brigadier of the heavy cavalry charging downhill into the French infantry on a well-trained warhorse. He was riding straight for a miskept English farmhouse. No enemy soldiers in sight.

The Andalusian balked, signaling its refusal to jump the rickety bridge. Nor would it obey Gabriel's belated urging to change course. He sensed by the bunching of muscled strength beneath him that he ought to prepare for a thorough bone-rattling.

The stallion stopped, shaking its heavy tail. Gabriel gripped his knees reflexively and exhaled through his gritted teeth, managing by habit of will to hold his seat. When the swimming in his head subsided enough that he could see, he noticed that someone had propped a warning sign on a wagon beside the bridge.

BEWARE
HELBOURNE BRIDGE IS BAD

As a former cavalry officer he understood the strategic importance of a bridge. Napoleon had ordered his *pontonniers,* his bridge builders, to construct bridges as a crucial part of his war campaign. Gabriel had helped his brigade blow up one or two to thwart a French attack.

Trolls hid under bridges.

So did homicidal French dragoons.

His horse, obviously possessed of more sense at the moment than its master, refused to make the crossing. Although Gabriel was not particularly superstitious, he had learned that life frequently whispered little cautions to those who listened. A warning sign, however, was hard to ignore. It was not as if he *had* to cross. He'd only won this estate so that he could gamble it off as a lark.

However, upon discovering that it was located in the village of his earliest years and youthful humiliations, he'd decided it was worth at least a visit in the hope of exorcising a few of his demons.

There had to be another way across. He could wade through the water in his black military boots, except he didn't fancy a soaking. He could walk around the blessed woods. He had hidden in them often enough as a boy to escape his stepfather's whip.

He had forgotten, though, that the outskirts of Helbourne Hall sat in the middle of a bogland. Pretty by day. Tricky at night. He supposed that at one time the peaked gables and overhanging bay windows of the farmhouse had pleased the eye.

Now the geometric carvings of Gothic influence in peeling white plaster and black timber danced tauntingly in his line of vision. Unless . . . ah, the eyesore could be merely the gatehouse. And the gatehouse keeper must surely be an eccentric who had allowed a wall of thorns and weeds to reach almost to the turret as a deterrent to anyone who bothered to intrude. Peculiar though. He couldn't imagine visiting here under any other circumstances than his own.

He stared down into the rushing water beneath the bridge. Perhaps he shouldn't cross it. Bridges played a symbolic role in poetry and paintings, didn't they?

A step to another world, another life.

And in this case it did not appear to be a better one.

He dismounted and slapped his horse across the rump. "What's your opinion? I trust your judgment. Shall we make a go of it?"

The horse stood like a memorial statue.

Gabriel could only laugh. "Ride straight into cannonfire and refuse to cross a country bridge? All right. There's no arguing with you when you're in that mood. I'll go first. Watch."

He tread gingerly with bent knees upon the wooded planking. The heavy beamwork creaked but held his weight. His mount apparently remained unconvinced of a safe crossing and did not follow.

"Look." He stomped on a warped plankboard. "Sturdy as a whore's bed. I—"

A rustle of leaves, the pounding echo of hoofbeats rose into the night. Somewhere in the distance a tawny owl hooted and took flight.

He pivoted and looked toward the woods.

He could hear a woman's voice, rising above the clamor. He waited in guarded curiosity, in expectation.

It never failed to amaze him how he could be virtually tottering with one foot in the grave, the other supported by a crutch, and yet be restored to all his strength when a female appeared on the scene.

Even his horse pricked up and swung its head at the tumult. Unfortunately, the unseen woman's frantic shouts for her companions to hurry did not raise Gabriel's hopes for a convivial association. He knew an upset lady when he heard one.

What had he done, promised, this time? It seemed he'd failed to deliver. He did not think he'd been followed all the way from London, or even from the last tavern. He claimed no current lovers, or as far as he knew, any who had a score to settle to bring them this far afield. He was rootless, irresponsible, unattached.

The boom of a blunderbuss into the trees rendered his reflections inconsequential.

He backed against the bridge railing. It gave a menacing groan.

A disheveled young woman burst forth from a grove of trees. "Sir, I implore you, do not—"

He held up his hands. "Put down your weapons. You have the wrong man. I have cousins all over England. I even have brothers somewhere. We all look alike. Black hair, blue eyes—whatever misjustice has been done to you, I can only apologize, but the blame—"

"—cross the bridge," she finished in a forceful shout. "Don't cross it, you babbling prattleplate. It is unsound."

He stared at her in a dawning amusement. Her warning went unheeded. Dear God, he *did* know her. That untamed cascade of curling hair, dark alluring eyes, and if that wasn't enough to stir a man's blood and dormant impressions of early desires, a deep bosom that her ugly cloak did not conceal, heaving in concern for *him*.

A bolt of awareness slid down his back. Lady Alethea Claridge, the local earl's only daughter and unattainable maiden of Gabriel's boyhood fantasies. Her memory had faded to an echo he had trained himself to ignore but that persisted upon intruding at the most inconvenient times.

Alethea had probably forgotten him long ago. Hadn't she married the village lord's son and moved to some nearby manor? Even if she did recognize Gabriel, he doubted she'd deign to acknowledge that she had once come to the defense of that wicked Boscastle boy.

God bless her, he remembered all too well. His mouth curved into a bittersweet smile. The distant image of their last encounter suffused him with humiliation. Most recollections of his early past did. He'd been put into the pillory and pelted with moldy cabbages, turnips, and sheep dung.

One of the shriveled stone-hard turnips had cut his forehead. Blood trickled into his eye. His assailants, most of them his alleged friends, laughed guiltily. Then the fancy carriage of Alethea's sire, the third Earl of Wrexham, slowed at the market square. Her father had ordered her to stay inside in his booming voice, cautioning her not to embarrass herself and venture where she ought not.

She did not obey, even though she was a proper young lady, presumably appalled that Gabriel's own stepfather had dragged him to the local lockup to punish his unruly behavior.

He'd watched her warily pick a path through the squashed produce to the stocks. She'd lifted her blue skirts up over her ankles and her low-heeled silver slippers. He hadn't seen a more comely sight in his life before or since. She knelt gracefully. Gabriel heard her mother, Lady Wrexham, gasping in horror from inside the cottage.

"I told you there was a wicked fairy in my chamber the day she was born, William."

"Yes. Yes," he retorted in an impatient voice. "A thousand and one times. But what am I to do about it?"

"Are you stupid, Gabriel Boscastle?" Alethea had whispered.

"I don't feel particularly academic at the moment." He recalled looking up from that sweet tempting bosom to her face and finding that his entire body suddenly hurt when he tried to breathe. Mashed turnip and warm blood dribbled in a blob to his cheek. He felt mean and ugly. "Are you going to give me an exam?"

"I just want to know," she said with a directness he did not expect, "why you keep doing things to anger your stepfather when he only punishes you in the end."

"It isn't your concern, is it?" he retorted, his attitude defiant. He could see a gang of clouts gathering up soggy tomatoes and rotten apples to throw. If they struck her, he would kill every one of them with his bare hands when he got free. He clenched his back teeth in frustration. He had finally met the prettiest girl he'd ever seen, and he felt like a pig. "You'd better get back in the carriage," he muttered ominously.

"I will." She glanced around with a disdainful glare at the grinning band until each boy and man melted back several paces. It occurred then to Gabriel that her aristocratic beauty was a more potent weapon than anything he wielded. "Shall I wipe off your face?" she whispered as she made to rise.

"No." His voice was fierce. "Go away, would you? I'm getting a pain in the neck looking up at you."

She drew a sharp breath. "Well, you look at me often enough on the way to church."

"Is that what you think?" He had hoped he'd been more subtle. "Well, you're wrong. First off, I don't go to church. Second, I admire your father's horses. I was looking at them, not you. Everyone knows I like horses."

Her full mouth firmed. Then, before he could avert his face, she wiped a blob of blood-streaked turnip from his cheek with the forefinger of her pearl-buttoned kidskin glove.

"My mother thinks you are going to come to a bad end," she said softly.

He flinched at her touch. She looked blindingly clean and pure. He reeked of cabbage and ordure.

"It isn't the end yet. Oh, bugger it. Your mother is

right. So is your father and your grandfather. Now do you mind leaving me to my misery? You're not exactly helping, you know."

"I'm not?"

He cursed to himself. "You shall only land me in more trouble."

She edged a few inches from the posts that imprisoned him. Her father's two footmen had leapt off the carriage, ostensibly to guard her. "But you're the son of a viscount. A Boscastle. How did—"

"My father is dead, and with him all the good and glory. Haven't you heard? Get away from me."

"I was only trying to be kind," she said, sounding hurt and indignant.

Trying to be kind.

Even then he could have told her that gentleness was not only a waste of time but a weakness that others would exploit. He'd learned that much in his early life, and the years afterward had done nothing to dispel that belief.

"Have I asked you for anything?" he asked in a dispassionate voice.

He dropped his gaze in an attitude of disinterest even though every muscle in his confined body coiled tight and something in him wanted her to stay. The two footmen were gently escorting her back to her parents. He could see her mother in the carriage window holding an orange pomander to her aristocratic nose as if Gabriel had been plagued with a contagious disease instead of an abusive stepparent and a bad temper.

He suppressed a rush of useless fury. Hell, hell, *hell*. He hated everyone, himself especially, having the prettiest girl he'd ever seen act as his champion.

Lady Alethea's embroidered slipper caught on a head of cabbage. A footman steadied her before she could stumble, and just when he would have expected her nose to wrinkle in distaste, she reached down, grabbed the drippy cabbage, and hurled it into his awestruck band of tormentors.

He stared past her. Well, now his humiliation had come to a boil.

What had she hoped to prove?

Didn't she know that boys were supposed to protect young girls? And women? Gabriel had done everything he could to protect his mother. It hadn't been enough.

"I *have* seen you look at me, Gabriel Boscastle," she whispered, pulling her shoulders free from the servants' guard.

His gaze drifted up from her dirtied slippers to her firm chin. He'd rather she think him belligerent than weak. Why had she bothered? It only made him feel worse. "What of it?"

"I've noticed, that's all. And I think—whatever the reason, it probably wasn't decent."

"I'll look if I want to," he called after her, his defiance the only weapon at his disposal.

She slowed, glancing around. "Pillory boy. I don't care if you do look."

Chapter Three

❦ ❧

Common sense, as well as past experience with her previous neighbors, warned Alethea that any man who had won Helbourne Hall in a card game could not be trusted. Still, one ought to grant even a gamester the benefit of the doubt, if not extend the hand of friendship. She might no longer hope that she would marry and become mistress of her own estate. She might have given up her belief in handsome lords and happy endings in the last year. But surely fate could at least consider sending Helbourne a decent man who would take advantage of his luck and settle down.

It seemed a small favor to ask. That for once, Helbourne would defy its bleak history and claim a reputable owner so that Alethea could continue to seclude herself from the world and its unpleasantness.

Her brother's gamekeeper, Yates, came bounding through the trees with three leashed wolfhounds barking furiously at the bridge. His green cap was listing over his left ear. His ancient blunderbuss, whose deafening roar proved it still functioned, rested against his shoulder. "We've got his name, my lady. His coachman ended up at our house by mistake. He's a Boscastle."

Alethea turned her head, a shock firing her nerves. "A—"

"The Boscastles are a well-known family," Cooper, the footman who'd accompanied her, added. "Every servant in London dreams of working for the marquess, and now one of the sisters has just married a duke. They always make the newspapers."

Alethea studied the sturdy figure who appeared to be conversing with his massive horse. A dark knight, she thought again. Apprehension intermingled with a poignant memory of the past. So, he'd returned home, and apparently with no more decorum than he'd had when he left.

The footman cleared his throat. "Did you hear what I said, my lady? He's not an ordinary devil."

"A special one, then?"

"He's a Boscastle from London."

"There are more branches of the Boscastle family than that notorious line in London," she murmured, stealing another look at the broad-shouldered figure at the bridge. Her heart had begun to race in an irrational rhythm.

"Do you know any of the Boscastles personally?" the gamekeeper asked carefully. He had not been in her brother's service long and therefore had little knowledge of Helbourne's history.

"I knew three of the young gentlemen a long time ago." She smiled despite herself. "We did not associate. Their family resided not far from here when I was younger. But this man—"

"Sir Gabriel Boscastle," the gamekeeper broke in, his gaze now also affixed to the man on the bridge. "That was the name his coachman gave."

"Gabriel. *Sir* Gabriel, is he now?"

"Aye," the gamekeeper said. "He was a colonel in the cavalry."

"That seems fitting. He always had a passion for horses."

"He's got other passions now, I hear."

"Really, Yates."

"Beg your pardon, Lady Alethea."

She drifted a little closer to the bridge. Her dark knight was watching her too, now. She doubted he would recognize her. In the old days she'd taken great pains with her appearance. Now her hair had grown an unruly length. She dressed in drabs for comfort and rarely remembered to wear gloves. Not that she cared to impress a rogue, which Gabriel, to no one's great surprise, had become.

From what she'd heard, her bad boy had been a soldier in Spain, a rakehell between regiments, and a gambler who heartlessly won properties from reckless young gentlemen.

She'd always prayed that he would not come to a bad end. Mama had been right . . . except, it *still* wasn't really the end yet, was it? His early life had not been easy. Perhaps he'd managed as best he could. His stepfather had had a reputation for cruelty.

She knew now what she hadn't known then. That other people, even those who claimed to care for you, could cause deep sorrow. Could hurt you in unspeakable ways.

"What do we do, my lady?" the footman inquired. "He looks a formidable sort."

"I believe he is."

She wasn't sure herself what to do. She could burst into giggles at the irony of it, or more wisely ride to the village church and beg the vicar's sanctuary. Sir Gabriel certainly exuded a devilish air that challenged her desire to see a decent owner take possession of Helbourne for a change.

Still, she was not responsible for his morals.

She walked slowly toward him. "Gabriel Boscastle? I do not believe it possible. Is that really you after all these years?"

He laughed a little uneasily, not moving but watching her so closely that she knew the rumors about him must be true. "If I admit to that identity, am I going to be shot for a crime I do not have cognizance of committing?"

"Have you committed many crimes?" she asked teasingly.

He smiled, his response bringing an unbidden blush to her cheeks. "Are you going to punish me if I admit to them?"

"No."

"What a pity."

She had come close enough to examine him in the tree-dappled moonlight. Ah, what a forbidding face. Those same hard sculpted features, the intense blue eyes that burned with inner fires, but now he stood older, edgier, all traces of boyhood hurt and humiliation buried if not dead. The jagged purple scar that bisected his lower jaw to terminate in a puckered gash across his throat looked hideous but did not disfigure him. She might have been frightened had she not known him before.

Gabriel's attitude had always given pause to those who approached him. Now he had a physical mark to discourage anyone whose presence he did not invite. She guessed he probably didn't mind one bit. Yet somehow he still tempted her, in the words of her late father, to venture where she ought not.

She stopped short of stepping onto the bridge. "I don't think you should cross here," he remarked calmly, his gaze assessing her cloaked form. "You might fall and I should be forced to save you."

She released her breath. His voice was rougher than she recalled, more cynical if possible, low with control. "You shouldn't be crossing it, either. Didn't you see the sign?"

He shrugged. He was taller now, too, his shoulders wide, his torso well-formed. "I thought it might have been to keep trespassers away. Whose bridge is it, anyway?"

"It's yours." She paused.

He had become an unusually attractive man, and appeared to realize it. Certainly he made no overt attempt to hide his interest in her female appearance, slowly examining her face and figure until heat stole up into her shoulders and neck.

"Tell me that you're only a trespasser," she said in an undertone. "Or a visitor to the person who now owns the hall. Oh, for heaven's sake, Gabriel—don't you remember me?"

He grinned, his eyes locking with hers. "Lady Alethea." He sketched a mocking bow. The bridge he stood upon creaked another unheeded warning. "The pleasure of our reacquaintance is surely all mine."

Wicked boy.

She struggled against a grin until at last, she burst into laughter. "I can only hope you're nicer than the last time I talked to you. Do you remember? I shall be offended if you've forgotten."

It was hard to believe she'd felt sorry for Gabriel once. He had been getting deeper and deeper in trouble in the months that followed his father's death. He had always seemed more mature than his age. To this night, she could still feel his fierce blue eyes appraising her when she rode past him on her dainty little pony. It had been rude of him to continue to stare at her. Her groom had even scolded Gabriel once for doing so.

But that hadn't stopped him.

Wretched boy.

Beguiling man.

He was still staring at her in that way that made her feel embarrassed and warm.

Yet there appeared to be something different in his eyes now. Knowledge. A guarded awareness she recognized from her own experiences.

"You didn't think I would ever forget you, did you, my beautiful champion?" he asked, his arms braced on the flimsy railing.

She glanced back at her entourage in embarrassment. "We barely knew each other. I think we only spoke on a few occasions, the last when you were confined in the village square."

"I remember our conversation." He lifted his hand to his heart. "The words are forever engraved in this empty cavity. That was not one of my best memories, I'm afraid. Not due to any fault on your part."

"Why did you come back?" she asked quietly.

"I came to claim my estate—Helbourne Hall. Can you direct me?"

She shook her head in disappointment. "It's across the bridge, right behind you. You cannot miss it." She pointed past him. "There."

His white teeth gleamed in a rueful grin. "The gatehouse, you mean—" He glanced around, giving a derisive snort. "Or is that the barn?"

She smiled slowly, thinking that of all the hall's past usurpers, Gabriel seemed most suited to the estate. "I will give another caution—this about the staff you have inherited. I have been told they are prone to be troublesome and derelict in their duties."

She heard her footman snigger at this understatement and cast a silencing look his way.

"The servants have been unsettled by the rapid succession of owners," she continued. "Without stability and correct guidance, they have learned to take advantage." Which was a polite way of informing him that his staff was comprised of drunks, former felons, and social outcasts.

For one satisfying moment she thought she had touched upon his higher principles. Then he raised his brow like a devil of enterprise and asked, "I don't suppose you come with the house?"

She gave a dismissive half-laugh and withdrew a step. "Pleasant dreams, Sir Gabriel. If the river carries you away, do not say no one warned you."

"Alethea—"

She hesitated. "Yes?"

"Nothing. Never mind."

Chapter Four

❧ ❧

Warned him. As if he'd ever heeded a warning, when a woman was concerned, in his life. He watched her graceful figure disappear down the tree-lined bridle path to where her horse awaited before he came to his senses. Even as a girl Lady Alethea Claridge had lured him out of his depths. Who did she think she was to come to his rescue? He could have told her he marked the day she had spoken to him in the pillory as the nadir of his public humiliation.

His stepfather had provided deeper humiliations in private, but Alethea's interference had only heightened the shame Gabriel had struggled to keep secret. He'd never sunk lower again in his own personal estimation, although others might venture an opinion to the contrary.

In fact, he was half-tempted to call her back again and state that she was absolutely out of her beautiful mind if she thought that either a broken bridge or a run-down estate would matter much to him after the things he'd seen and done.

Damned irritating, that she could still befuddle him.

He wasn't a complete ne'er-do-well. He had won his share of skeleton mortgages before. In his assessment, if the rickety bridge gave any indication of what lay beyond, Helbourne Hall would probably cost him a fortune in repairs without yielding a single pound of profit in return.

He reckoned he'd waste a fortnight or two here at most. His comely neighbor, Alethea, deserved a few days of his attention if only for auld lang's sake. After all, he could count on one hand the number of brave souls who had ever bothered to defend him. Three of his Boscastle cousins. His infantry commander.

A headstrong young girl who had dared defy her upbringing and dirty her gloves by wiping ordure from a hell-raiser's cheek.

Precious few were those persons who had dared to befriend him during his darkest years, for fear he would turn around and bite them.

Like it or not, even by a scoundrel's standards, he owed her a favor. Was there an undesirable suitor she wished would disappear from the face of the earth? Was there a recalcitrant one she hoped to make jealous? Perhaps the young lady found herself embarrassingly in need of funds. Perhaps her parents had died, and her brother—he seemed to recall that she had one—had brought disgrace upon the family name.

It was said that as part of their personal code, a

member of the Boscastle family never forgot an insult or a favor. Unsaid, but assumed, was that should Gabriel reap a reward in the course of repaying Alethea for her past kindness, he would be obliged to accept.

What kind of girl defied her father to help a willful boy whom everyone else in the village took precautions not to cross? It made him wonder about her sanity.

Her voice floated from the woods. "There are ghosts who haunt that bridge, Gabriel. A jealous lover drowned his sweetheart beneath and then took his own life. Try not to disturb them further."

He stared at her. Flirtatious curls escaped the hood of her cloak to caress her face. He had always wondered whether she had been as pretty as he remembered. She was, but seeing her again made him ache with the pain of dreams abandoned at the crossroads.

"Did you hear me, Gabriel? I don't know if you are superstitious, but a pair of unhappy spirits haunts the very place upon which you're standing."

He shook his head, snorting as he turned back to the bridge. There were ghosts who haunted him, too, but he wasn't afraid of them anymore.

He looked back at her with a smile.

Then he crossed the bridge.

And his horse followed.

Chapter Five

❧ ❧

Gabriel had first captured her attention when she had noticed him fighting one of the older boys in the village. Even seven years ago he'd looked strong enough to take care of himself. As she recalled, he had been getting the best of his bloody-nosed opponent until the pair of them noticed her. At once they broke apart and stopped their brawling. Then the other boy ran away, Gabriel shaking his head in disgust. She knew he had probably started the fight, but something angry and wounded in the way he acted made her wish to soothe him.

It had required all of her nerve, and earned her a lengthy scolding from her governess, to smile down at him one day from her pony when he suddenly looked up from the bench outside the public house where he'd gathered with his friends.

He glared back at her like a young dragon. Even though she had known she should be offended, deep beneath she'd felt a shocking thrill as his moody eyes locked briefly with hers. He hadn't always run wild, Alethea had overheard her mother explaining to the governess, although Mama cautioned her repeatedly to avoid him, hinting at the dire repercussions that befell girls who got involved with incorrigible boys.

Other times Mama had almost sounded sorry for Gabriel, reflecting that he and his brothers had been polite young gentlemen before their father had been killed and their mother had married that merchant who liked drink too much and visited the tavern maid. His three older brothers had left home. Alethea never knew what had become of them.

But she knew that every time she saw Gabriel there was trouble brewing in his eyes. She even knew why he'd been put in the pillory, and that he hadn't deserved to be punished. The apothecary's daughter Rosalinde had told her one afternoon while her father was compounding a toothache remedy for Alethea's brother.

"It wasn't his fault," Rosalinde whispered. Like Alethea and several of the other village girls, she was intrigued by Gabriel, and his misdeeds only enhanced this forbidden interest. "He threw the doctor's son into the street for making abuse of the old peddler."

Alethea would have done the same thing if she'd been able. The elderly peddler never sold anything of value. He had been a soldier once, and he did no harm. The villagers bought from him to be kind.

But even after Gabriel had dragged the doctor's boy out of the gutter, he'd pounded him until several of the village elders had pulled Gabriel off. The apothecary's daughter said there had been a great deal of blood, the peddler wept, and the apothecary had taken Gabriel aside to confide, "We all know he deserved it, but in private, Gabriel. You'll suffer for this, not him. Hold it inside, boy. We all have to hold it inside."

That might have been the end of it. The bully was too afraid to tell. But the physician had been driving by in his phaeton, and Gabriel's stepfather had stepped out of the pub to see what had drawn the crowd in the street.

"He was drunk as usual," the girl told Alethea. "And when he found out what had happened he shook Gabriel like a rat and mocked him. 'Aren't the Boscastles born to better? Isn't that what you think? Well, you're going to be punished as if you were my blood.'"

From the snippets of news she'd gleaned during her visits to London over the years, Alethea came to realize that Gabriel had only explored his attraction to trouble. She thought it was a shame, but no one else in the village seemed surprised that he'd pursued a hard path. It was hoped that his brothers had done better for themselves. His mother had returned to her native France when her second husband was murdered in a brawl one night. The last Alethea had heard, Gabriel had allied himself with his London family.

Still, no matter what he'd become or done, she had to wonder what life had served him in the intervening years to carve those cynical angles in his face. He was a fine-looking man whom she remembered with sad fondness, though he was certainly not the best-mannered gentleman she had ever met.

But then she knew well not to trust a man on his manners alone. And how easily they could deceive.

The gentleman to whom her parents had betrothed her before their deaths had violated her at a ball held in London the evening they announced their engagement. Lord Jeremy Hazlett had been due to leave for Waterloo on the following day. Forcing her into one of their host's private bedchambers, he had explained that since they were to be married anyway, he might as well enjoy an early honeymoon.

It was over before she could wage a fight. In fact, he raped her so quickly and efficiently, not even removing their evening clothes, that she suspected it wasn't his first time. When he was done, he warned her not to cry.

But she had cried a little, in the cloakroom, and a woman, a famous courtesan named Audrey Watson, had somehow guessed what had happened and insisted on taking her discreetly in a private carriage to her establishment on Bruton Street until Alethea felt better and could face the other guests at the ball again without giving herself away.

Two hours later, the shock of what Jeremy had done turning into cold anger, she had returned to the party and stood at his side while everyone congratulated them and wished Jeremy well in battle.

Jeremy laughed and held her hand as if nothing had happened, as if he hadn't utterly destroyed all her illusions or even noticed that she had spent the past two hours, ironically enough, in London's most exclusive bordello being consoled by its owner.

Jeremy went off to war, not apologizing for what he'd done. Alethea returned home and waited for him to send her a letter breaking off their engagement. She waited to find out whether his violation had resulted in a pregnancy. And while she was waiting, a French cannonball killed her betrothed and he became a hero.

Sincere expressions of shock and sympathy arrived at her brother's country house in the form of cards and callers. But all Alethea could think as she listened to and read these well-intended words was that now she would not be forced to marry the monster. Nor was she liable to marry anyone else.

In fact, she had been resigned to waiting for him to return and atone for what had happened. Yet when she stood at his ceremonial grave site, she could not make herself cry, and she felt guilty as the attendant mourners praised her courage when, in truth, she was wishing her dead betrothed a speedy journey to hell.

It was tempting to hope his demise had been divine punishment for his cruelty. But in order to accept this as a possibility she would have to believe that all the other brave, righteous men who had died in the war without dishonoring women deserved their fate.

She was well acquainted with too many friends and families who'd lost loved ones to credit this assumption for a minute. Jeremy was gone, a champion, an infantry dragoon at Waterloo, and she was suddenly free to withdraw from Society with sympathy for her position. She would perchance become a spinster, a governess to her brother's children should he ever work up the courage to propose to the young lady in London he desired.

Alethea's life had been forever altered. She bore a stain, invisible to others, indelible to herself. But gradually, as the months passed, she found her spirits rallying. She was still alive, and her practical nature could not tolerate a future of pointless self-pity.

Now Gabriel had returned to threaten not only her hard-earned peace of mind, but that of the village he had terrorized in his youth. She did not know what she felt for him, only that, after a long spell of dormancy, she had started to feel again.

He was not the first boy in Helbourne's history to be put in the pillory to learn a lesson. But what he had learned, she thought, was not as much how to behave as how to survive. At his age, it was probably too late to change.

And she was afraid the same could be said of her.

Chapter Six

❦

Gabriel laughed to himself at the notion of ghosts as he rode up the hill to his darkened estate. Wasn't he a man who gambled on chance? Ghosts? Well, a person learned to live with them. He thought the fact that Alethea had warned him not to expect much of Helbourne Hall was a rather misguided but sweet attempt on her part. He expected little of his ill-gamed winnings. Few men wagered away a property of any real value; he would be a fool to anticipate being welcomed to Helbourne Hall with cheers of joy. He understood himself to be a usurper, considered vulgar even by county standards.

He did not anticipate, however, the bullet that whizzed over his head and embedded itself in the door frame upon his maiden entrance to the house.

He swore and threw his saddlebags to the floor. His glance lifted to the indistinct figure that darted behind the gallery balustrade. "Stop right there, you bloody coward. I'll cut off your ears and pickle them."

"Sir, sir—have they shot you already? Oh, goodness. That was fast."

A pleasant-faced woman with unkempt white hair bustled toward him from the passage screens. At first glance she brought to mind the thought of a fairy godmother, waving what appeared to be a magic wand in her hand. On closer inspection the wand resolved into the deadlier aspect of a carbine.

He scowled as the figure abovestairs peered sheepishly through the railing. "And you are the . . . gatekeeper?"

She lowered her weapon with a startled look. "I'm the housekeeper, sir, Mrs. Miniver. Pray do not be angry that we have taken the liberty of defending ourselves. We've had no master to guide or protect us for months. But now that you're here, it will all change for the better."

"I wouldn't count on that," he said, staring past her. "Is it your custom, Mrs. Miniver, to greet all guests, especially your master, with a carbine?"

She bobbed a belated curtsy. "My apologies, sir, but you never know who's going to walk through the door these days. We've had all sorts of nasty visitors in recent months, gamblers and the like. Men one would not wish to acknowledge in the street, if you catch my meaning."

Gabriel walked around her. He definitely did not envision a future here. "Where is the rest of the help? My horse needs stabling and proper attention. I would like some brandy and the chance to explain what I expect from the staff during my stay."

She glanced up uneasily in the direction of the gallery. Gabriel reached back to wrestle the carbine from her hand and aim it at the balustrade. "One of my personal rules, as silly as it sounds, is that I am not to be used for target practice. Do you understand, up there?"

"Aye, sir," the rusty voice of an elderly man replied. "I thought you might be one of them village boys breakin' in again. I'm Murphy, your butler."

"We do have a time with the local lads, sir," Mrs. Miniver said. "What with no stable master to assert his rights, the riffraff are bound to take advantage. Of course now that you're here, we'll be protected."

"And who's to protect me from you?"

She hurried after him, wiping layers of dust from the hall stand with her apron. "A strong young lord like you is what we've lacked, no disrespect intended to the past sorry sods who ruled the house. I expect we'll all be put to rights now that you're here to show everyone what's what."

Gabriel could have laughed. God pity the ignorant souls who thought *he* would be the one to bring discipline to this house. Well, he would if he had any intention of staying.

"My horse needs water and food," he said firmly. "I am willing to wait until tomorrow to formally introduce myself and—how did you phrase it—put everyone to rights."

"Yes, sir."

"That brandy—"

"Right away, sir. Make yourself at home."

At home?

Who of sane mind in the past two centuries could claim to feel at home in this cobwebbed excuse for a crypt? He stared up at the dust-enshrouded portraits that hung upon the oaken walls. Good enough, he supposed, to impress those whose own ancestry did not claim substantial roots in English history. He stepped closer, noticing a dark object hanging from a wall sconce. "What on earth is that?"

"Damn me. It's one of them bats again." She banged her hand against the wall. The creature did not bulge. "I don't know where they come from."

He backed away from her. "Where do *you* come from? Bedlam?"

"Oh, no, sir. Newgate." She hovered behind him as he turned, shaking his head.

"We have prayed to be delivered, sir," she added. " 'Tis a good sign for us all indeed that you survived that accursed bridge."

He pulled off his riding gloves. "Are you acquainted with our neighbors, Mrs. Miniver?"

"Lord Wrexham? A fine gentleman, sir."

"And his wife?"

"Why, he's not married yet. Any day, we've been led to understand."

"Does he keep mistresses?" he asked bluntly.

"Good heavens, I shouldn't think so. Not with Lady Alethea living in the house."

"And Lady Alethea's husband lives with them, I assume?"

"She has no husband, sir. A heartbreak that. She lost her beloved in the war and has not been herself since. She used to be full of lovely mischief, that young lady, and now she either rides about the fields or sits in her brother's house alone with her books."

"I'll take my brandy now, Mrs. Miniver," he said quietly. "You may bring it out to me in the stable. I'm very particular about where my horse sleeps."

Chapter Seven

❦ ❧

Alethea slept better than she had in months, dreaming of epic heroes who wore billowing capes and rode thundering horses. For the first morning in almost a year she took the time to find her favorite forest-green riding habit in her wardrobe instead of the solemn black silk she usually wore. She brushed her hair one hundred times and wove a white ribbon into her braided curls. She rushed downstairs, full of energy, to play with her three dogs before she took her morning ride.

In fact, she had just walked her gelding to the courtyard when Mrs. Bryant, the long-legged and vigorous vicar's wife, pulled into the driveway in her gig. Alethea's trio of dogs started to bark, knowing there was always a treat in one of Mrs. Bryant's overflowing baskets. They gathered eagerly as she slid down from her seat.

"Don't go riding yet." Mrs. Bryant pulled off her straw bonnet and waved it across the pasture to Alethea. "I have a call for us to make together."

Mrs. Bryant had made no secret of the fact that

she was concerned about Alethea's future. She confided in anyone willing to listen that the young woman had become so withdrawn in her grief that she was liable to wall herself up in her brother's house. It wasn't a normal grieving seclusion, in Mrs. Bryant's opinion, although if she had ever guessed at the true reason for Alethea's self-imposed solitude, she did not say a word.

Alethea suppressed a sigh. "I've already got my horse saddled and ready to exercise. Has someone taken ill?"

"Not as far as I know. It's the new master of Helbourne Hall. I'm hoping I can persuade him to stay. Why don't you ride ahead of me? I'll catch up in my gig after I deliver some cheese to Widow Hamlin."

Alethea tapped her riding crop against her knee. "I'm not in a mood to make a social call. I'll only spoil your welcome."

"Well, I can't go alone," Mrs. Bryant insisted, even though she drove by herself day and night, over hill and stream, when one of the villagers fell sick.

The afternoon breeze stung Alethea's face, betraying a hint of an early autumn. She thought of a man with thick black hair, a twisted neckcloth, and blue eyes that drew her like a dark crystal. "Actually, I already met him last night—I had to warn him about the bridge and—"

"Good." Mrs. Bryant hurried back to her gig. "Then you can introduce me. And we'll stay together—just between you and me I think the servants are ruling the roost at the hall. It's high time it stopped. Do you think—I know you've only just made his acquaintance—but is it possible that he's the man we have all been waiting for to take control?"

A hundred devils were boring holes into Gabriel's dreams. One of them dug its talons into his shoulder and shook him without mercy; he ignored the aggravation. He was bone-tired after the hard ride from London and four hours of mucking out a decent stall for his horse in an Augean stable that hadn't seen fresh straw or a pitchfork in a month, if then.

Two bottles of brandy downed at dawn, his horse watered, brushed, and fed, he washed himself at the ancient pump, rinsed the travel dust from his mouth and hair, then dropped into a dead sleep. He couldn't say he remembered what he'd been dreaming about. A woman with dark eyes and silver slippers with a bat on her shoulder. He wanted to undress her.

He awoke with reluctance. His shirt hung unbuttoned off one arm. He groaned in protest, throwing his elbow over his face.

The sharp-taloned demon shook him harder.

Demoness.

He forced open one bloodshot eye, then promptly closed it upon recognizing the creature who was demanding his soul. Lord help him, if he had to surrender it to anyone, it might as well be her.

"Sir Gabriel, are you all right?" she asked in a voice so stricken that any man of good conscience would answer to put her mind at rest.

Instead, he played dead, wondering how she would react. His heart began to beat against his ribs. His male body awakened so abruptly he was tempted to pull his coat over that part of his anatomy that behaved as a barometer at the most inopportune times. But he didn't have his coat.

She stretched across his prone form. "Well, you're still breathing," she murmured, "and there's a brandy bottle—oh, two of them. Wake up, you wastrel. To think I was worried about you. Oh, *wake* up."

"I *am* awake," he muttered. "Come back later when I'm coherent. I want to stay in bed, if you don't mind."

"You aren't *in* bed," she exclaimed, wrenching at his arm. "The vicar's wife will be here any minute. Do sit up and at least pretend you are not insensible."

"The vicar?" That got his attention. He lowered his arm. "What vicar? Did I ask you to marry me during the night?"

"Yes." She tugged his rumpled cambric shirt up to his shoulder. "And we have a child on the way."

He grunted. "I'd remember *that* even if I'd soaked my head in a gin barrel all night."

"By the look of you, you came close. Please make an effort to present a decent appearance."

"What does the vicar's wife want with me, anyway?" he asked irritably, scratching his stubbled cheek.

Alethea studied him in chagrin. "She's coming to welcome you as the new master."

"Master of what?" He picked a piece of straw from her skirt.

"Of Helbourne Hall," she bit out, staring down at his hand until he lifted it away. "It might have escaped your notice, being as sober and alert as you are, Sir Gabriel, but your house is tumbling down rafter by rafter, the stables stink, and your servants are the most slovenly lot of misfits ever to disgrace the domestic profession."

"It isn't *my* fault." He frowned at her. "And I don't care."

"You have to," she said in a demonic voice that tore right down his spine like a razor. "You won the house. The responsibility for it falls on you. Now get up before I—"

"Before you what?" he asked, his eyes glinting in challenge. In fact, it was one of the few things she said that caught his interest.

She leaned down until her nose touched his. "I shall carry your drunken carcass to the horse trough and dunk you until your eyes cross."

Resigned that she would grant him no rest, he finally deigned to give her his full attention. His heavily lidded gaze wandered over her, returned to her dark gypsy face. It amazed him that after all these years she could still make him feel like howling at the moon.

"With all due respect, my lady," he said, "I have just returned from war. My moral obligations to Society have been met."

"*Moral?*"

"If I want to sleep in the barn all night, I shall do so. And if the servants of Helbourne wish to dance up and down the stairs naked while polishing the banister, I don't see why I should stop them."

"Then why did you come here?" she asked in frustration.

"You're not going to give up, are you?"

She bit the edge of her lip. "No."

"Why do you wish me to lord it over Helbourne?" he asked in amusement, wondering idly what she would do if he kissed her.

She drew back a little. "It's heartbreaking to see a grand estate fall into neglect—although not as much as to see a gentleman do so."

"Perhaps I could be persuaded to stay a month or two. Depending on how nice my neighbors are."

She gave him a hard look. "I always wondered what happened to you after you disappeared that last winter."

He cleared his throat. It was a pleasant shock to hear that she'd thought about him at all, but her concern was wasted. Suddenly, instead of feeling worldly and at the top of his game, he felt careworn, unworthy of her benevolent spirit.

"Well, now you know," he said with an unapologetic smile. "And don't tell me that I did not fulfill your expectations of what I would become."

"You do feel sorry for yourself, don't you?" she asked after a long hesitation.

"No," he replied in a clipped voice.

"Then if there's nothing I can do to persuade you to change your mind, I might as well leave."

He grasped her wrist without knowing why and drew her close. "I didn't say you couldn't persuade me. It's the least you can do after waking me up."

Before she could react or take offense, he clamped one arm down on her back and gathered her against him. He didn't allow her a chance to speak. He urged her down, onto the straw beneath him, and kissed her, his tongue easing between her parted lips. God knows if she hadn't been Alethea Claridge, he'd have taken a lot more than a kiss. She tasted like honey and fire and summer wine. Her body molded itself in soft enticement to his. He brushed his mouth over her lips, traced his hand over her well-shaped hip. She didn't move. He felt himself grow hard, gripped by an urgency he did not understand.

He pressed her deeper into the straw. She pressed back, the warm hollows of her body accommodating his heavily muscled frame. He didn't know what he'd done to deserve this unsolicited visit, but all of a sudden his head had never been clearer. Or his body more aroused. "Alethea." He eased onto his side, his hand still planted on her posterior. "May I—"

He felt the shiver that went through her. How easy to convince himself it was desire. The shadowed emotion in her eyes bespoke something less flattering. Still, his lips sought hers, craving every last drop of nectar.

"Gabriel Boscastle."

He eased himself onto his elbow. He traced his finger over her mouth to the tidy row of buttons at her throat until he reached the cleft of her breasts. His heart quickened as her gaze lifted to his. She was truly beautiful, in a dark, subtle way, with sculpted cheekbones and heavily fringed eyes that made him feel lower than the boy she had pitied years ago. He knew so much more now. Did that matter to her?

His thumb slipped beneath the lace banding of the chemise that bound her breasts. "Very pretty. And soft."

She gave a startled gasp. He went still, momentarily stunned at the intensity of his temptation to continue. He paused, his pulses surging.

"If you think I will be seduced in a barn, you *have* had your head in a gin barrel."

"I don't suppose you would invite me to share your bed?" he inquired, his grin impudent.

"Do you really need to ask?"

"If there is the smallest chance that you will agree, then yes, I do. And I'm not beneath begging, either."

He waited, gripped by a need that he wasn't sure he could control. And if he'd learned anything about himself, it was that he needed to be in control. "You'll have to forgive me," he said when it became apparent that she was not going to encourage further intimacies. "I'm not accustomed to being awakened like this."

She smiled archly. "Then I won't inquire as to your usual rituals upon arising."

He gave her such a guilty smile in return that she started to laugh. "The vicar's wife is *not* going to find us together. You are even worse than when I last saw you, Gabriel. I can't imagine why I'm bothering with you at all."

"Neither can I. However, in my own defense, I should state that when a beautiful woman awakens a disreputable man from a deep slumber, she should be prepared that he will respond with—well, that he will respond. Any man would react the same way, I'd wager, to find someone like you leaning over him with that look you were giving me."

She rose to her hands and knees, her riding skirt tangled around her dusty half-boots, her bottom in the air. It was such a provocative position, one of his amatory favorites, that he had to set his teeth to tamp down the rising tension in his body.

"I would expect a sleeping dog to react, perhaps," she said. "Or a—"

She lifted her left arm impatiently to push an errant curl from her shoulder. The gesture drew his gaze to the firm breasts molded beneath the buttoned bodice of her riding habit. He swallowed dryly, blaming his sudden sense of vertigo on bad brandy.

He glanced away. "Do you want me to help you brush the straw off your dress?"

"No. It doesn't bother me. Just keep those wicked hands to yourself."

He grinned. "Fine. Whatever pleases you. But in return I shall request that you not raise your voice. My head is aching like a swollen wineskin as it is."

She glanced in distaste at the bottles propped against the bale. "I wonder why. Hide those—and hurry. Get to your feet before Mrs. Bryant arrives."

"I did not ask for her welcome," he grumbled. "I have no intention of staying. She might as well be wishing me good-bye. Save her the trouble of bothering."

She reached behind him and picked up one of his discarded brandy bottles. Intuition cautioned him that she was contemplating conking him over the head. To his relief, she swept to her feet, her irritation seemingly satisfied by merely tossing the bottle into an empty stall. He decided their kiss had been worth this minor outrage. And she could hit him all she wanted if he could have her to himself for another hour.

"Why did you let yourself degenerate into darkness, Gabriel? You could have risen above whatever burdens you had to bear. None of us meet life without some sort of affliction. I'd hoped you would have become, well, something else."

Her criticism stung. But she did not understand and he refused to demean himself by trying to enlighten her.

"Perhaps my outcome was preordained by my bloodlines."

She shook her head, her lips temptingly moist from his kiss. His defense had sounded false even to his own ears.

He knew he could not blame the most twisted turns of his dark nature on his Boscastle ancestry. The scandalous brood had only extended the early lessons of love and a passion for life he had learned from his father. For a time he had resented the close bonds of his cousins and had concealed his envy behind taunts and rivalry, even as he hoped to prove himself their equal. None of his London kin knew much about his earlier travails. For years he had assumed they did not ask because they felt no true interest in what he had survived.

But now that he'd been accepted into the family proper, he realized they had been more likely respecting his privacy than showing indifference. He had concluded that if his proud French mother had asked for help after the death of Gabriel's father, the Boscastles would have offered their support without hesitation.

Yet his mother had been embarrassed, guilty, and afraid that the Boscastles would snub her for marrying so soon after Joshua's death. He wished he'd known then that the Boscastles were anything but a self-righteous family.

Passionate to a fault, yes, but strongly linked and loyal to one another. He wasn't ashamed to count himself in the clan.

He frowned at her. "What do you think I've become, anyway? Be honest."

"I don't know. Perhaps you ought to look in the mirror and ask yourself."

"Not this early in the morning, darling."

"It's past two in the afternoon."

"That's all? I shouldn't be up for five more hours. Let's have a nap together."

"You were a colonel in the cavalry," she said dryly. "Did you only fight at night?"

"No." He gazed at her with frankness. He couldn't tell her he had started to change for the better before Waterloo, and that inexplicably he'd begun to fall back into his bad ways after his last battle. "What about you? Are you still the paragon that struck every young man in Helbourne love-blind?"

"Hardly."

"Well, you wouldn't know it to look at you." He paused. She had to realize how beautiful she was. "I heard about your loss. It's a shame."

She stared at him, her face closing, and he wished suddenly that he had not brought up the subject. She was too easy to talk to. He had slipped into a comfortable conversation without even realizing it. But now, after he'd mentioned the death of the man she'd loved, she looked distant, upset, and he knew that this would be a barrier between them.

"It's all right," he said awkwardly. "I lost a lot of friends last year, too."

She nodded, glancing around. "I hear the gig at the gate. Where is your coat?"

"I gave it to my horse."

"Oh, Gabriel."

"Well, the others were filthy."

"What am I to do with you?"

He combed his fingers through his hair and surged to his feet only a second before a sprightly older woman came striding into the barn.

"Fetch your coat," Alethea whispered. "And don't tell her what just happened."

Chapter Eight

⚜

"Ah, there you are, Alethea," a genial voice cried at the door. "I should have known you'd be in the stables. And how clean it is in here. Our new neighbor has been hard at work, I see. It will be inspiring to watch this old house restored to what it used to be. That pasture begs for a thoroughbred or two, and surely a cavalry officer will take pride . . ."

Caroline Bryant, the vicar's wife, was an amiable blond matron in a calico dress with a bonnet tied under her double chin, and she chattered on with such focused energy it seemed she didn't care that the new master of the house had spent the night in the stable. From what little Gabriel knew, Helbourne had a history of dissolute owners, so his behavior was probably no different.

He reached down surreptitiously and picked up the riding crop that Alethea had dropped. "This is yours," he said in a wry undertone. "I'm not going to ask what you use it for."

For a moment he thought she would ignore him. Then with a smile she took the crop and answered under her breath, "It's a secret weapon to keep my neighbors under control."

He grinned back at her. "One never knows when a little discipline is in order."

He rested his arm back on a bale of hay and almost lost his balance. Alethea caught his sleeve with a disparaging sigh, then set him away from her with a frown of warning. The vicar's wife chattered on, oblivious to what she'd missed. He could have told both of them he was past hope, cavalry officer or not. The good possibilities in Gabriel had died before he was fifteen years old. During the war, when he had helped blow up a bridge over the River Elba, he'd all but given up the ghost himself. He'd had to cut off nearly all his hair because it was singed and had suffered an ugly scar on his throat. He really did look like the dragon the French officers used to call him.

He blinked, suddenly realizing that the vicar's wife had just passed her hand over his face. He wasn't sure if she was issuing him a benediction or attempting to raise him from the dead. He forced a response from his throat. "You were saying, madam?" he asked hoarsely.

"We are blessed in that we live removed from the evil influences of our times," she confirmed in a pious but overloud voice that resounded in the chambers of his skull.

He squinted at her. "London, you mean. Wicked place that. Ruins a person. I've just left."

She gave a nod. "Here in the country we live by faith, love, and charity."

"Amen," he said, earning another dubious look from Alethea. What was he supposed to say? "Let's start plowing then."

Mrs. Bryant looked at him for several moments. He caught Alethea rolling her eyes. Clearly he'd said something off. "We plow in October, Sir Gabriel."

"Ah. I'd forgotten. Then perhaps we should start in September." Not that he planned on staying in this bog that long. "To get ahead of the others who wait until October."

Alethea granted him a sly smile. "That's when we do our threshing."

"Could we not thresh earlier?"

He stared at her mouth. Her eyes teased him. He was going to do far more than kiss her if she gave him another chance. "Only if you know of a way to coax the corn to mature before its time." She paused, and he wanted to pull her down onto the straw again. "Do you?"

He grinned. "You'd think me a damned idiot if I said I did, wouldn't you?"

She laughed. "Yes."

"I'm not a farmer." He shrugged. "I never was."

Alethea studied him. "Perhaps you aren't a farmer, but you have tenants who are. Not many, I grant you. The few who've remained are your responsibility."

He shook his head. "I don't even know them."

"Shall we ride together so that I may introduce you?"

"Perhaps another day," he said, contriving to look sincere.

And not deceiving her for a moment.

She remembered what he'd been.

God willing he'd be gone before she discovered what he was now.

Mrs. Bryant gave him an encouraging smile. "We gathered you weren't a farmer. But may I ask what you are?"

"Well, I'm a gambler," he said without thinking. "And—"

"Isn't that helpful?" Alethea murmured.

"—and a cavalry officer. Well, I was. I know horses. I do."

Mrs. Bryant appraised his strong form. "That's a good start."

"Horses and women," he amended.

"And I suppose to your way of thinking there's not much difference," she said with an admonishing look.

He smiled at her. "Of course there is. A well-bred horse can make a man a fortune. A well-bred woman can spend the same amount ten times over."

Alethea vented a sigh. "I think it's time for us to leave, Mrs. Bryant. Poor Sir Gabriel was up all night tending to his horse."

He blinked again as the three of them walked outside. The sun was enrobed by a sullen bank of clouds. It was a typical gray English day with a glare that set off a pain behind his eyes.

And made him realize again how truly beautiful Alethea had become. Perhaps she'd grown a little too tall to be called a London beauty. Her features, that patrician nose, her overgenerous mouth, and angular chin, were not delicate by a classical standard.

But he'd kissed that imperfect mouth and she was still talking to him. The fact cheered him considerably. After all, she had beheld him at the lowest ebb of his life and even if he hadn't become a better person over the years, he wasn't worse. Or at least he hadn't been *caught* at anything. And he had no other plans for the rest of the summer unless he visited some old friends in Venice.

Mrs. Bryant thrust a heavy basket into his hands. "On behalf of the parish, please accept this small token of our esteem. Welcome to Helbourne, Sir Gabriel."

He swallowed hard. "Thank you," he said, realizing she expected some response. "What—exactly what is it?"

"Violet jelly. Three jars of it. A succulent ham. And a book of prayers."

Violet jelly and prayers. He wondered when he'd be fitted for his false teeth. "That's too kind of you," he said politely.

Mrs. Bryant looked him in the eye. "You'll need to keep your strength up if you're to take over Helbourne. You must not allow your staff to intimidate you," she said forcefully. "You must take charge of your estate."

Gabriel hazarded a glance at Alethea; her eyes danced with laughter. "Must I?"

Mrs. Bryant stamped her foot in the straw. "Tell the varlets who's in control."

"I did last night. At least I think I did."

"Then why, may I inquire, did you sleep out in the barn?"

"Well, because I—"

Mrs. Bryant nodded in understanding. "Because you were afraid to sleep in the house. Afraid that one of those scalawags would do you in during the night. I do not blame you for taking the precaution."

"I believe I shall have them in hand soon enough," he said, although the thought had crossed his mind after that potshot from the long gallery that he had been dispatched from one war only to fight another.

"I assume Alethea told you about the man who took possession of Helbourne three years ago?"

Gabriel shook his head. "What happened to him?" he asked cautiously.

"Nobody knows," Alethea answered. "He was seen running through the hills in his nightwear and was never seen again."

"But that won't happen to Sir Gabriel," Mrs. Bryant said with an encouraging smile.

Alethea arched her brows in curiosity. "Why not?"

"Because I don't as a rule wear nightclothes," he replied bluntly. "And because nobody is chasing me from this house until I leave of my own accord."

"Then it's settled," Mrs. Bryant said with a nod of satisfaction. "Helbourne has a new master, and he is no namby-pamby who will allow anyone to drive him away."

Chapter Nine

❧ ❧

Namby-pamby he was not, Alethea thought. Not even in his early years could he have been termed as such. Tough, disrespectful, defiant, stubborn to his own detriment. Those enduring faults she would not deny, and most likely neither would he. But he was an unabashed reprobate if ever she had met one. She mounted her gelding and rode past the broken pasture fence with what composure she could summon.

Gabriel was leaning against the stable door, his rumpled black coat retrieved and slung over one broad shoulder. His expression betrayed only a detached amusement as he regarded her. Mrs. Bryant had gone off to pay her daily visits and pray for her parishioners.

"This fence needs to be mended," she called back at him on impulse.

He nodded. "I can see that. It looks sturdy, though."

She shook her head in disparagement. He wasn't looking at the fence, at all. He was looking right at— She straightened her back. She'd never thought of herself as beautiful. Her nose had a bump. She was almost as tall as her brother. But she did take pride in her posture, the result of wearing a whalebone corset throughout all her school days to correct her rounded shoulders.

She frowned. "I hope you enjoy your violet jelly. It's nice on toast."

A smile crossed his face. "And my prayers."

The only prayer Alethea could manage at this moment was that she pay attention to her leave-taking and not ride off in the wrong direction. Or worse, turn full circle and return to his tall, sultry figure, that lean mocking face. She couldn't believe his uninvited kiss could have so pleasantly unbalanced her after what Jeremy had done. She would have expected to feel dirty and insulted. Instead, she was trembling deep inside from a not entirely unpleasant perception.

And when he'd kissed her, she really had not tried to stop him. She felt almost guilty that he'd apologized for it. The entire time his mouth was on hers she had been laughing and crying inside; she'd wanted to tell him that she was every bit as bad as he was, but she'd never let anyone know.

She'd go straight home and drink a half-pint of distilled dandelion and burdock. And then—she straightened her seat in the saddle. Brazen man. Putting those bold hands on her backside as if he were testing its softness.

Of course, *he* hadn't felt soft at all. The brief contact with his muscled body had given an impression of rock-hard strength. She might have been more upset had he not stopped the instant she made it clear that he ought to behave. She had begged Jeremy to stop, pleaded until her throat was raw, but he'd gone ahead and hurt her. She was surprised that Gabriel's kiss had been wickedly sweet in comparison and dealt her no lasting offense, unless one counted the strange compulsion she'd felt to bid him continue.

She rode slowly, wondering idly whether he had ever forced himself on a woman and knowing he had not. He was more likely to hurt himself in some misadventure. Still, he seemed like a rough sort who could turn dangerous if he were provoked. Alethea's governess had claimed that he and his brothers had inherited from his mother that blood affinity of her Bourbon background for plots and intrigue. From his Boscastle blood had come his striking looks and magnetism.

She could not decide what to make of him. He hadn't mentioned the three older brothers who had disappeared before he had. Alethea's mother had confessed once that she'd breathed a sigh of relief for their benefit. It had been the countess's belief that whatever misfortune the missing brothers encountered in the world could not equal the evil of what they'd endured in the privacy of their home.

But Gabriel had stayed behind with his mother to protect her from his stepfather. It wasn't until later years that Alethea had come to understand how miserable life must have been to a young boy who had lost a gruff but loving father only to find a hostile stranger standing in his place. In learning to defend himself he'd become understandably hard-hearted.

Which suggested that while he might indeed prove a benefit for Helbourne, a formidable master to supervise for once, he wouldn't necessarily contribute to Alethea's peace of mind.

Still, it was hard to completely avoid one's neighbor. It was maddeningly hard when one harbored an inexplicable and long-standing interest in his fate. They had known each other before, before he'd lost his father, before she'd lost her self-worth and all that a future as a married woman would have provided. She could only hope that the two people they had once been could agree to a polite association. She had no reason to be afraid of him.

In a way it was such a relief to be ruined. She no longer had to pretend that she never felt mean or impatient or that she could not meet a man like Gabriel on his own ground.

Chapter Ten

❦ ❧

Light rain began to patter down a few minutes after Alethea rode from his sight. He had not made a secret of watching her. Nor would he pretend that he aspired to be the fine gentleman she desired as a neighbor. He wasn't going to deceive her. He would have taken her if she had given him any encouragement. But he would never dishonor a woman unless it was part of their decadent love play. In fact, he would never wish to distress Alethea at all. She was apparently still trying to bring out the best in others. Perhaps she'd met with success before him.

He grimaced as rain from the stable roof splashed upon his cheek. He turned, nearly stumbling over the basket delivered by Mrs. Bryant. Alethea's riding crop lay beside it. He picked both up with a grin.

"Violet jelly and—"

The whickering of his horse from deep within its stall interrupted him. He glanced around sharply to perceive a shadow stealing behind the bales of straw that had formed his bed. The indistinct figure soon passed from his detection, but not, however, before Gabriel recognized the costly bridle and cavalry sword it carried beneath one gangly arm.

Blood rushed to his face. He was a man of few possessions, but those he kept, he treasured.

"You, thief!" he shouted indignantly. "Don't take another bloody step unless you wish to find yourself impaled on that weapon you would steal."

This warning, roughly delivered as it was, only served to give the thief impetus to escape through the back window of the barn. Cursing beneath his breath, Gabriel dropped the crop and heavy basket to the ground and gave chase, via the same route as the agile sneak who thought to rob him. A young lad in a soiled yellow jerkin and the patchwork trousers of a parish lockup case. He knew the garments too well.

"Drop that bridle and sword before you hurt yourself, you stupid little bastard!" he roared.

The commotion drew a crowd of curious servants from the direction of the scullery, though none ventured forth in the rain to assist their raging master. Gabriel flung them a look of disgust that sent all but one young kitchen girl scurrying for cover. She stood, mouth open, to witness the excitement.

By now the nimble thief, motivated no doubt by the fact that he had robbed a lunatic lord, had scaled the paddock fence and headed for some unseen footpath.

Soon enough Gabriel ran him down, these byways not unfamiliar to a man who'd raised worse mischief in his day. For a disorienting moment he might have been running away from someone to whom *he* had given offense, instead of the other way around. He'd acted in this play before, the roles reversed.

The intervening years had flown by. Why had he come back? What had he hoped to prove? That he was better than a lockup boy who'd had the guts to try and trump him? Or that he was worthy of kissing the only girl who had ever dared to stare the dragon in the eye?

He reached out, grabbed the boy by the scruff of his jerkin, and wrestled him to the ground. The sword fell in the mud. The bridle flew from the thief's bony arm and landed in a thicket.

He stared down into an angry red face and a pair of blue eyes that burned with the hatred of hell. "Eff off, you scruffy sod," the boy said with a sneer.

"Do you know where little arseholes like you end up?" he asked coldly.

"Yeah. But tell me another time."

Gabriel raised his fist, knowing it wouldn't do any good, that no one could beat the demons from another, that violence only made a rebel grow stronger. But he meant to—

A firm hand gripped his shoulder. He turned his head and glanced up in disbelief into Alethea's face. "Don't, Gabriel," she said. "Don't hurt him—he's half your size."

"Do you know this little thief?" he asked in an incredulous voice.

"I've seen him about the village, yes."

"He was stealing from me—my sword and bridle, most likely at the same moment the vicar's wife was instructing me to pray and—"

"Here." Taking advantage of his captor's inattention, the boy squirmed loose, shooting to his feet, only to have Gabriel jump up and block his path. "The lady said you should let me go. I was only taking the sword and bridle to polish them up as a surprise for you."

"You damned liar," Gabriel retorted in amusement.

"It's true," the boy insisted. "I was lookin' for work and thought I'd prove myself first. You'd have had 'em back by nightfall. I'm fast."

Gabriel glanced back, distracted by the woman who stood behind him. The rain fell harder now, filtered through branches that arched in a tangle above them. Several tendrils of Alethea's hair lay plastered to her throat. A deep-bosomed wench with dark hair and a gypsy's face. She made him forget what he had been thinking, and God knew what was going through her head. He felt a flash of panic, his footing unsteady. What was he supposed to say next?

"You do realize he is lying?"

She nodded, her gaze shifting past him, bright with guilt. He heard a twig snap behind him and knew his prisoner had taken flight.

"You ought to retrieve your possessions and go in

from the rain," she said. "You're not wearing a coat even now."

He stared at her in frustration. He didn't feel the rain at all. But what he felt made it hard to breathe. "I thought you wanted me to demonstrate discipline in my role as master."

She smiled and swept around him, plucking his sword from a pocket of mud. "But you did demonstrate discipline," she said as she handed him the weapon. "You mastered your own anger. And I have every confidence that you realize even a thief deserves at least one chance for redemption."

He laughed and stopped short of asking her what she thought *he* deserved. Up until now he had never really cared about anyone's opinion of him. From what he knew of Alethea, she would give him an all-too-honest answer.

He spent the rest of that day taking his errant staff to task for their countless misdemeanors. He berated the groom for the moldy straw in the stables and the dark water troughs. He ordered the stalls mucked out thrice a day, the pasture checked for rocks and holes, and the paddock fence repaired. He might not intend to stay, but neither would he wallow in the previous owner's filth, and he liked putting his shoulder into hard work.

The kitchens smelled as foul as the devil's furnace, the rafters blackened with soot and ancient splatters of grease. He suspected that any man fool enough to consume a full-course meal prepared by the cook's hands would die in agony under the dinner table.

"I want these caverns scrubbed from top to bottom and clean enough that one could eat off the floor."

"We eat off the floor all the time," the scullery maid informed him. "Ain't never sickened any of us yet."

"You're upset, sir," the housekeeper said unhelpfully. "It's a big responsibility taking over someone else's home. All that worry over whether one of the old masters will sneak back one night and murder you in your sleep."

Gabriel snorted. "I was nearly murdered in the entry hall by one of my staff."

"Well, that won't happen again, sir," she promised. "We've imprisoned the offender in the cellar for a spell. Why don't you take a good bottle of gin into the garden and get yourself all calm while I see what I can do about supper?"

"Home?" he muttered as she scurried off toward the kitchen. "Not bloody likely."

He couldn't imagine lording over this place. The walled garden where he was supposed to becalm himself was a tangle of thorny roses, shoulder-high weeds, and pungent herbs that released the scent of bitter memories beneath his bootsteps.

How could anyone prefer the rustic life over the bustle of London? The air here knocked him dead with the pungency of cow ordure and growing things. The stillness alone gnawed at his nerves.

There was no one with whom to gamble or even smoke a cigar. Most of all, though, he detested the quiet because he could hear his own thoughts, loud and angry with too many unanswered questions from a time upon which he chose not to reflect. He was a man of the present. Perhaps coming back had been a mistake. The revenge he'd hoped for might be served upon himself.

When evening fell, he even found that the moon shone too brightly in the country. He had forgotten how often he had stared up at the stars and hoped. He wasn't sure when he'd lost hope and the stars now had ceased to glitter, but he was too old for that nonsense.

He washed, rinsed the taste of bad gin from his mouth, and wandered back into the dining hall. His stomach growled. He hadn't eaten since he'd devoured Mrs. Bryant's ham hours ago.

Mismatched Wedgwood plates and pewter knives sat upon the damask-covered tablecloth. But there was nothing edible in sight. Nor could he hear the rattle of plates on their way to the hall.

Hunger drove him to the kitchen outbuildings, where he found the sorrowful lot of Helbourne's staff playing a game of hazard at the table.

"Where is my supper, Mrs. Miniver?" he asked as he lifted the lid from an empty pot on the stove.

Hiding the pair of dice in her apron, the housekeeper rose to curtsy. "I was about to make a fresh pie, sir, only to realize we've run out of flour. With your permission I shall walk to a neighboring manor to borrow a bowl."

"Don't you market, Mrs. Miniver?"

She pulled off her grimy apron. "When there's money to spend, sir. I shouldn't be long. Lady Alethea understands."

"Does she?" he asked, frowning.

"Oh, yes, sir. She keeps an eye out for her neighbors, poor lady. I expect it eases her grief now that she has no expectations of raising a family of her own."

"I'll ride over, Mrs. Miniver. It will be faster."

"You, sir?" she asked slyly. "The earl isn't at home, you know."

He ignored her perceptive look. He wanted to ask more but resisted. Alethea had not struck him as being overly mournful, but sorrow that ran deep did not have to be shared. He tried to picture her sitting alone at her table, a vacant place opposite her. Perhaps she saved a spot in memory of her late fiancé. For all he knew she had invited someone else, a bloody stupid lockup boy who caused trouble in the village.

"Are you sure, sir?" The housekeeper stared at him in interest.

He wasn't sure of anything, except that if he stayed here he would probably lose his mind and that there was no point in he and Alethea both sitting alone. Furthermore, since he had already crossed the bridge of no return, he had little else to risk by going over it again.

Chapter Eleven

❧ ❧

Alethea was sequestered in the library of her brother, Robin Claridge, the Earl of Wrexham, when the under-footman appeared in obvious agitation to report that a stranger had come to the door.

"A stranger?" She put down her quill.

"A gentleman who claims a prior friendship with you," he added with a mysterious air.

Alethea sat numbly in her chair. She had already unpinned her hair, made use of her toothbrush and toilette, and taken her nightly glass of sherry. She could not remember anyone calling at this hour, although it took little imagination to conclude who her visitor was.

She rose, suddenly imbued with purpose. Gabriel may have enjoyed his midnight amusements in London, where the young bucks refused to go home until morning. But in the country one enjoyed quiet evenings, with the occasional party to attend. Of course, she did ofttimes wish for a few livelier pursuits herself, but the annual masquerade assembly would soon be held before the autumn chill kept everyone by the fire at night.

Prude. Spinster. That was what she was becoming, one of the pitied gentlewomen she and her friends had secretly made fun of not long ago. Gabriel must think her dull in comparison to his London ladybirds, and she had to admit that *he* invigorated his surroundings and that . . . she hoped it *was* him. She laughed softly at the thought, at herself. She couldn't believe she was looking forward to telling him off for coming here this late at night. She couldn't remember the last time she'd looked forward to anything.

Still, it was not Gabriel who stood awaiting her in the entrance hall. And when her visitor turned, she felt not only a great disappointment, but stark panic and an impulse to run for her brother's pistols.

A ghost. Jeremy's ghost.

Then he lifted his face into the light. The illusion vanished, and she realized with a shudder of relief that her caller was only Jeremy's older brother, Major Lord Guy Hazlett. Unsmiling, he was gaunter of countenance than his deceased sibling. She had barely exchanged more than three words with him at the memorial service. Yet she had felt him observing her with unnerving intensity, as he was now.

She'd hoped she would never see him again. He and his family maintained a grand estate in nearby Ashwell. What brought him here? What could he want? The engagement ring that his brother had given her?

She'd thrown it off the bridge for the two lovers who had died there. She had nothing else of value to give the man who might have been her brother-in-law.

She met his stare. The same green eyes as Jeremy, the same chiseled features and arrogant demeanor. Guy had not deigned to visit Helbourne in years. He considered the village beneath him.

What *did* he want?

He rushed forward and warmly embraced her. "Forgive me for intruding at this hour, Alethea. I had personal business in the area, and promised my wife I would inquire about your welfare. This has been a difficult time for all of us, with Jeremy gone."

He hung his head in a moment of solemn silence. His short speech should have relieved her. It made sense when she remembered his wife Mary's sympathetic looks at Jeremy's memorial service. The fact that Jeremy had proved himself a monster did not mean that his brother shared his penchant for cruelty.

"I am well, my lord."

And yet as she stood before him in her heavy burgundy robe she felt inexplicably exposed and ill-at-ease. She assumed her discomfort stemmed from the realization that he closely resembled his brother in physical appearance.

His honeyed voice sent an unpleasant spark down

her spine. "Mary wondered if you were indisposed for good reason. We wish to offer our support to you."

"How is your wife?" she asked, thinking of the pleasant if rather plain heiress who doted openly on Guy.

"She's expecting another child. A girl again, the midwife has warned us." His pale eyes drifted over her, calculating, unsettling. "May I speak frankly with you?"

She hesitated. Why had she not asked the footman to stay? Because she had expected her visitor to be a different man? "There are servants within hearing. If this is a personal matter, perhaps we should wait until my brother and cousin return. I do not think it proper to—"

"Come outside," he coaxed. "Walk with me through the garden. The country air is safe for sharing confidences."

It was not safe for other purposes. Her heart lurched against her ribs. In her mind she saw Jeremy forcing her into the dark, covering her mouth with his hand.

"It's too late to walk—"

"Alethea," he said gently. "I know what happened between you and my brother."

Her head jerked up in alarm. "What did you say?"

"I know that you became his lover the night he left."

His lover. A twisted version of the truth. Not an act of love at all.

Her temper rose. "Is that what he told you?"

He gripped her gently by the elbows. "If you have borne a child in secret, Mary and I have discussed how best to help you."

"Pray do not touch me, my lord. That is the last time I shall ask you. And to satisfy your curiosity, there is no secret child."

He released her arms. She backed away.

"You retired to the country for over a year. I would have thought if grief had—it does not matter. What matters is that you need a protector, Alethea." Yet the manner in which he began to circle her did not make her feel safe. "A woman in your position—bereft, vulnerable. It is an invitation to certain ugly realities of the world."

How much did he really know? Had he guessed? Or had Jeremy confessed to him to clear his conscience? Guy must have thought it odd that she did not weep at his brother's service.

"I wish you had asked for my help, Alethea." He paused. "Should my brother have married you, you and I would have become close, I'm sure. You would have trusted me. Trust me now."

"I have told you the truth."

But not that she had hoped she would never see him or any of Jeremy's family ever again. The time of uncertainty over a conception had long passed. Her flow had come, a nerve-racking week after her nightmare. She would have found the strength to bear that cross had it been laid upon her shoulders. Now she merely had to make peace with her ruined status and what that entailed. She held little patience for grieving her stolen virtue. She had been shamed, but she still had her brother and their cousin to care for her, her friends in the village.

"Lord Hazlett," she said resolutely, "is there something else you wish from me? Your brother's engagement ring? I regret to say I lost it the day I learned of his death."

"No, my dear," he said. "I can well afford to buy you another. Is that what *you* wish? Do you desire jewels? Some pretty clothes?"

She forced herself to look steadily into his face. "I have nothing of value to give in return, except advice on manners which I suspect you would not heed."

"You're wrong, Alethea."

She held his regard with cynical reluctance. His green eyes seemed to offer her only sympathy; her instincts did not trust him. And yet she was more angry now than afraid. She would not suffer further violation.

"I fear you don't understand me," he told her. "I do not possess my brother's, let us say, temper and tendency to aggression."

So he did know.

"Your composure is admirable," he added. "I don't know that I would be as forgiving in your place."

"Perhaps there isn't anything to forgive."

He smiled knowingly. "Another woman would have gone into hysterics. My fool of a brother was afraid you would tell half of England what he did."

Her mouth tightened in revulsion. "Well, let the dead rest in peace. I have no confessions to make."

"But I am worthy of your confidence. I shall keep your secret for you. And, if you allow me, I shall make your life better than it would have been otherwise. I know what a little swine my brother was. Spoiled, taking everything he ever wanted."

She swallowed tightly. She need not panic. There were servants within the sound of her cry.

"My primary concern is your future, Alethea."

"*My* concern," she said. "Not yours."

"There are only so many options open for a woman in your fallen state."

She felt her stomach turn, yet managed to say, "If I fell, I have since found my footing."

"Just between you and me, I see no shame in passion. Jeremy swore that you encouraged him—that you sought to give him pleasure the night before he left."

"Did he?" she asked faintly, for "pleasure" was the last word to describe what she had experienced.

"If so, it was a generous gift, one that—"

"I say that there *was* shame."

He shrugged, slowly nearing her again. "Then that ill memory must be supplanted by a more desirable reflection. Perhaps even by desire itself."

"Is this a proposition on behalf of your late brother or for yourself?" she asked in distaste.

"You are unclaimed, Alethea, secluded in this place. There are arrangements for women like you who no longer fit into the polite world."

"I know what I am. And what those arrangements are," she said, her voice shaking with anger.

"Then you know what I am offering you, and why it is a sensible solution for a beautiful young woman who was never meant to be a governess."

Chapter Twelve

❧◦❧

Gabriel had begun to feel like a bit of an idiot as he approached the quiet manor house. He'd forgotten that in the country all the yokels dropped into bed at an ungodly hour. It certainly did not offend his rules of behavior to visit a young lady unannounced, using his housekeeper's bare pantry as an excuse. However, he could not recall when, if ever, he'd called upon a beautiful woman to beg a bowl of flour for his supper.

It was a ridiculous pretense. He wouldn't be able to keep a straight face when he presented it, and Alethea would see right through him, as he suspected she always had. It was a pleasant thought, sharing a laugh with her at his expense. But when he reached the end of her drive, his amusement vanished. There was a carriage parked in front of the entrance steps, although only one or two faint lights glowed behind the windows. Alethea had apparently not yet retired. And, apparently, she was not alone. He should not have been surprised, but he was.

But he was not naïve. To deny the implication of a late-night visit would be gullibility in the extreme. Alethea was unclaimed, inviting, a beautiful woman. It was not difficult to imagine other men desiring her or being lured as he was to her door.

He dismounted and tethered his horse to the post at the curve of the drive. The two footmen standing against the carriage nodded as he passed. He ignored them.

A gentleman, of course, would not intrude on a liaison. But he was curious. He was a gambler. An unprincipled beggar with an empty bowl.

He ran up the front steps. He knocked softly, waited a few seconds, then let himself inside.

Restrained voices drifted from the end of the entrance hall that led to the main staircase. He cleared his throat.

"Anybody home? The butler, the baker . . . Alethea? Lady Alethea, are you here?"

He paused. He heard her deep, well-bred voice. From the sound of it she was not engaged in pleasing conversation.

"That must be one of your footmen calling for you, my lord," she was saying. "I shall bid you good night."

"You will reconsider my offer?"

Gabriel's hackles rose. He walked toward the two candlelit figures. What kind of offer did a man make at this hour?

"Well, there you are," he said heartily. "I've been knocking for ages."

"I didn't hear anyone knocking," the other man said.

"I did," she said quickly.

He studied her tautly drawn face for a sign that he was unwelcome and decided she felt relieved at the intrusion. The realization awakened his aggressive instincts. Her visitor had not been invited. He glanced past her in open appraisal of the tall man in the florid brocade jacket who stood beside her. No local squire, by the look of him, but not entirely unfamiliar, either. Was he a suitor?

Not one whose company she'd sought, judging by the enthusiasm with which she rushed forth to draw him into the hall.

"Sir Gabriel," she announced with such strained gaiety that he wondered fleetingly if she had become one of those midnight tipplers. "How good of you to come! I had given up all hope."

He could have sworn that when they had last met in the woods, they had parted on unstable terms. "Well, it's really—"

She grasped him under the arm and dragged him between her and the other man. "You're an hour late, sir."

"So I am," he said smoothly, deliberately nudging her back behind him.

"Better late than never, though," she said with a nervous laugh.

The other man straightened. "Then it must be later than I realized, and I should be on my way if I'm to have a meal before bed."

Gabriel braced his hip against the sideboard as if he had no intention of being the first to leave. Indeed, he would not go until assured that she was rid of her unwanted guest. Alethea had not moved, except for a small involuntary shiver when the visitor glanced at her.

"What I have offered you still stands," the gentleman said to Alethea, at the same time turning his back on Gabriel. "I do not like to think of you bearing your grief alone."

"I have had a year to grieve," Alethea replied.

Gabriel snorted lightly. He'd like to get this man alone in a dark alley and give him some grief. He hadn't arrived a moment too soon by the look of it.

"Better hurry," he said. "The bridges in this area can be murder. There are ghosts, too. And bats."

The older man glanced around to give him a long, hard stare. "You are not a person I recognize, sir. Have we met?"

"Not unless you frequent the gambling hells."

The man's upper lip curled in a sneer. "Fortunately, I do not. But I have seen you— Boscastle?"

Gabriel stared back at him. Now he knew who this pompous ass was. The elder Lord Hazelnuts. The heir. Gabriel's older brothers had stolen Guy's horse and given it to the gypsies when they'd caught him whipping it in a tantrum. "You have the advantage. I do not know your name."

"Major Lord Guy Hazlett."

"Ah." Gabriel responded with a dismissive smile, signifying that the name meant nothing to him. "And you're Lady Alethea's—uncle?" he asked, as if questioning the age difference between the two were a sign of respect and not a blatant insult.

Hazlett frowned. "I would have been her brother-in-law had misfortune not befallen my family." By which he clearly meant that this gave him the right to pop in on her at late hours.

Her brother-in-law, his arse. Gabriel laughed inwardly. He knew a darker quest when he saw one.

Hazlett lifted his shoulder. "And your business with her, sir?"

He plopped down on the hard oakwood hall chair. He hadn't been invited to sit. It was bad manners. However, as Alethea voiced no objection, he decided it was up to him to send Hazelnuts packing. She could lecture him on his deportment later.

"We're neighbors," he said succinctly. "In fact, I have something for her." He slid his bowl to the floor and withdrew from under his arm the riding crop she'd dropped earlier in the day. "You left this in the straw when you woke me up today," he said guilelessly.

Alethea's brows rose. "How thoughtful of you."

"Well, since I *was* coming anyway—"

"All that way to deliver a whip," Hazlett muttered. "As if it could not have waited until morning or been brought by a servant."

Gabriel grinned as she took the crop from his hand. "You never know when a little discipline will come in handy," he said. "I understand one cannot safely open one's door at night even here in the country. Who knows what nasty people might be lurking about?"

Hazlett smiled without humor. "Indeed. May I drive you home, now that your good deed has been discharged? My carriage is right outside."

"No need," Gabriel said airily. "I've got my horse, thank you, and as a matter of fact, I have been sent by another agent on a different matter. A private one, I should add."

"A private matter?" Alethea and Hazlett echoed in chorus.

Gabriel gave a solemn nod. "It's rather embarrassing. I'm not at liberty to reveal it to anyone but Lady Alethea."

Alethea pressed her lips together and did not comment. Hazlett shook his head in defeat.

"I should be on my way before the inn fills for the night," he said. "I shall take it upon myself to check on you from time to time, Alethea."

Gabriel surged to his feet. "I think that between her brother and the parish, we shall be able to keep her safe from evil influences . . . don't you, Alethea?"

She muttered something under her breath. He smiled back in shining innocence. He had a feeling he was going to catch hell from her for playing about. Perhaps she really did like this Lord Hazelnuts. However, when finally the man took his leave, Gabriel did not feel the least bit guilty. Not at all.

Not even when Alethea looked up at him and

asked, "What *are* you doing here this late at night, Gabriel?"

"I saw a light in the window—"

"And a light drew you from your house? Liar."

"I thought you just said I was invited."

"Oh, honestly."

"'How good of you to come!'" he quoted. "'I had given up all hope.'"

"That was . . ." She bit her lip. "It was an excuse."

He laughed quietly. "Then I'm not really welcome?"

"Gabriel, I am usually abed at this hour."

The powerful sense of protectiveness he already felt now mingled with lust. "Better late than never?"

"Is that the private matter you have come about?"

He hesitated. "My housekeeper sent me over for a bowl of flour."

She shook her head in resignation. "I should have known. Mrs. Miniver is the worst housekeeper in the world. Follow me."

"My bowl—"

"Never mind. I'll send over a sack."

It was a long walk to the kitchens. For once Gabriel blessed the old-fashioned architecture of bygone days that separated one building from another. The arrangement caused certain discomforts, but it gave him a few moments alone with Alethea, although she did not seem inclined to appreciate the opportunity herself.

They entered a dark low-beamed hall at the end of which firelight glowed through an arched doorway from a kitchen hearth. He put his hand on her shoulder.

"You did not like that man," he said softly.

She turned, her dark eyes evading his. "I didn't. Thank you."

"For—?"

"Your welcome intervention."

"Did he upset you?" he demanded, his anger flaring. "By God, did I arrive too late or just in time?"

She shook her head. "You came at the perfect moment."

"Were you distressed because he brought back memories of his brother?" he guessed, suddenly feeling awkward and not wanting this moment to end. He sensed that she was reluctant to answer, that she probably wished he would leave.

Her voice was barely audible. "It was upsetting to see him, that's all."

He frowned, realizing she had escaped a truthful response. "Do *I* upset you?"

She laughed unexpectedly. "Yes. *Yes*. From the very moment I laid my eyes on you, you have been a disconcertment. I had always hoped—"

"Alethea."

He caught her by the waist, his eyes locked with hers, and slowly molded her to his length. For a moment neither of them moved; he thought it better to act as if he were contemplating their situation than to confess his desire for her had bedeviled him.

"Gabriel," she whispered, "it's—"

"Don't make me go yet. Please, please."

She shifted indecisively, then subsided into acquiescence, her hand rising to rest lightly on his arm. His body hardened in unashamed anticipation. He needed to kiss her as desperately as he needed air. But this time he braced himself for what she would make him feel, and determined that she would feel a similar turmoil.

He gazed down at her in brooding silence, waiting, until her lips parted on the sheerest of sighs. His invitation. He slid his hand up her back, between her shoulder blades, to her nape, to support her head. She said nothing, her dark eyes undoing him, questioning what his next move would be.

He bent his head in answer. She tensed; he settled his other hand firmly on her hip as his lips teased hers. Her eyes drifted shut. Her guard dropped, and his heart pounded in excitement until every pulse in his body echoed with the unmerciful refrain of his desire.

She was his for that moment. He knew it as he kissed her. She was his until she made an indistinct sound that brought him to his senses. Even then he could not move, his mouth still touching hers so that he tasted her exhalation of breath, the sweet aftertaste of sherry. "I'm sorry. I believe I've lost the thread of our conversation."

She smiled, stared up into his eyes, and gently slapped him across the back of his thigh with her riding crop. "And I believe *you're* the one who mentioned the timely delivery of discipline."

He closed his eyes, indulging in a delicious moment of self-torture. "I asked for that."

"And I asked what you were doing here at this hour," she said softly. "You *could* have sent a servant for flour."

He opened his eyes. "I was rescuing you, wasn't I?"

She drew the crop up to his chest, delicately caressing the scar at his throat. "Unless you have been peering through the windows, I cannot imagine how you'd have known I needed to be rescued."

She turned, only to discover herself drawn back and trapped again in his arms. Her heart fluttered in unbidden excitement as he looked into her eyes. She did not, could not, find the strength to look away. He smiled, then pulled her into his chest. Without a word, he lowered his head to kiss her again.

She drew her breath and tried to count to ten to clear her thoughts. She lost track of her numbers at three. His kiss rendered any effort to ignore him useless. Heat shimmered down her shoulders, her arms, her spine. She felt suddenly unfettered, on fire. Light as a flame, capable of scorching anything she touched. Gabriel. The one man she should run from at all cost. But he had come to her rescue, her knight-errant. For that one act alone she could convince herself he deserved a kiss, even if she had no idea who would rescue her from him.

She leaned away from him. He followed, his

hands expertly skimming the shape of her breasts, her back, then abandoning this wicked foray before she could mount a protest.

Who would have known that his thick, calloused fingers could evoke this tender yearning? "Why?" she whispered in bewilderment. "Why am I letting you kiss me?"

He laughed. "I've no idea. My advice, the rule I follow, is to enjoy now and repent later."

"That is not a rule at all."

"No?"

"No," she said firmly. "It is a lack of one."

He ran his hand down her spine again to rest in a proprietary manner on her bottom. "Do I have to let you go?" he asked her with a playful smile.

She shook her head without hesitation. "Yes."

"I thought so." He studied the floor as if there were inspiration to be found in the vicinity of his feet. Indeed, she glanced down herself. As to be expected, when he looked up again, the dark gleam in his eye revealed his motives to be more devious than innocent. "And may I return?"

She took her time considering her reply, although he must have sensed that she would agree. "Yes, but only for supper. And with a full complement of guests. My brother is due to arrive home next week."

"When?" he asked, after another pause. "When may I come back? Do I have to wait for his return if I promise to behave?"

"You don't know how."

"I'll practice."

She bit the edge of her lip, laughter in her eyes. It was almost midnight, and all she knew of this man, aside from the fact that his kisses muddled her wits, was that he had not only misspent his youth, but that his present and future appeared to be no brighter. She was not sure how inviting him to supper would benefit either of them. But she wanted to see him again. Just the way he smiled at her made it worth the risk.

She said, "On Friday evening." So much could happen before then. He could run away. Or reform. Or—

He nodded solemnly. "Five days hence. Yes. I shall be honored to come."

"Do you want your sack of flour, Gabriel?"

"My— I don't care."

"That's what you came for, isn't it?"

"Why don't you give me a crust of bread instead?"

She grinned in delight. "To go with your ham and violet jelly?"

"I ate the damn ham," he said gruffly.

Chapter Thirteen

❧ ❧

Two days later Gabriel was thundering in the Tuesday predawn gloom back to London, leaving turnpikes, quiet hamlets, and temptation behind him. He had awakened before dawn, looked out the window across his weed-choked garden toward Alethea's house, and realized he was in danger of losing himself. When he was younger he had known exactly what he was up against. His lot had seemed unfair but at least he had understood it.

He wasn't a country gentleman. He was a gamester, a soldier, and if circumstance had shaped his character in undesirable ways, he'd had no reason to change it. He couldn't possibly put down roots, even in the soil that had spawned him. God only knew what he might grow into. It would be a discourtesy to Alethea to stay any longer. In fact, it was a sign of his true affection for her, removing himself from her life.

He'd dressed and pounded down the stairs, bellowing for his horse, his breakfast, his coachman. Bellowing to a negligent staff who would not bestir themselves unless the very roof collapsed upon the house. He bridled and saddled his mount in the dark, and truth be told the Andalusian seemed as eager to escape, for action, as its master. His coachman, accustomed to Gabriel's restless ways, quietly agreed to follow.

He could not stay here another day, another hour, his entire life. This was what he had escaped. He'd told himself so many times over that it was a kindness to Alethea to leave that he believed it. Last night, if she'd given him any encouragement at all, he would have proved to her that he was no better than her other visitor. He would have promised her whatever she desired and not meant it.

Or, he would have meant it, an even worse possibility, which suggested that he wasn't running back to London to save Alethea's honor as much as to save himself.

It was a heartening sign, Alethea thought. An indication of respect for her feelings that Gabriel did not visit her in the next two days. If he'd appeared unannounced at her door again, after the displeasure she had expressed over Guy's unheralded visit and subsequent offer, she might have refused to receive him. Then again, she might have been persuaded to ask him to tea.

And allowed him to kiss her again.

She could only hope, however, that he had taken her advice to heart and was setting his estate in order. She, on the other hand, was letting the dogs run around the house unrestrained, wearing her hair loose like a pagan, and opening her window at night to watch Venus rise in the sky. The fact that a new owner had moved into Helbourne Hall had nothing to do with her sudden penchant for evening air or the energy she felt after months of melancholy. She thought of herself as a late-winter tulip, poking through layers of crusty earth to enjoy the sun.

Even her brother, Robin, noticed her uplifted spirits when he arrived home, dusty, disheveled, but in his usual agreeable mood. "Did the gypsies cross your palm with silver while I was gone? I haven't seen you smile like this in ages."

"Have I become that morose?" she asked in chagrin. She hadn't forgotten how to laugh, she wanted to add. It was just that there had not been much to amuse her these days.

He regarded her fondly as she preceded him into the drawing room, where the table had been set with a light breakfast of bacon, muffins, and strong hot coffee.

He was only an inch taller than Alethea, lean, with silky brown hair that constantly fell over his left brow. "I wish you'd come to London with me. Your friends begged me for news of you. Cassandra Waverley has just been delivered of twins. It would do you a world of good to visit her."

It wouldn't have, though. She would have felt envious, afraid that she would only ever know the closeness of children as a governess. He chatted on.

Her thoughts strayed until he paused and then, to her embarrassment, she blurted out, "We have a new neighbor. An old one, actually. It's Gabriel Boscastle." Now that she had finally spoken his name aloud, she realized she had not banished him from her mind but only admitted that he dominated her thoughts. It did not help that after the blank expression faded from her brother's face, he stared at her in amused horror.

"You do remember him?" she prompted. "His father died—"

"Gabriel and his brothers beat the guts out of every boy in school. I think he was even put in the pillory once for—"

Alethea slid a plate of muffins toward him. "You've gone far too thin since you left. Didn't you have a decent meal in London?"

He glanced down at the table. "I've just eaten three of those. Now back to—"

"Well, have another. They won't keep. Or have another slice of bacon—and eggs. I'll ask Mrs. Sudley to make some."

"He was put into the pillory," he continued, pushing his plate aside. "Mind you, he—"

"He never walloped you, did he?" she asked, taking a breath. "I mean, I don't recall you ever coming home from school battered and bruised. You had no fights with him that I can remember."

He tapped his long fingers on the edge of the table, eyeing her with suspicion. "No. I didn't, and I always wondered why. Do *you* have any answers?"

Alethea picked up her cup, pretending not to notice his wary scrutiny. "Perhaps he liked you. You're a rather pleasant sort even if you are my brother. I know Emily thinks so. Speaking of Emily, you didn't happen to visit her in London? Or propose, as you have been promising for the past five months? Or is it five years? It isn't fair to keep her waiting this long. I don't think you want to get married at all."

He regarded her steadily. "I think you should come with me the next time I go."

"When will that be?" she asked, exhaling in relief that the subject of their notorious neighbor had been supplanted by talk of Robin's love interest. Every time he worked up the courage to propose to Emily, he was besieged by an attack of nerves. Alethea had begun to fear they would grow old and unloved together with no children to enrich their future. She would probably be hand-feeding him muffins forever.

"I'm leaving again on Friday morning," he said with a grin. "And if all goes well I *am* proposing that night. Would you like to hide behind the sofa and prompt me in case my resolution falters?"

"Friday? I was planning— I've invited Mrs. Bryant and a few other friends over to dinner. It's been a long time since we've reciprocated."

He sighed. "It's all right," he said after several moments. "I understand. You miss him, and you're still in mourning."

Him. Jeremy, he meant. That blazing bastard who had become canonized in local memory.

She felt tears sting her eyes. Not tears of grief, but rather of bitter amusement and frustration. How she wanted to tell Robin the truth. But her brother would never recover if she did. He would blame himself for not protecting her, for not confronting Jeremy that night in London. Still, the words bubbled up inside, like a slow-festering poison, and she ached to release them.

Instead she said, because it was the easiest manner in which to distract him, "And I've invited Gabriel Boscastle here to supper, too. I thought you would be home to serve as host, or I might not have done so. But it would be rude now to explain that he can't come. I've invited him, and that's all there is to it."

Chapter Fourteen

A rolling stone should gather neither moss nor memories. Gabriel was accustomed to hasty exits and unplanned escapes from both battle and bedroom scenes. It was practically habit by now to throw himself over his horse and ride half-asleep to parts unknown.

But he was only three hours onto the Great London Road before he realized that the heaviness in his chest wasn't the usual relief but regret. He would live the rest of his life wondering what he had missed by leaving.

Damnation, a man could not miss what he'd never known, could he? And he'd never had an affair with anyone like Alethea before. Who was to say that she wouldn't be the end of him if he stayed? Besides that, he couldn't imagine having supper at her house without doing something to merit banishment forever.

It just seemed easier to bow out, as rude as that might be, than to humiliate himself in her presence.

It seemed easier to dream of her, knowing his

yearnings would never be realized, than to face the end of his most cherished fantasies.

At least that was the thought with which he consoled himself as he arrived at the Mayfair town house of his older cousin, Lieutenant Colonel Lord Heath Boscastle. He could have turned up like a stray cat at the door of any of the London Boscastles and been invited to stay. In fact, he had done so more times than he could count since he had made peace with this side of the family.

The fact remained that of all his male relations, Lord Heath seemed the one least likely to judge or ask questions—a presumption that the most reserved of the Boscastle men turned upon its ear the very minute that Gabriel let down his guard in his cousin's study.

It was a room of mystery, hushed and reverent with the ambience of ancient knowledge and secrets never revealed, not unlike the raven-haired former spy who sat half-shadowed in silent appraisal behind his military desk. Books with broken spines and vellum-leather bindings, many in archaic languages, filled the shelves that lined the walls. Several maps of Egypt and Europe, military campaigns in relief, hung between the curtained bow windows.

Gabriel gathered that not only had Heath read all the obscure books in his library, he most likely possessed the intellect to have written them. He was the family sphinx, the calm one said to be capable of coaxing a confession from the stoniest adversary. His silence played upon the nerves.

Gabriel laughed. "What have I done? What's wrong? I've only been gone a few days. What could have happened in a week?"

"In this family?" Heath gave a wry smile. "I should not need to explain. The Boscastles barely require an hour to disgrace themselves."

"True. Isn't that part of their charm?"

"Where have you been, Gabriel?"

"In Enfield, lording it over a country manor I won in a card game."

"Enfield? Was that not where you were born?"

By damn, what a memory. Gabriel never spoke of his past to anyone. "Yes."

Heath glanced down at the orderly piles of letters and documents on his desk. "And has the prodigal son found what he sought? Escape? Diversion?"

"Hardly," Gabriel said in amusement.

"No secret jaunts back to London?"

He straightened. "Not in the last week."

Heath looked up.

Years ago, while Gabriel had waged war against his private demons, he had isolated himself from the Boscastles proper, the London trunk of the notorious ancestral tree. But in the recent past he'd carved a comfortable niche for himself in the family, and while Gabriel's code of conduct still might have raised eyebrows in the stuffiest homes, he had never broken a confidence or engaged in any true disloyalty toward his cousins.

"What manner of secret jaunts are we discussing, Heath?" he asked, more at ease now that he'd made a hasty assessment of his conscience for some obscure misdeed.

It couldn't have anything to do with Alethea. Hell's bells, he'd been on his best behavior—at least by his former scoundrel's standards. He had kissed her. That was not a black mark in the Boscastle book of sins. It was only a beginning . . . and the mere thought of kissing her again reinforced his desire to return.

Heath merely smiled.

"Devil take me," he said in annoyance. "I forgot Grayson's natal ball, didn't I? The one where tickets are to be auctioned off for one of Jane's charities? I cannot believe anyone would even miss me in a squeeze like that. I shall atone. What can I buy Jane? She likes shoes and jewelry—what if I have a pair of dancing shoes specially fashioned for her dainty feet, ones with diamonds on the toes?"

Heath shook his head. "Grayson's birthday falls at the end of the month. You're invited. You are always invited."

"Not always," Gabriel said before he realized what he had admitted. Therein lay the problem with Heath. One simply had to sit alone with him and exchange a few meaningless comments, and secrets began spilling out like a fountain.

Still, there'd been a time when Gabriel had not been in close harmony with his cousins. He had deliberately antagonized them during the few family gatherings he'd attended. It had seemed easier in the midst of all that Boscastle esprit de corps to pretend his own family had not fallen apart and that he had not regarded the rambunctious lot of them with envy.

"That was your choice, Gabriel," Heath said without any trace of condemnation. "We would have welcomed you at any time. As I recall, you were invited to every important function. You and your brothers refused us more often than not."

"Those were trying years for *my* family. I was not exactly fit company for the ton."

Heath met his gaze. "So I understand. Yet you never told us. Nor did your mother."

What else did Heath know of his past? Things that Gabriel himself had forgotten or had never been told?

"I don't understand," he said. "If it is not a family matter that I've missed, why am I under your suspicion, for that is what underlies this conversation."

"Not *my* suspicion. But I will admit that I have associates in London who have come to me in private and inquired about your recent whereabouts."

By which Heath could be referring to any number of informants in the lowest wards, including constables and runners, politicians and prostitutes. As a retired intelligence officer, he claimed a list of loyal supporters who befriended him to this day.

"Well, are you going to tell me why they wish to know my whereabouts, or is this some form of Boscastle torture?" he asked genially.

He could not believe that his gambling had aroused Crown suspicion. And for the first time in many years, his conscience was actually clear, unless one counted his desire for Alethea Claridge.

Heath picked up his pen. "I was hoping you'd tell me."

"I might, if I had a bloody idea what you're nattering on about."

"A man of your description has been engaging in some housebreakings across London that involve sleeping ladies in Mayfair."

Gabriel shrugged. "That's nothing new. I'm hardly seeking a papal dispensation for my sins."

"You seem to be seeking something. Look at this, please." Heath slid across the desk one of the comical caricatures that circulated in the streets and salons of London.

"Oh, no, you don't," Gabriel said, holding up his hand. "If this is another drawing that your wife did of your private bits, I don't want anything to do with it."

"It isn't *me*," Heath retorted in annoyance.

"Well, it certainly isn't—" He glanced down at the print, suddenly falling silent. It depicted a man climbing out of a window with a pair of lady's drawers in his teeth and several silk stockings draped around his neck.

As caricatures went, Gabriel had seen cruder, including the one that Julia Boscastle had drawn representing Heath's tallywag as an organ of cannon-size proportions.

No. What was disturbing about this particular drawing was that the subject bore a remarkable resemblance to Gabriel. But it wasn't him. In fact, he was amused that Heath even considered it a possibility.

"You're assuming that this handsome rogue is me," he said with a dark scowl.

"You're assuming that you're handsome," Heath countered. "And are you saying this man isn't you? I will not doubt your word, but I do need to ask."

"I confess I have no idea what you're talking about. What exactly has this Mayfair scoundrel done?"

Heath settled deeper into his chair. "Broken into the bedrooms of several young ladies—"

"Welcome or unwelcome?"

"Unwelcome, definitely."

"Well, it wasn't me. I never break into a bedroom without an invitation."

"And he's rifled through their drawers, searching for some unspecified object—"

"That was *not me*," Gabriel said with confidence. "I've never gone through a woman's drawers without knowing exactly what I was looking for."

"Nobody has actually accused you. Or even named you."

Gabriel folded his arms over his chest. "That's not surprising, considering it wasn't me."

"I never said it was."

Gabriel glanced at the door, his attention diverted. He thought he heard footsteps outside the room, which was not surprising since Heath housed a small academy for young ladies who were awaiting a new location. His sister Emma had opened the school, and although now married to the Duke of Scarfield, she had not abandoned her charges.

He stood up, restless, and increasingly offended. "Did you honestly think I'd break into a woman's bedroom?"

"Not without good reason. Oh, and there are purportedly a few gentlemen's offices that were searched, too. It must be a coincidence, Gabriel, that the intruder matches your description. I pray you accept my apologies."

"Whoever he is, I hope he enjoys himself."

"Where are you going?" Heath said.

Gabriel turned. "To enjoy *myself*. Perhaps I can invent a few novel crimes to stir up some legitimate accusations."

Heath trailed him to the door. "I could come for a few hours to keep you company."

Gabriel laughed. "To keep a watch over me, you mean. Your informants must be quite persuasive."

"Not necessarily. But they do tend to be reliable, and, they say, where there's smoke—"

"—there's usually a Boscastle," Gabriel finished. "Or more than one. Stay home with your wife, Heath. Treasure the peace you have earned. I shall be fine alone. We can meet at Tattersalls tomorrow if you have the time."

"In the market for a new carriage?"

Gabriel paused as Heath's butler opened the door

to the London night. More than ever he wanted to see Alethea again. "I thought I might breed thoroughbreds."

Heath nodded in approval. "A cavalryman could make a worse choice for his future."

Chapter Fifteen

❦❦

He spent two hours at Arthur's Club on St. James's Street, not engaging in play but offering advice to a few old friends. He wasn't in the mood for gaming. His concentration felt off. He was relieved, in fact, that no one noticed when he left the club and took a hackney to a disreputable establishment in Pall Mall that catered to high-ranking players. The same hell in which he had won Helbourne.

Several gentlemen glanced up to acknowledge him. A waiter brought him a glass of porter and took his coat. "Good to see you back, sir."

"Have I been gone that long?"

"The tables have missed you. And more than a few ladies in London, I've been advised."

"It's only been what—a fortnight?" Gabriel said wryly.

"Is that all, sir?" The waiter hovered at Gabriel's side, dropping his voice. "Your plucked pigeon has come home to roost on his empty rafter every night."

"Has he met with any luck?"

"No, sir. As the rumor goes he got into family trouble for staking Helbourne Hall and wants to win it back."

"Does he now?"

"He's gone to his annuity-broker and attorney to try to arrange a sale," a man approaching him remarked. He was an old gambling friend, Lord Riverdale, a happily wed father of five who shared Gabriel's attraction to the tables.

"I suppose he's found out that the title deed is ironclad and I am indeed the owner of the unfortunate property?"

"You don't want a farmhouse edged in a quagmire, do you?" Riverdale asked in a droll undertone.

Gabriel shrugged. "It might be of use one day. I'm of a mind to begin breeding thoroughbreds."

"Ah. Who is she? Does *she* like the house?"

"She's a neighbor and she detests it, with good reason."

"A place to breed horses," Riverdale mused. "Well, why—"

"Has Sir Gabriel chosen corruption or the country?" a slurred male voice interjected from a corner table. "We took odds. I am relieved to see corruption won out."

Gabriel looked up in irritation. Damn if it wasn't Oliver Webster, the jinglebrains who had gambled Helbourne Hall away. "What are you trying to lose tonight?"

Webster took Gabriel's question as an invitation

to challenge him to a game of écarté at his table. Gabriel accepted, and the two men cut to decide who would deal. Webster lost.

"I'd like to win Helbourne back," he announced. "I've missed that old bat."

"Mrs. Miniver?"

"No. The one on the wall."

Gabriel grinned. "Interesting. There must be buried treasure in the family crypt."

Webster frowned. "There's nothing valuable there of which I'm aware. It's a hideous old place, but losing it has made me look like an idiot."

"Helbourne isn't in the pot," Gabriel said. "How about three thousand?"

Webster shrugged, watching Gabriel deal them five cards each.

"Why don't you go home?" Gabriel asked mildly, glancing down at the table.

Webster flushed. "Easy for you to say when you're up. I'm not exactly welcome there right now."

Gabriel laughed, although he was no longer paying attention. He dealt the king faceup as the eleventh card. Webster snorted.

"Point," Gabriel said, without inflection.

Webster called for new cards and motioned the waiter for another bottle. Gabriel's advantage stood. The game continued, Gabriel winning most of the tricks, concentrating until suddenly he glanced around, sensing that he was being watched.

Two familiar gentlemen wearing demonical grins

flanked the doorway. His cousins Drake and Devon Boscastle, not in this hell by any coincidence. He nodded in wry acknowledgment. "Don't tell me your wives have unleashed you for the night."

Drake approached first, his smile cynical. "They're the ones who sent us to keep an eye on you."

"He won my house," Webster complained. "It seems only fair that I have a chance to win it back."

Gabriel shook his head. He'd lost interest in the game, more pleased to see his cousins than he would show. They'd blazed through enough hells in their bachelor days, but he knew it was Heath who'd likely sent them— Heath didn't *really* believe he was the man raising mischief in Mayfair?

"I'm going to Tattersalls tomorrow. I've my eye on an Arab to enhance my country stables."

Devon, the youngest Boscastle of the London brood, leaned against the heavily draped window, his long frame relaxed. "Is it true you're rusticating?"

"Trust me," Riverdale said, studying his glass. "There's a woman involved."

Webster vigorously shook his head. "Trust me. There aren't any beddable women in Helbourne. Not any worth mentioning—well, except for Alethea Claridge, and she might as well live on Olympus."

Drake Boscastle circled the card table. He and Gabriel shared an alike darkness of brooding countenance and broad-shouldered strength. "Why doesn't she count? Is she married?"

"She was betrothed to poor Hazlett," Webster said, "until he got his guts blown out by a cannonball. She hasn't been herself since, from what everyone tells me. All she did when I was there was ride her horses and walk her dogs. Didn't have the time of day for me. Don't know why."

Drake regarded Gabriel's downbent face. "Well, sometimes all a mournful lady needs is a little consolation, a sympathetic shoulder to cry on."

Webster made a rude noise. "Are we playing cards or having a tea party to benefit the bereaved?"

"Five points. Game." Gabriel leaned back in his chair. "And may we change the subject?"

Webster narrowed his eyes. "Don't tell me that Alethea Claridge has caught your eye, Gabriel. She's above every man in this club."

Gabriel raised his hard stare from the table. He realized his cousins were awaiting his reaction, as were the other men within earshot. "Lady Alethea is merely my neighbor, and an old acquaintance. I would not refer to her as if she were a courtesan."

"Perhaps that's what she'll end up one day," said a slender barrister who had sauntered up to the table. "I saw the lady pay a visit to Mrs. Watson's house late one night last year. She caught my eye. What a beauty."

Gabriel stood, his face taut with anger. "You do not value your life, do you?"

Drake's hand fell on his shoulder. "Caution, cousin," he murmured. "If you engage the moron in a duel over the lady's honor, it will only give people cause to wonder if his words bear merit."

"But he won't be saying anything if I kill him," Gabriel pointed out. "And do not play the hypocrite, *cousin*. You've fought more than one duel over a woman in your time."

Drake's eyes glistened. "Of course I have. But it's much easier giving another advice when one's own heart is not involved."

Gabriel felt a shock go through his body. "My heart is not involved," he said quickly. "I hardly know the lady well enough to risk my life on her account."

"I thought you met her years ago," Devon said with a guileless smile.

Gabriel scowled. The devils knew him too well. "We spoke but a few words."

Devon nodded sagely. "Ofttimes an affair is all the better for not speaking. I have learned the wisdom of holding my tongue when Jocelyn is upset."

"Would you both stop trying to be so bloody helpful? I want this slack-jaw to take back what he said. And to never say it again."

Drake and Devon turned the full power of their intimidating Boscastle presence on the other man, for whether they agreed with Gabriel or not, he had thrown down the gauntlet, and Boscastle blood was thicker than brandy.

A sheen of perspiration broke out on the barrister's upper lip. He pulled a silk handkerchief from his pocket. Every eye in the room was now trained upon him.

"Perhaps I—I made a mistake."

Gabriel exhaled. "Perhaps?"

"Well, it was dark."

"It usually is at night," Drake said.

The barrister's voice cracked a little. "Come to think of it, the woman I saw was wearing a hat with one of those veils."

"Are you even sure it was a woman?" Devon asked, his arms folded across his chest.

The barrister took pause. "Well, of course—I'm sure." He swallowed as the power of their combined stares conspired against his nerve. "No. You're absolutely right, and as a man of a legal mind I should have reconsidered. In retrospect, it could have been the prime minister's wife—"

"Or the prime minister," Devon said.

"It might have been," the barrister said.

Drake forced a laugh. "There you have it, Gabriel. All's well, isn't it? You've won. Shall we enjoy what's left of our night? I do not travel abroad often since I am married."

Chapter Sixteen

❧ ❧

Less than an hour later the three Boscastle men were sitting in Drake's parked carriage in front of Audrey Watson's exclusive brothel on Bruton Street. Drake and Devon had watched in dispassionate silence as Gabriel loosened his cravat and downed half a bottle of fine French brandy.

Mrs. Watson's guards had emerged from the house to investigate. Upon recognizing the Boscastles, the bordello sentinels had immediately withdrawn, only to return a minute later with another bottle of brandy and a personal invitation from the proprietress herself to come inside. The three men politely declined.

At length a wind blew up, bringing fine rain. Gabriel, staring through the window, appeared not to notice. One of Drake's two footmen coughed in a subtle bid for consideration. The coachman, an older man who had spent many more years in his master's service and was less inclined to subtlety, stamped his heavily booted feet upon the box.

Gabriel slumped back against the carriage seat,

one hand covering his face. Of course the barrister had been mistaken, or there was a perfectly good explanation. Perhaps Hazlett had kept a mistress through Mrs. Watson, and the two women had wished to meet and, well, do whatever two females did when they realized they had been sharing the same man and that now he was dead. He wasn't going to insult Alethea by asking about it.

In fact, it wasn't in his best interest at all to remind her she had loved another man. He would be a gentleman and pretend he'd never heard anything about the mysterious visit she may or may not have paid to the exclusive seraglio on Bruton Street.

The problem was, unfortunately, that Gabriel had never cared until recently whether he was seen as a gentleman or not and had himself sought entry into this establishment. But he'd never seen a lady like Alethea in any of the rooms.

Certainly Alethea had not since her betrothed's death embarked on the merry life of a courtesan. Gabriel would have claimed her on the spot had he sensed that she was in the market for a protector. No. For his money she was what she appeared to be: a pretty young woman whose sensual potential would be buried in the country unless some sharp-witted squire won her attention.

Devon, not the most patient of the Boscastle males, finally nudged Gabriel with his foot. "Well, go on. Audrey's given you the invite. See what you can find out. We can't sit here like gawking school-boys."

"I don't want to go inside," Gabriel said stubbornly.

Drake snorted. "Well, that's a chapter for the history books. You never refused before, as I recall. Just go in and get it over with. When a man's heart is involved in these things, it is useless to evade the truth."

Gabriel shook his head indignantly. "Why do you insist upon saying that my heart is involved?"

"If this isn't a matter of the heart," Devon said, "it must be something corporeal, and I don't doubt Audrey's got an answer for that, too."

Gabriel's mouth thinned. "You're so glib and well liked, why don't you go inside and do the honors?"

"Me?" Devon held up his palms. "I'm a devoted husband, and I got into trouble once before over a visit to Audrey's. Jocelyn would crown me if it happened again, as innocent as I was."

Gabriel turned to regard Drake, who said bluntly, "No. My days of private sessions at Audrey's are over. The fact that we've been sitting here for an hour will probably be reported in the papers, and I shall be hard-pressed to explain it. What do you say, Gabriel?"

He smiled in resignation. "I say there's no balm in Gilead or in London for me. We leave."

Chapter Seventeen

❧ ❧

A simple roast beef with buttered potatoes and blancmange? Leg of mutton with braised cabbage and fruit compote? Alethea had reviewed the menu for Friday night's supper a dozen times over. She'd heard from Mrs. Bryant, who'd heard from Mrs. Miniver that Gabriel had gone to London for a few days on some unspecified business. And when on Thursday morning the blue September skies darkened and angry thunderheads amassed above the hills, she tried not to take it as an omen or to be concerned that he had not returned. Or to wonder whether he would come back at all.

She brought the cows in and, despite her brother's steward Wilkins protesting, helped hammer up all the holes in the chick house and dovecote. She also made certain that Wilkins posted another sign on the bridge to Helbourne Hall—a good rain would wash out the stream, the local road, and anything else, living or not, that happened onto its path. The physical activity settled her nerves. A country gentlewoman could not afford to sit in idleness.

On Thursday afternoon a storm swept in from the coast. Alethea barely had time for her after-tea ride, which included a run past Helbourne Hall, and no, she was *not* checking on whether Gabriel had returned. She rode by his house every morning as part of her daily exercise.

But the rain broke in earnest just as she galloped up the drive. By nightfall Gabriel's fields, fallow and unplanted, would be awash in mud. She doubted he cared.

Once upon a time she had believed in fairy tales. She had trusted the handsome prince her parents had chosen for her until he stole not only her virtue but her faith in happy endings. Therefore, it made no sense that she hoped to tame a man who had never pretended virtue at her table. And yet she did.

She was drenched to the lining of her cloak when she returned home. Shivering yet determined to stay in good spirits, she ordered the servants to carry to the dining hall two Gothic candlesticks that stood over seven feet high. She bought a basketful of flowers from the gypsies who came to the door even though Mrs. Sudley chided her gently for the extravagance and muttered that they'd been stolen from Alethea's own garden.

And if he did not return by Friday, Alethea would know he was a lost cause once and for all.

She had done her best. She had even invited a handful of their mutual neighbors to supper to make Gabriel's acquaintance and to play a friendly game of cards.

If Gabriel chose to decline her invitation, it would only reflect badly upon his manners and prove what everyone in Helbourne privately thought of him.

Everyone, unfortunately, except her; she did not understand why she persisted in trying to prove the rest of the parish wrong.

Chapter Eighteen

✤◦ ◦✤

On Friday morning, during a steady downpour, two messages arrived separately for Alethea. One was sent by her brother, explaining that he had been forced to stay another day due to the inclement weather and would likely return on Saturday morning. He would not worry Alethea by riding in a storm.

The other came from Gabriel and informed her that she should expect him at the table, storm or clear skies, and please, would she forgive him if he appeared a little the worse for wear? He expected to arrive directly at her house and would not have time to change into fresh attire.

Alethea drove her long-suffering cook to distraction. "What do you think, Mrs. Hooper? Is Sir Gabriel an epicure or not?"

The ruddy-faced servant frowned at this question. "Well, that's hard to answer. He was born in England, wasn't he, and he rode in the cavalry. So I'd guess—"

Alethea restrained a grin. "Are you of the opinion that he's not a fancy eater?"

"I don't have to make turtle soup, do I? I'm not at all partial to these foreign dishes."

"Good heavens, no. I was thinking of a tasty rump and one of your delicious plum puddings."

Mrs. Hooper nodded in agreement. "Hearty English fare. I draw the line at serving snails at my table. Sir Gabriel appears to be a healthy young man who would not appreciate grubs for supper."

"I can't imagine Sir Gabriel would eat snails, either," she said.

"Well, soldiers have to make do under tough circumstances. Trust me, my lady, to set a proper table."

"Your culinary talents are not in question," Alethea said. "Only whether our guest of honor will be here to appreciate them."

Gabriel had made good time from London, determined the miserable weather would not deter him. He'd set out before sunbreak Friday and arrived at Helbourne Hall with barely an hour in which to bathe and change into his evening clothes. With luck he would cut a presentable figure at supper. At any rate, it was a short ride to Alethea's house, the rain had eased, and he wasn't going to embarrass himself by showing up late.

Still, it took a deucedly frustrating half hour he had not anticipated to travel the long way through the woods. He wished belatedly that he had taken the time to have the bridge reinforced. As he cantered past the ominous point of crossing, he half-fancied that he heard the unsettled spirits of the

young girl and her murderer who had perished
there a century past.

"Fool," he said to himself.

When had he started believing in ghosts?

When, in fact, had he ever given a thought to star-
crossed lovers at all? Or to love, for that matter?

Alethea hurried through the hall, opened the front
door, and stepped out onto the rain-splotched steps.
The small park that enclosed the estate glistened
darkly in the moonlight as if it had been sprinkled
with diamonds. She breathed in the dampness with
a shiver of pleasure. Something magical sparkled in
the air. She thought it might be hope.

"You'll ruin your hair, my lady, and your dress,"
warned the housekeeper. "No sane person is going
to come to supper in this weather. A shame, though,
all that good food going to waste."

Alethea wasn't paying the least attention. She was
staring in delight at the dark-clad rider who'd just
emerged from the woods. Gabriel, more handsome
than she could bear, but *here*. He'd kept his word.
She ran down the steps to greet him, lifting her
hand to her mouth when she saw the muck stains
on his black Hessian boots and silk-lined evening
cloak.

He grinned, dismounting before her. One of the
grooms dashed across the grass to take Gabriel's
horse. "Someone ought to repair that bridge," he
said. "I shall have a firm talk with the property
owner."

"Oh, dear," she said in sympathy, lowering her hand. "You've ruined your fine clothes."

"You're getting wet, too." Although it was obvious that she would look elegant in anything she wore. Or nothing. Especially nothing. His breath hitched at the thought of rain sluicing over her nude body, of being invited to warm her with his hands, his mouth. He supposed he couldn't kiss her outside without the risk of being seen.

"Gabriel?"

He cleared his throat. "Yes?"

"Is there any reason that we're standing out here?" she asked with a fleeting smile that hinted that she guessed what he was thinking. No. Not likely. Alethea was as pure-hearted as they came, one of those innocents who always gave the benefit of the doubt to men like him who did not deserve it.

"Are we waiting for your brother?" he asked, looking past her to the house.

She smiled. "My brother won't be joining us, unfortunately. He sent his regrets. And he does remember you."

Gabriel hid a grimace. He could imagine that what Lord Wrexham remembered of him was not flattering—all the fights at school, the pranks he played. The more the earl reflected upon those days, alas, the less liable he would be to encourage Alethea to invite Gabriel's company.

She bit her lip as if she were tempted to laugh. "Come inside. Vickers, my brother's valet, is home." She wheeled, taking his hand. "He'll brush off the mud. It's not as if he isn't used to it. And if you're going to stay—"

She stopped, suddenly releasing his hand. "You grew up in the country. I expect I'm not telling you anything you don't know."

He smiled. "I don't mind. I've probably forgotten what I knew. My life here was—"

"—not pleasant? That I remember. But things are different now."

He brushed his gloved fingers across her cheek. "You're getting soaked."

"I don't mind the rain," she said, her voice as soft as smoke.

"Neither do I." He tracked a damp rivulet of raindrops down her neck to her shoulder. "We can have supper out here if you like. All we'll miss is the candlelight."

"Oh, Gabriel." She shook her head as if coming to her senses. "For a soldier I do believe there's a bit of the poet in your soul."

"You're joking."

"Can you never accept a compliment?"

"I don't know. I might the day I deserve one."

Come on," she said. "I can hear a carriage coming down the road."

"You really did invite other guests?"

She stared at him in astonishment. "Did you think you were coming to supper here alone?"

A smile crossed his hard, sun-bronzed face. "I wouldn't have minded."

Chapter Nineteen

❦ ❧

She gave him directions to her brother's chamber, summoned Vickers, and escaped to her own room to tidy her hair. Naturally it had taken on a life on its own, curling wildly in every direction that defied her comb. She had never seen Gabriel in evening wear, but his dark elegance had left her breathless and determined to look her best. She began to ring for her maid, then stopped to regard her bedraggled reflection in the mirror.

"This," she said in distaste, "is what becomes of young women who spend too much time with horses. Oh, bother, look at that dress. Only a feather-brain would stand in the rain wearing light green silk. *I'm* the scandal of the parish, not Gabriel."

She'd have to change, and hurry. She could hear voices conversing belowstairs, her invited guests having braved the rain to sup with her. She ought at least not to look like an urchin.

She removed a thin lemon-gauze dinner gown from her wardrobe, reaching back to unhook her dress. The door behind her opened. She muttered,

"I was just about to ring for you, Joan. I've three minutes to look presentable, and if you could help with these hooks—"

"I can do it in two."

She pivoted in shock, staring up into Gabriel's laughing blue eyes. His cropped black hair had been brushed to a crisp sheen, his cloak discarded, the mud whisked from his tailored evening coat and tight-fitting pantaloons. Gabriel, a devil of beauty as she had never seen him. And what did she look like? A half-dressed slattern with hair like a haystack.

What *was* he doing in her room? And why did she not order him out immediately?

"Allow me," he said.

"Allow you to what?"

"To make you look presentable." His warm perusal warned her that presentability was not foremost on his mind, a suspicion he proved by adding, "Although I'll be damned if I have ever seen a more fetching sight than you right now."

A wave of wicked excitement swept over her. He was gorgeous, arrogant, amusing . . . and alone with her in her bedroom.

She said, "You shouldn't be seeing me at all."

"Do you have a stocking I may use as a blindfold?" he asked, the glitter in his blue eyes belying his polite inquiry.

"A stocking?"

"I am trying, Alethea, to be a gentleman."

She had never heard such an absurd claim in her

life. And while she stood there utterly immobilized, he reached around her shoulders and expertly unhooked her gown.

She choked back a cry of indignation. "Gabriel Boscastle," she said in a breathless voice that made her sound like some silly chit greeting an admirer at her first assembly.

"That was *not* the act of a gentleman."

He shrugged casually. "I only said I was trying, not that I would succeed."

"Well, try harder." She glanced around for a shawl with which to cover either herself or his handsome, mocking face. "Go downstairs and have a brandy."

"Shall I bring one up for you?"

"*No.* Go and introduce yourself to anyone who may have arrived."

"Do I look tidy enough for your party?" he asked with a boyish grin clearly designed to disarm her. He was wearing a loose ruffled muslin shirt beneath his long-tailored jacket.

She sighed.

He feigned a frown. "Is it the ruffles? I've never been much of a man for frills and furbelows."

"You are in my bedchamber!"

"I must have gotten lost." He ran his hand lightly over her half-bare shoulder. "Or else I have unerring instincts."

"You have the devil's instincts," she muttered.

"Darling," he chided. "Is that any way to talk to a guest?"

"The door is right behind you." She shivered delicately. His fingers were wreaking lovely havoc on her shoulder. "Do the dressing table and the bed give the impression of a dining hall?"

He glanced around distractedly. "Come to think of it, no." He drew her closer to him. "I must admit, however, that you whet my appetite more than anything I've ever been served at a banquet." His voice deepened. "Is that your bed?"

She took a breath, tried not to think of what he had in mind. Tried not to picture herself lying beneath him on her bed, his strong body over hers. "Yes."

He paused. "Where you sleep?"

"I should think that would be obvious."

"Right under that window?" he asked, peering past her.

"Do you want a description of the roof? The eaves?"

"I can see your room from mine."

"How do you know it's mine?" she asked unthinkingly.

A grin curved his lips.

"Gabriel," she said in a whisper. "You are in my brother's house, and as such—"

"I love your hair loose," he said quietly. "I never dreamt it was that long and lustrous. Why don't you wear it down more often? You look like one of those Italian princesses in a painting."

"A lady of our time observes certain rules," she

managed to get out, "and a gentleman today does not—"

"—take advantage?"

Which he did, rubbing his closely shaven cheek against hers before he claimed her mouth in a hard, unapologetic kiss. And then another until her mouth softened under his gentle aggression. His hand locked around her waist, pulling her against his body until she felt herself yield to his strength.

Dangerous? Without a doubt.

But like a fire in the midst of winter, the heat he offered beckoned. And if she burned herself, would that not be better than the cold isolation of the past year?

Overwhelming, the warmth of his mouth on hers. Surely winter did not last forever.

"Gabriel . . ."

When she parted her lips it was with the intent to object, but then he teased his tongue deep into her mouth. His face blurred in the candlelight. She was slipping, unstable, caught between dark and light, between surrender and self-protection.

"I rode all the way back from London in the rain to be here," he murmured.

"For supper," she reminded him shakily.

"I'm sorry." He dragged his mouth against her cheek. "I can't help myself. You're everything lovely and pure, and—"

She shook her head in bemusement. "Then why am I kissing you?"

He traced the curve of her hip with his fingertips.

"Because I'm everything dangerous and bad, a temptation to the pure, and I always have been." He paused, his eyes glinting. "Do you want me to help you take off your dress?"

"What?" she asked, giggling as if she'd misheard him.

"I know it isn't proper, but as I am here, I might as well prove I'm capable of the deed. I hate to stand about being useless."

Alethea placed her hand against his firmly muscled chest, wondering why his low voice thrilled her when it should have sent her running. Proper. Improper. Once the lines that delineated her behavior had been clearly etched. She had known whom to marry, to befriend, to trust. Now the image of what should be was tainted. She could not judge by the past.

Nor could she ever go back to what she had been in her Eden years, although she doubted she would ever become what a man like Gabriel would inevitably desire. Ruined or not, she could not give herself to a life of pleasure without love.

She drew an unsteady breath. He had already pried free the impossible hooks of her dress. And while she had been lost in thought, resting in his embrace, he had also untied her chemise at one shoulder.

Wicked, enterprising man. Perhaps she had not invited his seduction, but had she done anything to discourage it?

"Gabriel," she said sternly.

His beautifully sculpted mouth grazed the tops of her breasts. By some dark magic he had unfastened those bindings, too. She gave a gasp, her knees folding in unwilling submission. Sensations, forbidden and thrilling, cascaded over her. Her nipples tightened. Deep in her belly a pulsing warmth pooled. She savored the strange pleasure for several moments more.

"The devil, Gabriel," she whispered, feeling his arms support her. "I did *not* invite you here for this."

They stumbled back, sank to the chair beside her wardrobe, his outsplayed thighs supporting her. She raised her hand, her earnest intention to push him away. Instead, she draped her arm over his shoulder in a gesture that spoke more of surrender than assertion.

It was a subtlety of language he understood all too well.

"I do apologize," he muttered, his eyes feverish, a bright hot blue.

"I should think so."

He looked up briefly from her unfastened bodice. "If you were not a lady in the truest meaning of the word, the most decent one to ever grace my pathetic life, I would—"

She pressed her finger to his lips. "I hope this is not meant to be an example of your restraint."

"Trust me, Alethea. For you I have locked shackles around my desires and swallowed the key."

"You've grown into a man without principle."

"Do you think I could change?"

"Not in time for supper." She reached back awkwardly to draw her gaping corset together. "*Oh*. How am I going to explain arriving late to my own party and barely able to—"

His mouth flattened in a cynical smile. "You seem to be having difficulty breathing. Perhaps I should further loosen your stays?"

"If I cannot breathe properly, it has *nothing* to do with the tightness of my lacings."

"Ah." His sensual voice sent a shiver down her arms. "Then I may assume that there is only one other reason?"

She gave a slight shake of her head. Far be it from her to admit that he had managed to unravel more than her bindings. And if she did not gather her wits, she would find herself completely undone in every sense of the word.

"Do you know why ladies are so tightly laced into their corsets?" he asked, proceeding to pull together her short corset, her gown. "It is not to enhance your lovely forms. It is to keep rakes like me at bay."

She looked away, her reply barely audible. "It doesn't stop the worst of them, though."

Strange response.

He wondered for an unsettling moment what she could mean. If he had not been so caught up in restraining his rakish instincts, he might have had the insight to question her. Weak man of the flesh that he was, however, he was wholly absorbed in her earthly allure. He wanted any excuse to continue.

He'd had some experience with innocence.

He was better versed in darker pleasures.

I saw the lady pay a visit to Mrs. Watson's house late one night.

Yet Gabriel would swear for all he was worth that she was innocent. Alethea had probably never even heard of Mrs. Watson, and even if she had, she would be too well-bred to admit it.

"I hear someone coming," she whispered in alarm.

He didn't. Or perhaps he did but was hoping to ignore it. He was painfully aroused. He couldn't hide it from her. Through the layers of their clothing his erection reared against her in rampant demand. If he did not regain his self-mastery, he would— God, he'd do anything if she would grant him her favor, invite him to her bed.

His frank gaze met hers. "Is there any chance that you desire me as badly as I do you?"

Her slight hesitation gave him hope.

"Please, Gabriel," she said, her eyes dark with emotion. "Do not embarrass us both when I have invited my friends to make your acquaintance. I have spoken well of you. Let me not appear to be deceived."

"Later then?" he asked after a moment. "Will you at least reassure me that I have not made you angry? Will you promise—"

She laughed unwillingly. "I shall not promise you

anything except supper and an evening of country entertainment. And I'm not angry."

"Fair enough." He drew away, his expression amused. "I've no choice but to behave myself and appear a well-mannered guest."

"I shall accept nothing less."

She was a little wary of how easily he had conceded. Weren't scoundrels of his ilk notorious for their seductive persuasion? And indeed, as he allowed her to rise, she noticed the obscure smile that tightened his mouth.

"Beware of false retreats," he said in a mocking voice.

"What do you mean?" she asked, her heart beating in uneven palpitations. Perhaps it was better she did not know.

He stood. He looked as elegantly gorgeous as she did disheveled. "I'm leaving now. If I meet anyone in the hall, I shall simply explain that I lost my way in the dark."

Chapter Twenty

❧ ⚶ ❧

Gabriel walked from her room in bemusement, thinking that his last utterance was not a lie. He did feel lost, and all points of his personal compass directed him to her.

It was the first time in his life that he had abandoned an attempt at seduction because he wanted a woman desperately enough to care what she might think of him afterward. He hoped it meant nothing. Alethea had been interwoven in his past for as long as he could remember. The one woman he'd always dreamed of possessing. If she had known what he had been thinking while he kissed her, how he had ached to coax her, she would have been justified in taking her crop to him again.

He paused as he reached the top of the stairs. No guests in sight. She was safe from discovery. She wasn't safe from him, though. His entire body pulsed with primal sexuality. He wondered if he would survive supper without giving himself away. He would look a bit peculiar if he crossed his legs all night. Was that how the custom of placing a napkin across one's lap had originated?

"Sir," an anxious young male voice inquired. "Is anything wrong?"

Gabriel glanced downward at the under-footman who'd appeared at the bottom of the stairs. "I'm fine, thank you."

He wished he could reassure her that he wasn't anything like the rebel pillory boy she remembered. Unfortunately, *he* wasn't convinced that he was much different now. Apparently, she hadn't heard that he'd half-murdered his stepfather a week before the nasty bugger had ended up getting himself killed in a tavern brawl. A good thing, too. Gabriel knew it would have only been a matter of time before he murdered John for the numerous abuses to which he had subjected Gabriel's mother.

There was something different about Alethea, though, and it wasn't anything he could identify.

She still flustered him. And he thought he flustered her.

But he'd begun to notice at certain moments a cynicism about her that he would not have expected. Well, she had lost her true love, the man chosen by her parents, who had guarded her from little beasts like Gabriel. And with good reason.

He didn't want to believe that the sadness he saw in her was simply grief over the man she had chosen first. That she was the sort of woman who could only love once.

But it was the obvious answer.

Chapter Twenty-one

✤ ❦ ❧

Alethea's older cousin, Lady Miriam Pontsby, a likable busybody in her early forties, detained Alethea before she made her entrance into the formal dining room. Lady Pontsby had not been officially invited. However, she was a beloved relation, with the instinct of a bloodhound for change in the air, and the minute she'd heard that her cousin was entertaining one of the notorious Boscastle men, she'd driven herself and her husband in her creaky carriage the entire five rainy miles that lay between her home and the earl's.

Lady Pontsby shivered melodramatically as a footman divested her of her damp cloak. "I came as fast as I could, Alethea, when I learned who was to be your guest of honor. Blackguard, Boscastle, gambler. And your dear brother is not here to protect you. Why didn't you let me know earlier?"

Alethea smiled with fondness at her short, plump cousin. "I think I'm safe enough. The vicar and his wife are here. And there wasn't any need to alarm you."

"Did your brother propose to Emily yet?" Miriam asked.

"I believe he's still working up the courage."

"It has been a year!" Miriam exclaimed. "Whatever is he waiting for?"

Miriam smothered the impulse to ask the same of her young female cousin. To her practical way of thinking, a woman did not fail if she made a less-than-perfect marriage. She only failed if she did not marry at all. Alethea's plight drove her to distraction. Neither a widow nor a spinster, not exactly fresh on the marriage mart, she presented a problem not covered under the rules of good society.

It was bad luck that Alethea's betrothed had met his end on the battlefield. The well brought up could not bring themselves to discuss the vulgar details of Jeremy's undignified demise. He was gone, unfortunately, and nothing could change that.

But what to do about the lady he had left behind? Miriam was at her wit's end. Alethea spent her spare hours riding horses and tending farm animals instead of searching for a new husband. Never mind mourning. Nobody in Helbourne observed all of Society's silly dictums.

And now her pretty young cousin, through the hands of an unfathomable fate, had attracted a Boscastle male to her supper table. Was Alethea already bewitched? She had not shown an interest in another man since Jeremy's death, or even before, that Miriam recalled. What had come over her to invite a member of London's roguish family to the house while Robin was gone?

Miriam had not wasted a moment in speeding to Helbourne to oversee this perplexing state of affairs. The very least she could do, as a dutiful country relation, was to ensure that her heartbroken cousin was not lured into an illicit arrangement with a man of Sir Gabriel's indecent charm.

"I understand your desire, my dear, to offer hospitality to a neighbor," Miriam went on as her husband escorted them to the dining hall. "But what if he intends to turn Helbourne into one of those hamlets where men debauch unwilling—or willing—maidens and hold an orgy every full moon?"

Alethea and Lord Pontsby shared a smile over Miriam's head. "Single-handedly?" Pontsby murmured.

"I imagine there are more scoundrels where he comes from," Miriam said. "That family is full of them."

Alethea lifted her brow. "Did you know that he and I were actually born less than a mile apart? And that his—"

"The good people of this parish, you included, Alethea, would expire of embarrassment were you to gaze out the window one moonlit night to witness noblemen chasing naked ladies up and down the hills."

"Why don't we wait to address that issue when and if it occurs?" Alethea bit her lower lip. "Although I daresay it would be a less alarming sight

than that of Squire Higgins running about in the altogether after his broody hen."

Miriam whitened. "Your darling mama is frowning down at me from her heavenly abode for being
remiss in my duty toward you."

Alethea paused in the doorway. Never one to
stand upon formality, she'd encouraged the footman to seat those guests who had arrived early.

She had not, however, expected that every person
she'd invited to supper, and a few she had not,
would brave the rain to grace her table. She had a
full house on her hands. Wilkins had already
brought in a half-dozen chairs from the music
room.

The main attraction strolled up behind her, wide-
shouldered, hair and soul as dark as midnight, a
man who had not only addled the wits of his hostess, but had also apparently unsettled the collective
composure of her five suddenly attentive female
supper guests. Make that six, she amended silently
as Miriam turned to Gabriel with a chastening
frown that quickly dissolved into a look of dumb-
foundment. In fact, her cousin appeared so befud-
dled by the sight of Sir Gabriel in the flesh that
Alethea almost wished for her prior disapproval.

"Miriam." She wiggled her elbow into her
cousin's side. "*Blackguard, Boscastle, gambler.* Remember?"

"I don't believe *everything* the gossips tell me,"
Miriam breathed, pressing herself against the door
with a sigh as Gabriel bowed.

"Madam," he murmured, his voice deep with irony, "I have not had the pleasure—"

Miriam glanced distractedly at Alethea. "One of England's finest families," she whispered from the side of her mouth. "Pray do not faint and spoil the evening. I see possibilities in your future I had not expected. My previous remarks derived from ignorance, and I admit it."

Alethea caught firm hold of her cousin's arm, speaking in an undertone, "Think of wicked noblemen, Miriam. Imagine yourself naked—being chased into the blackguard's arms."

Miriam's gloved hand fluttered in a spiral to her shoulder. "What if Society has misjudged him?" she whispered with a thoughtful smile. "Do we have proof that he is a rogue? Shall we stoop to scandal and slander those who may most benefit us?"

Gabriel directed a guileless smile at Alethea. "Have I done something wrong?"

She glanced away before her guilty blush betrayed her. "I do hope you like ordinary country fare, Sir Gabriel. A well-done roast and pudding."

He studied her for a few reckless moments, then offered her his arm. "It is what I grew up on."

"And it did not do you a bit of harm, by the look of it," Lady Pontsby said, striding forward with her husband.

Alethea released the faintest of sighs and fixed a smile upon her face as she and Gabriel prepared to separate and take their respective seats. When her cousin looked back at her with a sly grin, she pretended not to notice and said, "Sir Gabriel has dined at many tables since his early life. I do hope our country hospitality does not bore him."

He smiled gallantly. "I need only a peaceful evening to entertain me."

Alethea's lips parted. "I shall remind you of that if you start to fall asleep."

"With you in the same room?" he asked, grinning wickedly. "Your presence would raise a dead man from his grave."

She shook her head. "Do not dare to say anything like that at supper."

"Why not?"

"Oh—just sit down, Gabriel. Eat your supper and be a nice guest."

His grin widened. "Will you be a nice hostess if I do?"

Chapter Twenty-two

❧ ❧

At her silence, he took his seat between a widowed baroness and Lord Pontsby. The baroness immediately engaged him in conversation. "The previous owner of Helbourne Hall was planning to have a grotto built where the oak grove now stands. He consulted a foreign architect for the design."

Oak grove? Gabriel lowered his soupspoon, striving to appear respectful as he racked his brain. He wanted desperately to make a good impression. But where the bloody hell on his estate was the oak grove? "Ah," he said, trying to catch Alethea's attention. "The oak grove. Not a bad idea for a grotto, is it?"

The silver-haired baroness looked sweetly distraught. "We understand that your predecessor meant for this edifice to be used to entrap young women into—well, I expect you know."

Gabriel dropped his spoon. He'd spoken only a few words. How the devil had seducing virgins been laid at his door? He looked across the table again at Alethea for help. Pretending to be unaware of his dilemma, she gave him a vague smile and proceeded to butter her slice of bread.

He coughed lightly. "Well, according to the ancient Druids, an oak grove is a sacred haven for . . ." He didn't exactly know what. He did recall, however, he and his brothers awakening on the occasional midsummer sunrise to watch the village girls gather to greet the dawn. If there had been oak trees in the background, none of the boys had noticed or cared.

"You're rather tall to be a Druid, aren't you?" the baroness ventured after a few moments of silence. "Dark enough, but not at all diminutive."

He met Alethea's amused gaze. "I don't think Sir Gabriel is admitting to any pagan tendencies, Lady Brimwell."

"Well, what is he admitting to?" the Reverend Peter Bryant joked. "Speak up, Sir Gabriel. I've heard all manner of sins confessed."

Alethea shook her head. "Not at my supper table. You may have my guest at another time, if you please."

"What I'm saying," Gabriel continued, realizing that he was actually enjoying himself without gambling, drinking heavily, or accumulating more sins upon his mortal soul, "is that the trees are pretty and despoiling innocents is not."

Not that Gabriel had ever given more than a fleeting thought to the innocents. However, if God struck the guilty or hypocritical dead, he would soon be felled by a righteous lightning bolt through the roof. He glanced up in expectation from the table. Luckily no such divine retribution occurred. Perhaps God was saving his vengeance for a time when Gabriel least expected it.

A gambler at heart who could not resist taking a risk, he added and actually meant, "There shall be no grottoes built for any illicit purposes as long as I remain at Helbourne." An ordinary bedchamber was good enough.

"And how long shall you remain, Sir Gabriel?" Alethea asked, her fingers tracing the stem of her goblet.

Damned if he knew. It was on the tip of his tongue to reply that his decision depended on her. But he had already resolved to put Helbourne on the market and return to London, hadn't he?

He said, "I'm sure you shall all be tired of me before I leave."

And if he eluded a definite response, he was certain he had not deceived Alethea. She carefully changed the subject and looked up as the main course arrived at the table. Gabriel should have been relieved that she had released him from having to lie.

Instead, he struggled to understand. Why had she shown any interest in him at all? For old times' sake? Because she had a tender spot in her heart for errant boys? He hoped she was not one of those ladies who believed a bent nature could be straightened by a few kind gestures.

The conversation turned from rakes ruining young women to farming. Gabriel talked, as if he had the faintest interest in scaring off crows from cornfields, the fate of country craftsmen, and the upcoming Michaelmas hiring fair; he was reminded to buy his geese early before the good ones went. As if he'd know what to do with them.

At length, fortified with wine, candied nuts, sweetmeats, and cheese, the guests moved into the music room for a game of Slap the Slipper, Gabriel standing shoulder to shoulder with Alethea until it was all he could do not to disgrace himself again. It was almost a relief when he was partnered off to play whist.

He and the vicar sat against Alethea and Mrs. Bryant. As the thirteen cards were dealt, he was hard-pressed to restrain a patronizing smile. It was unfair to wager against these amateurs—and then Mrs. Bryant took the trick, forcing him to drop his condescending attitude and pay attention.

He lost.

"We won against the London gambler," Mrs. Bryant crowed. "Can you credit it, Alethea?"

Alethea feigned a frown. "Aren't we supposed to be ashamed of ourselves for encouraging his pursuit of gambling? At the very least, it doesn't seem right to boast that we took a shilling from him, a man whose activities we criticize."

"Tell him we'll raise the stakes next time," the vicar said in a jovial voice as he rose to leave.

"Will there be a next time?" Gabriel asked casually as he and Alethea walked through the front door into the wet night.

"We haven't bored you?" she asked in surprise. "You would actually come back?"

"Only if I'm welcome. Am I?"

She gave him an artless smile that sharpened the aching desire he had subdued for hours. "Yes," she answered, mischief lighting her eyes. "We shall play more games. Do you like Hunt the Thimble?"

He stared at her, stricken with a sudden need to kiss her throat and all the creamy skin below half-hidden by her curls. "Can we play it alone?"

"I don't think it would be as much fun."

He held her eyes. "I think you might be surprised."

"We'll have to see," she said carefully.

"That sounds promising."

"I'm bringing my two older sisters next time," Mrs. Bryant said behind them as she waited for her cloak. "They won't believe I beat Sir Gabriel."

"Did you let her win?" Alethea inquired under her breath.

"No," he and Caroline answered in unison.

"I suspect, however," Gabriel said with a feigned scowl, "that Mrs. Bryant is an expert cheat."

Mrs. Bryant squared her shoulders. "Can you prove it?"

Gabriel grinned. "Probably. I shall watch you

more closely next time for bent cards and subtle winks. Come to think of it, you did cough quite a bit, and we never riffled the deck for markings."

She looked delighted. "Are you going to challenge me to a duel of honor if I'm caught?"

"What will the weapons be?"

"Bible verses," she said with a wicked chuckle.

"Then I think," he said, laughing helplessly, "that I have just been tricked into making a donation to the parish."

"Never mind the donation," Mrs. Bryant assured him. "It shall suffice that we meet at the table again to give you the chance to redeem yourself."

And Gabriel had no doubt that she did mean at cards, not of a great redemption. The trouble was, which he could hardly admit, that being in close proximity to Alethea might subdue his need to gamble, but it certainly did not lessen his other impulses.

For when he at last departed her company, he realized that of all his past and present pleasures, of all the wages he had won, none equaled the satisfaction of being invited to be in her company and basking in her laughter.

Alethea ran across the paddock in the wet grass and watched him canter off into the mist. What a beautiful sight. He had been a gentleman tonight, after that amorous interlude in her bedroom. Kind to her friends. Even so, she understood that not all gentlemen were gentle in the dark. And that Gabriel most likely thought her resistance to his pursuit was old-fashioned compared with the behavior of the ladies he knew in London.

Everyone knew what he was, and yet everyone in Helbourne liked him, wanted him to prove the rumors wrong. And none more so than Alethea.

He'd reminded her that she still enjoyed a good laugh, that even though Jeremy had violated her with unspeakable cruelty, she would recover.

Gabriel had proven that she was still capable not only of feeling desire but also of suffering from all its incautious urgings. Considering his reputation as an accomplished master of love's art in London, she knew he understood well how to awaken hidden passions.

But that he could make her fall in love with him when she knew what he was—well, she would stop herself.

She refused to fall for another true-love prince after the last one had turned into the king of toads before her horrified eyes. Her first heartbreak.

No. That wasn't exactly true. She had known Gabriel before she'd been introduced to Jeremy at a local christening. It was only fair to grant Gabriel the dubious distinction of being the first boy to break her heart. For he had deeply injured her feelings when she'd risked angering her parents to help him at the pillory.

No one had ever refused her tender gestures before, and so rudely, too. She had always been praised for her ability to show compassion to others. But it had been prideful of her to think a young girl's words of sympathy would be enough to uplift a boy like Gabriel.

And it was probably more so to think a woman could lead him from the path he had chosen.

Chapter Twenty-three

❧ ❧

Thus became established a pattern during the final weeks of summer. Every Friday evening, come fair weather or foul, a light supper party entertained the local gentry at the Earl of Wrexham's country home, his sister Alethea acting as hostess when Robin could not do the honors. Few guests invited failed to attend this lively affair, for it had evolved into naughty fun to challenge Sir Gabriel at cards and claim that one had beaten a professional gamester.

In between he invented one reason after another to meet Alethea on her daily rides until she stopped teasing him about surprising her and he stopped making excuses. Twice he escorted her and Mrs. Bryant on parish calls. This was a practice he vowed not to repeat when one elderly widower they visited informed Alethea that the village schoolmaster had once caught Gabriel writing rude Latin rhymes.

She laughed about this the entire ride home. So did Mrs. Bryant.

"It wasn't me," he insisted. "It was my brother Colin. He had talent."

"For trouble?" Alethea guessed, the ribbons of her bonnet dancing across her white throat. She was sitting awkwardly next to Mrs. Bryant, who drove her gig like Cybele's chariot of lions.

Gabriel rode alongside on his Andalusian, enjoying the view. He'd never been good enough at Latin to think of rhymes, and he couldn't think of one now. He didn't care if she made fun of him. He liked being with her, listening to her voice. But when their eyes met, something sharp went down his spine. And he didn't know if he could stand it.

He looked away, toward the woods.

"Are you coming back for tea?" Mrs. Bryant asked blithely.

He blinked. He thought he saw a figure standing in the trees, so furtive he could have been staring into his past reflection. Tea. He didn't want it, but he would drink it.

By the conclusion of the fifth supper party, each one having ended a little later than the previous, Gabriel could not bring himself to go home. The Earl of Wrexham had gone to visit the parents of the young gentlewoman he wished to marry in London. Lady and Lord Pontsby had departed early, complaining of a bad rheum and each other.

Gabriel politely took his leave.

But like the impolite person he was at heart, he rode around the house in circles until he was certain that every other guest had gone. And then he returned. Alethea came to the door, holding Lady Pontsby's cashmere wrap. "I knew you'd be back for—"

"—you?" He glanced down at the expensive shawl, pursing his lips. "It's not my style. All that fringe and pattern. I'm more of a—"

"—scoundrel?" She crossed her arms across her chest as he invited himself back into the hall, closing the door onto the quiet night. "Or is it housebreaker? Gabriel, I do ask myself what has occupied your time in the intervening years—"

He walked her backward down the hall, beneath armorial shields, his footsteps muffled by the clatter of servants bustling to and fro to clear away the supper dishes and extinguish the wax candles that had illuminated the dining hall and salon.

Now, in smoky darkness, he had returned. "I've changed my mind about dessert."

She shook her head, on the verge of a smile. "You're too late."

"For everything?"

"I suppose there is still some brandy and cake—"

"That isn't what I want," he said with a directness that widened her eyes.

"I don't know how to respond, Gabriel," she said after a pause. "Surely I am dull company in comparison to the ladies you knew in London."

He grinned ruefully. "You're joking. Do you know how empty-headed those women are?"

"They are not all empty-headed. Some of them are quite brilliant."

He frowned. "Well, none of my acquaintances know how to play Slap the Slipper."

"That is hardly an intellectual pastime."

His eyes gleamed with humor. "Not one of them has ever beaten me at whist."

"You let us win, Gabriel."

He paused, reduced to playing upon her sympathy. "Do you have any idea how lonely London is for a man like me?"

Her answer took him off guard. "No more so than my life here."

He stared at her, realizing what she had admitted. "I can't replace him, can I?"

She flinched. "I would never compare *him* to you," she said in a startlingly fierce voice.

He straightened. Why hadn't he learned to keep his mouth shut? Now he had spoiled their mischief, bringing up that other man. "I'm sorry. I know how deeply you loved—"

"I didn't."

"What?"

She had not loved Jeremy? Is that what she meant? Surely not.

She turned, obviously distraught. It occurred to him that she was hesitant to speak Jeremy's hallowed name aloud for fear of some emotional collapse. Disgruntled as he was to think her grief was so profound that she sought solace in a gamester's seduction, he was not, however, discouraged enough to refuse what fate had dealt into his hands.

He gathered her against him and kissed the back

of her nape. She shivered but did not shy away. His blood heated in anticipation. *Please, whatever I do, let me not ruin this chance.* For as desperately as he desired her, she was still his sweet, bold-hearted girl from the most painful days of his past. He would die himself before bringing her dishonor.

Slowly he drew her closer.

He clasped his hands under her breasts, swallowing a groan at how good she felt. Her voluptuous curves molded into the hard angles of his body. His senses flared. Delicious. He loved how she leaned into him, as if there was more than ordinary desire between them.

"I warn you," he whispered against her neck, "do not invite me to your bed unless you mean it."

"Do you desire me, Gabriel?" she whispered, turning slowly until she faced him, her smile uncertain, his arms locked around her waist.

"My deepest desire is you."

She sighed. "How pretty."

He kissed the corners of her mouth, tightened his hold on her. "Are you impressed by pretty words?"

"No."

"I thought not."

Her eyes lowered briefly. "Do you wish to impress me?"

"More than I wish for the sun to rise in the morning."

She laughed, looking up again. "Silly, pretty words. But . . . he is gone."

He did not know what to say to that. When she

mentioned the man she had been meant to marry, she became visibly upset. Yet she claimed she had not loved him. He brushed back the curls that over-shadowed her face. "May I stay?"

She studied his hard, forbidding face. "You've been a good sport this last month."

He managed a smile. "We both know why."

"I never thought you would take to our simple pleasures."

"Can a man not change his ways?"

"Some ways, I suppose."

She knew who he was. But did he know her? He didn't, but he wanted to. He took her hand.

"Take me inside."

"Not to my bedroom. My maid sleeps next door. There is a private parlor upstairs where I read."

He wasn't about to argue. Her hand felt soft and firm in his, and he wasn't sure why she was leading him inside, only that he didn't want to draw her into any of the dark places he had known.

He followed her up a side staircase. She'd said she was lonely. Was he preying on her vulnerability? She could not bring herself to speak Jeremy's name more than a year after his death. In the past he had never felt compelled to plot out his affairs. Wher-ever he had been had presented the perfect time and place.

But now he was dying inside, not in control.

The small fire-lit parlor seemed to be her private retreat. Books, letters, a basket of knitting. A place of peace, of reflections. "Perhaps you should not have invited me here, Alethea. I know I cannot replace what you had once hoped for."

She closed the door, her eyes bright with anger. "How do you know?"

He shook his head. God forgive him. He did not wish to take advantage of a woman so immersed in grief she would offer herself to a rogue for momentary comfort. But if he could make her forget her pain, even though on the morrow she would despise him, he could not resist.

"I have never been a saint," he said. "I will take you no matter what your reason. Even if it is only to ease your sorrow."

He waited for her to protest. And when she did not, he guided her toward what in the dark appeared to be some manner of overstuffed sofa upon which sat a shawl, a spyglass, and a pile of papers. She laughed as he swept them onto the floor.

"Alethea," he said, and started to laugh himself. "I have imagined this moment in a hundred fantasies—"

"—but in a tidier room."

"It doesn't matter." Nothing but her mattered now. He pulled her down beside him, whispering, "Please, may I undress you?"

She gave another laugh, this one uncertain in the darkness. "Why? You can't see anything in here."

"I can touch you. And I *am* going to make love to you." How easily his hands unmoored her, how right it seemed as he released her from the constraints of her stays and chemise. He caressed her, gave her time to relax, to anticipate what would soon come. When he went down on his knees to slide off her stockings, he felt her stiffen in alarm. *"Gabriel."*

"Don't change your mind," he muttered, gazing up at her starkly. "Don't make me stop or I shall die."

She gave a shaky giggle. "You sound so intent."

"Oh, I am."

He gazed up at her, fascinated by the beauty of her naked body. Dark nipples that protruded from her sweet breasts, a rounded belly and full hips, a thatch of curls that crowned her cleft. His throat closed at her self-conscious smile.

He smiled back. "I would think this was a dream did the carnal demands of my body not tell me otherwise."

"I stopped believing in dreams." She ran her fingers lightly through his short black hair. "Until you came back."

She gave him so many hints that night. She revealed herself to him in subtle ways that a man of perception would have recognized. He missed every clue. His only excuse was that desire rendered him incapable of following all but his baser instincts. There would be tomorrow to reflect on nuance. It was all he could do to follow her lead, to master his desire.

He kissed her ankle, her calf, the soft hollow of her knee until the perfume of her secret flesh stole into his senses. He got up from the floor, working off his jacket and neckcloth, the buttons on his shirt and trousers. "You'll never forgive me for this," he said ruefully as he removed his boots.

For a moment, as he turned, his heart and body bared, she did not speak. Yet she didn't seem offended by his scars and blatant arousal. He could only hope that she found him half as desirable as he did her.

"How do you know what I will forgive?" she said at length. "Do you know me at all?"

He sat beside her. "I want to know." He caressed her face, and slid his hand around her neck.

"I'm not what I was," she whispered.

"You're so much better," he murmured, and bent his head to kiss her.

With another lady he would have attributed her remarks to teasing, to false modesty. But he wanted her too desperately to ponder what she was trying to say. Arrogant fool that he was, he assumed he had a monopoly on heartache. He assumed what appearances told him, that while the world had dealt him one blow after another, Alethea had remained intact, the perfect young lady, safe from sin, from harm. As she was meant to be.

"What I know," he said, "is that I will not leave now until you're mine. And that I don't intend to ruin you."

"Isn't that what rakes are meant to do?" she said, and she *was* teasing now.

"Not necessarily." He brushed his fingers down her throat, her breasts, then her belly, stealing lower until she trembled. But she did not draw away. He felt the pulse of her blood beneath his palm. "Some of us merely ruin ourselves."

"Do you think that those who care for you are not affected?" she asked, gasping as he slipped his finger into her sheath. Her body tightened, not in resistance but in desperate need. He stroked. She opened, slowly melting.

His voice roughened. "Does that mean you care for me?"

She moved her hips, aching, seeking more. "Can't you tell?"

"You've chosen me?"

She suppressed a moan. Whatever he was doing to her, this gentle invasion was too much, and yet she craved more. But how did he know when she had not been aware of this herself?

His hand stilled. She tried to clench her thighs, to catch her breath. "I'm sorry," he said, his voice low-pitched, compelling. "I had to leave, but . . . would it have mattered if I'd stayed?"

"Yes. I'm not sure—*yes*."

"Why?"

"Because—because then I might not have been betrothed to . . . him."

What *was* she telling him? That her loss had been so deep she wished she had never loved Jeremy? "Was there another man besides Hazlett?" he asked slowly, his breathing, his heartbeat suspended.

She wrapped her hand around his neck. Her fingers smoothed his raised scar. "Did you come back tonight to record the history of Helbourne or to make love to me?" she asked lightly.

He pressed her down onto her back. "I would be a fool to refuse an offer like that when I can barely see straight in your presence."

"He's gone, Gabriel," she said in a ghost whisper. "And," she added, her voice so low he was not sure he'd heard it, "I wish he had never existed."

"Are you certain that you want this?"

"No. But do it anyway. What I want is to forget."

She saw the surprise on his face and prayed he would not probe for an explanation. What she said was true. When she was with Gabriel she forgot the parts of her life that seemed ugly, unspeakable. And whatever happened between them was of her own choosing. Yes. *She* would choose tonight.

She buried her face in the notch of his hard shoulder. He smelled faintly of musk and cologne. So wonderful. His skin felt warm, the sinew and muscle woven beneath a shield of strength. How tempting to give him power over her. To unthaw. Winter's end.

"Once we are joined," he said, kissing the top of her head, "there are certain consequences we shall have to face."

"Such as the conception of a child?"

When had she become so frank in the ways of life? In the mirror of time she had remained innocent, untouched. Was he the one who had missed the deeper lessons of life? Were all his reflections distorted? No. Not of her.

"Yes," he said, swallowing. "That is one concern we must accept."

"Do you have any children, Gabriel?"

"No. I—" What could he say? That he was a man who had eluded commitment and escaped a fate he probably deserved? He had not always been careful but now, suddenly, so many things he had always scorned seemed to matter.

"Have you always desired me?" she whispered. "I know that once you liked to look. I never understood what it meant. What were you thinking?"

"I'm not sure that I thought at all in those days. Perhaps I wanted what I could not have." He pressed his face between her breasts, inhaling her scent. "I've never lost a game once I set my mind to it."

"I'm not a game, Gabriel," she said in mild indignation.

"I know, but if you were, what would I need to do to win you?" He raised his face, his smile beguiling. "I have relied on fights and wiles all my life to survive. I don't know of any other way to live."

"Isn't it possible that you could learn?"

"Would you be willing to help me?"

She laughed wistfully. "I always thought you managed well enough on your own."

"Because I knocked down anyone who stood in my path?"

"You fought your stepfather. That was brave of you."

He swallowed. He was ashamed that she should

know of that. "I was never viewed as the white knight of the village."

Her eyes flashed with mischief. "Some ladies are attracted to the darkness."

"I never took you for one of them."

"Don't you want me, Gabriel?" she asked with a catch in her voice.

"Yes. But for more than just one night."

"Isn't that forbidden in the rake's book of rules?"

"Can you think of me in any other terms?" he said in annoyance.

"I should ask the same of you."

"You have always been perfect in my eyes."

"But I'm *not* perfect. And if that is the only reason you desire me, then you are deceived."

"You're going to change your mind—"

"Oh, *Gabriel*. You don't understand."

He shut his eyes. "I don't want to hurt you."

"Then don't leave me."

How could he leave? His body absorbed her heat, her invitation. His breath shivered across her mouth. He lifted himself above her. He'd taken her in a thousand unfulfilled fantasies. Envisioned her beneath him when other women shared his bed.

He told himself that there would be time afterward to discuss whatever matters weighed upon her mind. In truth he did not wish to give her another moment to reflect or refuse. His every instinct bade him to seal their bond.

Don't let her change her mind. Don't let her real-

ize how wrong I am for her. Surely I do not deserve anyone so pure and perfect, but I swear, I shall never ask for anything again in my life if I am given the chance to love her.

"You're staring at me the way you used to," she whispered, her eyes suddenly wide open. "What are you thinking now?"

"That I have never seen a woman more beautiful." He kissed her, his hand tangling in her hair. She moaned in her throat. At this uninhibited utterance of encouragement, deep shocks of pleasure ran down his shoulders to his legs. Alethea, naked, opening her thighs to offer him pleasure. The lush sensuality of her body mesmerized him.

He bracketed her within his arms, arching his back, his gaze fastened to hers. Contrary to what was said of him, he had not made a habit of despoiling virgins. He understood, however, that the first time would not be as pleasurable for her as it would be for him.

Yet the hollow between her thighs felt moist, her flesh ready, enticing. He parted her plump folds and speared her with two fingers, penetrating as deeply as he dared.

She took several sharp breaths. He could not imagine a worse terror than having to stop, nor a more desirable fate than thrusting inside her.

He kissed her eyelids, her face. "I think I have been yours forever."

"Gabriel." She breathed his name, her fingers

pressing into his shoulders, as of its own volition her body opened beneath his.

"Do you want me?"

"Please," he said hoarsely.

"Is it passion that makes us burn, or love?" she whispered.

"Can it not be both?" He stared down into her face, his eyes piercing her. Her breasts rose temptingly with her indrawn breath. "Can it?"

"Yes, although I wonder—"

He did not give her a chance to finish, to think her answer through. His heart soared. At that moment he did not particularly care what terms she demanded. "Tell me later," he muttered, and slipped his left hand under her smooth hip. "Take all of me inside you—"

She released a groan that broke the chains of his control. He reared back, ignoring the little gasp of vulnerability she gave, and penetrated her to the full. It caught him in the chest, the shock of pleasure. To be buried in her tight passage, to feel her shiver in relief beneath him. Sweetest of fantasies come true. It gripped his mind, his senses until he knew nothing but reflex.

She arched into him. Although his body strained to respond in kind, he ground his teeth and slowed the tempo of his thrusts. Her first time. There would be nights of sensual exploration together. He would learn what pleased her and share his secret desires. Most assuredly he could have chosen a place better suited to lovemaking than an old sofa, as sturdy as it fortunately proved to be.

He heard her ragged whisper as if from far, far away. "I waited for you to come back."

"I'm here now."

"Make me forget, Gabriel."

Chapter Twenty-four

When Jeremy Hazlett had violated her, Alethea had not realized that it was the innocence of her heart he'd broken, not her ability to love, nor her body's capacity to know sexual pleasure. The carnal appetite that Gabriel had awakened, and proceeded to satisfy, at once embarrassed and excited her. She was convinced that no other man could have aroused her passion.

Whereas the same act, or rather its violent parody, had brought her only revulsion before, she now felt her natural desires return with an intensity she could not subdue. In her heart, he was her first lover, her only love. And for a man who was undeniably well-versed in sin, there had always been a valiance about him to balance his darker aspects. She savored every feeling, pleasing and uncomfortable, that he summoned, until, in the end, she gave herself up to him completely.

He led her past shame, forced her not only to submit but to acknowledge her hunger. Virile. He made her feel alive and strong, unafraid to reveal what she craved. He demanded. She surrendered, scarcely aware of the instant that his large body ceased to move. She knew only—in her own unexpected burst of pleasure, her release—that the trembling of his shoulders, the warmth deep inside her from his seed, meant he had found fulfillment.

And if even for a moment she was afraid that this act had been motivated only by desire, he lost no time reassuring her otherwise.

"You are the most desirable woman, the *only* woman I have ever truly wanted," he said as he lifted his head.

"Am I?" she whispered, stroking her finger down the deep crease in his cheek.

"I remember the first time you touched my face."

"You're considerably more attractive now."

He tugged one of the dark curls that had fallen across her breast. "So are you."

"I think—"

"My cousins in London will want to meet you."

"Your cousins?"

"My family. The other Boscastles. The boys."

She made a halfhearted attempt to sit up, her thoughts suddenly moving from their distracting nudity to the implications of meeting his infamous male relatives, not as his neighbor, not as a debutante, but as his lover.

"They will accuse us of impulse."

He raised his brow. He was heady, full of confidence, prepared to take on the world to impress her.

"Seven years is not exactly what could be called an act of impulse."

She regarded him keenly. "It wasn't as if we had a courtship all that time."

He grinned. "Yes we did."

His playfulness was contagious, and yet the secret that stood between them overshadowed her heart. He had not known, had not guessed. Would it change how he felt? She could not bear to spoil this magic intimacy, but intimacy could not survive without trust, and trust was built upon truthfulness.

She would have to confess. But how, when? Would he view her differently, still desire her as he did now? She glanced up at his dark sardonic face.

"Seven years," he said again.

"We had no contact!" she exclaimed.

"Yes, Alethea. We did."

She knew she was right because she would have remembered. She'd seen him only once since their early years—in London, flirting in the park—although he had not seen her. If she had been tempted to wave in greeting, his battalion of lady admirers had more than discouraged her. She had, however, frequently scanned the papers for news of his activities, until it had become painfully obvious that he'd fulfilled her parents' prophecy of a decadent life.

"I don't recall that you ever wrote to me or made any effort to see me," she said, frowning at him.

"I asked Jeremy about you whenever I saw him."

She looked away. "He never said."

He kissed her bare shoulder. "Perhaps he meant to protect you from the bane of the village. And if I did not see you, you were so often in my thoughts that it was as if we still knew each other." He paused, his voice beguiling. "Did you not ever think of me?"

"Of course I thought of you," she said without hesitation.

"I dreamt of you, too."

She turned her head, smiling wistfully. "You might have thought to tell me once in all those years."

He reached down for their scattered garments. "You were betrothed to another man. Do you hold that against me?"

"No."

She held it against that other man, and only wished that Gabriel had been dishonorable enough to challenge his claim. But how could he have known? Even now he assumed what she had allowed the rest of the world to believe. That she had loved her betrothed, that Jeremy had not only died a hero but had lived as one. No one wanted to think that a polished gentleman, a man with pristine manners and impeccable bloodlines, would dishonor the woman he claimed to adore.

But tonight she had needed Gabriel, to hold her, to exorcise the memory of her disgrace. It was as if by choosing him, she had defied the ghost of the man who had pledged to protect her.

If only she dared to be honest with him about what had happened.

They dressed slowly, pausing to share kisses, to assist each other. Alethea should have been weeping in regret, planning her penance. Instead, it was all she could do not to ask him to stay. Would he commit his heart to her? There was no guarantee that he had not spoken in passion, no assurance that by tomorrow he would not feel regret. But at least for now she felt hopeful, and wickedly happy.

She had trusted Gabriel with her body. And she would be honest. Surely he had heard more unpleasant stories from his half-world women. If only he hadn't put her upon a pedestal of her past virtue.

His husky voice distracted her. He stood, lifting her with him. Her heart caught at his cheeky grin. "I forgot something." He produced an expensive vellum envelope from the pocket of his evening coat. "I meant to deliver this when I saw you earlier tonight. It's an invitation."

"For me?" she asked in surprise. "Who is it from?" She had declined every social offer she had received in the past year until they had stopped arriving at all. "Are you going to give it to me?"

"Only if you promise you will come with me."

"Come with you where, you devil?" She reached for the sealed missive, only to find herself entrapped against his hard chest.

His dark eyes teased her, warmly seductive. "It's only an invitation for my cousin Grayson's annual birthday ball in Mayfair. And if I do not let you go right now, I will still be here by the date of the party."

She smiled up at his shadowed face. She could still feel him inside her, the pleasure of his possession.

"In London," he said, handing her the invitation, "at the party, I will show you off."

"I trust you won't mind if I bring either my cousin or brother as chaperone."

He bent to kiss her. "Even if you bring the entire village of Helbourne, you won't be kept from me again."

It crossed Gabriel's mind for only a split instant that he had not encountered the barrier of her maidenhead during their lovemaking. Not that he'd gone about seducing virgins or shouting hallelujah at the loss of a lover's virtue. Sexual pleasures were enshrouded in myth and mystery. He understood instinctively what pleased a woman without having dedicated himself to a study of the subject.

Young ladies, it was said, could injure certain delicate tissues during the course of a vigorous horseback ride. Certainly Alethea was an ardent equestrienne. And for all he knew, he had caused her discomfort, and she had refrained from expressing it. He wanted to think that she had been so swept away by passion that any hurt he had inflicted was immediately forgotten.

He, on the other hand, would never forget or be the same afterward. And he could not wait to see the reaction of his cousins in London when he told them he had fallen in love with Alethea Claridge and that—yes, he knew she would not have given herself to any man otherwise—she loved him, too.

Chapter Twenty-five

❧❧ ❧❧

Alethea lingered in bed long past her usual hour, half-listening to the servants bustle below. She had not dreamt it, had she? The warm decadence, his affection. She rolled over, clasping her pillow. Slowly she became aware of her body's deep awakening, the tenderness that gave adequate testament to Gabriel's prowess.

She felt thoroughly like a woman taken.

Swived. Seduced. Done one proper. All those naughty words one should only speak in hushed whispers, if at all. Gabriel had implemented each of them, in the wickedest sense.

"Lady Alethea?" a woman's familiar voice called from behind the door. "Are you ailing?"

She sighed, subsiding back onto the bed. She knew she had something to do. She always did. "No, Joan. Did you want something?"

"I don't think you'll have time for a decent breakfast if you're to be at the assembly rooms before ten."

"Assembly rooms?"

"It must be my mistake. I thought—"

Alethea flew out of bed. How had she forgotten? She was the patroness of Helbourne's annual ball, the person who oversaw suppers and world-shifting decisions such as whether the ladies committee should buy a new pianoforte or put in a polished ballroom floor so that their slippers would not catch in the middle of a quadrille.

And today she had promised to inspect the drawing room where the ladies took tea before dancing. Her brother had made a substantial donation, to be spent as she desired on curtains or chairs. Last year the vicar's mother had gone right through a seat of the ancient oak settle onto her hindquarters.

She rushed through her morning toilette and was still putting on her gloves as Wilkins drove her to the assembly rooms. No one else had arrived yet, only the old caretaker who lived down the lane. She would ask him to boil tea and take a few moments to catch her breath.

In fact, she did not even need to ask. She had only just reached the small upstairs drawing room when she heard cups rattling on his tray. "Mr. Carson," she said, "you are so thoughtful. How did you guess I was too rushed for my tea this morning? I overslept."

"No need to apologize," a deep voice drawled from the door. "I myself had quite an active night. I trust your evening involved nothing *too* strenuous."

"Gabriel." She whirled around, laughing at the

sight of him walking toward her with a tray of tea and crumpets. "I had no idea you harbored domestic talents. What a pleasant surprise."

He frowned. "Do you mind not looking so lovely until my hands are free? I'm afraid I shall drop your tea and disprove my domesticity." As evidence of this statement he deposited his burden on the table between them, the cups rattling precariously in their saucers. "There." He gave her a dangerous grin. "Now my hands are free. And you still look lovely, I see."

She shook her head, happier to see him than she could show. "How did you know I was here?"

"I went to your house right after you left, apparently, and asked your housekeeper where you were. She gave me directions and another sack of flour."

"I didn't notice anyone following me."

"I rode ahead. And brought up your tea. I can be a good boy when I try."

But he hadn't been good last night. Neither had she. The knowing smile that stole across his face reminded her of how wonderfully bad they had been together.

She swallowed, her eyes riveted to his. Her devil-may-care lover. His short black hair had been tousled by the wind. His dark gray riding coat and snug buff trousers molded in such a sinful manner to his rugged frame that she suddenly felt the need to crumple into a chair.

He regarded her closely. "Do you want your tea?"

"Not yet, thank you." She smiled. "I'm surprised Mr. Carson allowed you to carry the tray. He doesn't care for many people."

He walked around the table. "He worked once for my father." For a moment his expression revealed a chink of vulnerability. "And he cares for you—which doesn't surprise me in the least."

"He likes to serve my tea. I wonder why he didn't come with you."

His shoulders lifted in a guileless shrug. "I sent him off on a small errand."

"What sort of errand?" she asked in a skeptical voice.

"To buy some cheese in the village."

"Cheese?"

"Well, I've run out of ham."

She folded her arms in amusement. "But not audacity."

His gaze slowly raked her, stirring her nerves into sizzling awareness. "Why are you here alone, anyway?" he asked.

She forced herself to retreat a few steps toward the windows. "I'm inspecting the curtains for moths and mildew." Although with Gabriel in the room she wasn't sure she could tell one from the other.

"How exciting." He advanced on her. "May I help?"

She narrowed her eyes. She did not believe his act of innocent gallantry for a moment. In fact, the sparkle in his eyes was unequivocally dangerous. A well-behaved woman would be on guard. While one with more wicked tendencies would be— tempted.

She was definitely one of the tempted.

He closed in on her one step at a time until at last she stood against the windowsill, his hands planted on either side of her.

She held her breath in expectation. "Well, what do you think?"

He looked down at her in undisguised satisfaction. "I think you're trapped—you can't possibly go any farther."

"Curtains, Gabriel. The *curtains*."

He blinked, then cast a disinterested glance at the faded draperies that flanked them. "Yes. Motheaten. Mildewed. Didn't we already establish that?"

He kissed her softly on the mouth, his hands still enclosing her on either side. Her heartbeat escalated. "What I meant to say is that—"

"—you're going to marry me," he said, easing his tongue between her parted lips. "We can talk about curtains all you like then."

Her blood flared at the intimate heat rising between them. How easily his brief kiss unbalanced her. "Marry you?"

"Your answer?"

She could not breathe.

"Where there are curtains," she managed to continue, "there is usually a window. In case you haven't noticed, we are in view of the carriage drive."

"I understand your concern," he murmured. "Do me a favor, darling. Turn around."

"What—" She had no notion why she obeyed, but she did. "And now?"

His warm mouth traveled down her nape. "Don't move."

"Why not?"

"Please. Just humor me. Do you notice any suspicious activity outside?"

"No. Only directly behind me."

He laughed.

She stared down at the sinewy arm locked around her midsection. How male even his wrist looked, his brown skin a sensual contrast to the pristine white cuff of his sleeve. She remembered his hands upon her body last night. Gentle but unmerciful. She gave a shiver and closed her eyes, waiting in delicious anticipation for—

"Your answer," he said. "I'm waiting patiently."

She turned, looking up. "It's yes."

His hard mouth curved into a smile. "Passion," he said, lowering his head to kiss her again. "*And* love."

She sighed in anticipation. But their lips barely touched before he lifted his head and swore softly. "The *window*."

She breathed out another sigh. "You're right—it can wait." She wasn't certain that *she* could, however.

"There's a curricle parked in the drive," he said. "I thought you were keeping watch."

She glanced around in chagrin. "It belongs to the Shrewsbury cousins. Three married women who adore creating little scandals out of nothing."

He laughed. "Well, I'm only here to bring up your tea."

The *click-clack* of three pairs of slipper heels on the old stairs of the assembly room resounded in the quiet. Alethea stared at the door in dread. Half of Helbourne had already realized that she had not been inviting Gabriel to supper for his card-playing skills alone.

The other half would know the truth soon enough.

"We'll have to be married in London," he said hurriedly, releasing her. "My cousins will insist upon a family wedding. And a party to announce our engagement."

"You are serious."

"Aren't you?"

The clatter of footsteps grew louder. He glanced around thoughtfully. "Would you like me to hide behind the curtains?"

"As if *that* wouldn't appear suspicious. You might as well pour that—"

The door opened. A flurry of feminine whispers crept into the silence.

"Lady Alethea certainly doesn't appear to be mourning Jeremy much these past few weeks."

"Would you?" the youngest cousin asked. "Boscastle is wickedly handsome."

"And handsomely wicked from what I understand," the eldest one said with a sigh.

"That's quite a contrast to Lord Jeremy," the middle one said as they walked into the room. "He was so polite."

Then all three of them looked up at the handsomely wicked subject of their debate. He bowed.

"May I fetch a few more teacups to whet those wagging tongues?" he inquired with a smile that Alethea knew from experience would send every thought out of their heads.

"We *are* sorry, Alethea," the eldest Shrewsbury cousin said. "We had no idea that Sir Gabriel was here—"

"—to help," Alethea said hastily. "He's helping me take down the curtains."

"And pour tea," he added.

Alethea eyed him closely, as did the three other women in the room. She was not surprised that they had compared him favorably to her late fiancé. But while their comments had secretly pleased her, while she had longed to announce that he was hers, their whispers had also cast a shadow upon her mood.

Jeremy was still a threat to her happiness. Her shame ran deeper than she had realized.

❧ ❧

Chapter Twenty-six

Alethea feigned sleep during the long carriage ride to London, too absorbed in thoughts of Gabriel, of the upcoming party, to care for conversation. Her cousin, Lady Pontsby, and her brother, Robin, spoke in whispers around her, commenting on how distracted she appeared of late and how it would do her a world of good to attend a party again with the bon ton of her birthright. They couldn't guess that she and Gabriel had been meeting in private for days and that her distraction stemmed from a cause she had not yet revealed. Her brother had not altogether overcome his doubts about Gabriel, while she was so hopelessly in love with the man she could not sleep nights for staring out her window at his house.

"She's lonely," Lady Pontsby said in concern. "She has secluded herself to the point that she surely will become a spinster. And while Sir Gabriel has proven to be a charming visitor, one cannot help wondering how long he will stay."

"She needs time to grieve Jeremy," Robin said quietly. "She's not been herself since he's been gone."

"Nonsense. She needs a husband. I never cared all that much for Hazlett, if you must know."

"I thought you adored him," Robin said in surprise.

"I only pretended for Alethea's sake," Lady Pontsby confided in an undertone. "In all honesty I thought him to be a petty young man, always ordering his family about."

Alethea managed to suppress a sigh. She wondered if she could pretend to be asleep the entire way to town, and to maintain the pretense when she met Gabriel at his cousin's party. Soon everyone would know.

"Dear God above!" Lady Pontsby exclaimed in such a tone of genuine horror that Alethea was forced to have done with pretense altogether. "Brigands! Protect us, Robin."

Alethea opened her eyes as, indeed, the vibration of hoofbeats approached the lumbering carriage. To her delight the horseman who cantered up beside them, dark cloak draped upon his broad shoulders, was Gabriel.

"My friends," he said, lifting his leather-gloved hand to his forehead. "Allow me to offer you escort. These are"—his eyes twinkled, although he avoided looking directly at Alethea—"dangerous times for the traveler."

"They are dangerous times for everyone," Alethea murmured as she settled back against the cushions.

Her brother studied her for several moments. "Indeed. I think there are dangers around us of which I have been unaware."

A party to celebrate the birthday of Grayson Boscastle, the Most Honorable, the fifth Marquess of Sedgecroft, was an occasion that the crème de la crème of Society could not refuse. A few of the haut ton had already returned from the seaside or country for the Little Season.

One could not imagine a more entertaining way to launch back into London life than to brag an invite to Grayson's magnificent redbrick mansion on Park Lane, once, although it was not mentioned, home to the gallows. Now its close proximity to Hyde Park gave it unquestionable elegance.

Cattle drovers en route to market and curious city folk peered through the main armorial gates under the watchful scrutiny of several attendant footmen in powdered periwigs and formal knee breeches. Weed, efficient senior footman to the marquess, oversaw the more personal details of the celebrations, from supplying the Italian opera singer with champagne to playing peekaboo behind the marble hallway columns with Grayson's son and heir, Lord Rowan.

By the time Alethea arrived, the majority of the guests had already drifted from the numerous reception rooms into the side pavilion and from thence into a garden pleasantly shaded by stately plane trees and classical statues of weathered stone.

There was no sign of Gabriel. "But in this fashionable crush who can spot one's favorite friend?" she murmured without thinking to her cousin.

Lady Pontsby smiled in agreement, although she was too dazzled herself by the parade of aristocrats they passed to give Alethea's comment any deep reflection. "One would not acknowledge him, anyway, without an announcement from the majordomo."

"Half of London has already been announced, by the look of it," Alethea said. "Still, it would be nice to see—"

"How good to see *you* here," a deep teasing voice said from behind them. "I trust your travels were as pleasant as our rustic highways allow."

Alethea restrained a gleeful smile and revolved slowly to face her dark knight. "As if you did not follow us through every turnpike, Sir Gabriel."

"And gallant of you it was, indeed," Lady Pontsby said. "A lady cannot claim too many escorts in these hazardous days."

Gabriel granted her a genial smile. Before she could continue, however, he had fastened his gaze upon her cousin. He had been waiting—no, pacing like a condemned prisoner—for Weed to alert him to her arrival. He drank in the sight of her. She had swept her dark curly hair back into a loose knot that he ached to undo and spread over her beautiful body. He could not believe he had won her.

He wanted to announce it to the world, or at least to his family, and keep it secret at the same time. Could he spirit her away to some secluded spot and resume their heated intimacies? It wasn't as if his cousin's house had not witnessed its share of amorous scandals.

He continued to stare at Alethea until she raised an eyebrow in subtle reprimand. Fortunately, Lady Pontsby seemed unaware that he desired nothing more than to be alone with her cousin. By the end of the party or as soon as he could gather the other Boscastles in one room, he would be able to reveal that she was his. Until then he'd have a deuced time acting as if he cared about anyone in attendance other than this one woman who could unravel, chastise, and uplift him in one negligent glance. There was no one else for whom he would discard his prior life without a twinge of regret.

He had sated himself on sin. Now he wanted only her, and if they played whist in the country every night before he took her to bed, well, he couldn't be happier.

"You don't mind, do you?" Lady Pontsby said, her voice raised.

He shook his head. "Mind what?"

She scrutinized him with a thoughtful smile. "If I leave you both for a few moments to chat with Lord and Lady Farnsworth. I haven't seen them in years. Robin is right over there, with Emily's father. Don't interrupt them, will you? I am hoping that this is the day we have waited for."

He shrugged in an attempt not to announce his pleasure at this opportunity. "I suppose we can manage for a few moments."

"Good. Now do enjoy yourselves."

Chapter Twenty-seven

❧ ❧

Gabriel extended his arm. "Shall I give you a tour?"

"Shall I trust you?" she asked, as if it were not evident that there was anyone she trusted more.

"Of course not. But your cousin did instruct you to enjoy yourself. And by the way, I have missed you."

The wicked glitter in his eyes tempted her. "Where are we going?"

His magnificent shoulders lifted in another shrug. "Here and there."

"And for what reason exactly?"

"Oh, this and that."

She laughed. "In that case I don't think we should be seen walking arm in arm."

His diabolical grin set off a delicious swirl of sensations inside her. "As you wish. I do feel compelled to remind you that as of tonight it won't matter. Our families will know we are engaged."

"Which doesn't mean we can indulge at will in—"

"—this and that?" He guided her down the endless high-columned hallway, seemingly impervious to the appealing glances of the ladies who recognized him and waited for acknowledgment.

"You appear to have a string of admirers," she said dryly, stealing a look at his hard, chiseled profile.

"Do I?"

"Yes. Didn't you notice?"

He glanced around. "Where?"

"They were—" She hesitated, staring behind him in surprise. While she had been paying attention to the stir he'd caused, he had led her down another corridor to a reception room warmed by a small coal fire. A royal-blue silk chaise occupied one corner. A rosewood table held a basket of imported fruits, two goblets, and a bottle of sparkling wine. "We can't go in here. It's clearly meant for—"

"—family." He swept her through the door and locked it behind them. "You're going to be part of the most infamous family in London."

"How can you be sure they will accept our engagement that easily?"

He walked her a few steps into the center of the room. The smile that curved his chiseled mouth made her pulses jump. "If they accepted me into the fold, they will absolutely embrace you as my wife."

She edged toward the fireplace. He moved casually to her left, his blue eyes dancing with mirth. "Why do I feel as though we're playing Puss in the Corner?" she said with a frown.

He shook his head, took another languid step in her direction. "Do you prefer another game?"

She nodded firmly. Had the chaise moved toward her? She noticed a card table on the other side of the room. Cards. That might keep his mind occupied. "Whist is fine. Let us sit over—"

"What about Trump?" he asked, unbuttoning his charcoal-gray jacket.

"That is a lovely waistcoat, Gabriel," she said as he gently took her by the hand. "It—did you say Trump? Is that a game of cards?"

"Oh, have you played it before?" Suddenly they stood at the edge of the chaise until he pressed his mouth to hers, and her knees gave way. "My goodness," he murmured, standing over her for only a moment. "Are you feeling light-headed? Shall I loosen your gown?"

"Yes. No. No—don't you—not a—"

He lowered himself over her half-reclining form, kissing her until she had forgotten what she was trying to say. His muscular torso and thighs hindered her faint struggle to dislodge him. When she recovered her wits, as well as breath, to look up at him, she felt her heart miss several beats at the sultry passion that darkened his face.

"I don't know when we'll have a chance to be alone together again. Once the Boscastles realize you're going to be one of them they'll invite you everywhere."

"I haven't even met most of your family yet," she whispered.

His eyes traveled from her mouth to the tiny bows that laced her puffy rose silk sleeves and bodice. "Aren't *we* going to be family?"

She leaned back, her voice catching. "We shall be starting our own family at this rate."

He shrugged out of his jacket. To distract herself she took it and folded it neatly on the scrolled mahogany rail of the chaise. The pleasing hint of cologne on the well-tailored garment teased her senses, and she glanced up slowly. He looked gorgeous in his pleated cambric shirt, ivory vest, and snug pantaloons that emphasized his masculinity. No wonder those other ladies had stared at him in the hope of attracting his notice. He exuded a dangerous elegance, a promise of wicked pleasures, that made a woman abandon caution and propriety. And yet for all his unreserved sexuality, he had shown *her* more concern than the man her parents had chosen for her. Still, she shouldn't let him seduce her at his cousin's party.

"I think—" She started to rise. "Is that someone in the hall?"

His thumb traced her jawline, then slowly dropped into the deep hollow between her breasts. She slid back down onto the chaise, overcome, unable to remember why she had wanted to get up in the first place. "It doesn't matter. The door is locked."

Her breath quivered as he caressed her swelling breasts. Warm tingles of excitement stole down her spine. She stirred, her nipples distended, her body restless. "I thought—you don't even have a pack of cards, Gabriel," she said with a sniff of indignation.

His eyes gleamed as he settled alongside her. "You don't need any for this game. It's called Boscastle Trump."

"You fraud," she whispered, the power of his hard body weakening her. "There is no such game. You made it up."

A roguish grin spread across his face. He dipped his head and pressed hot kisses across her décolletage. She felt a throbbing heat between her thighs. "I didn't." He blew softly on her breasts. Pleasure flooded her. "It's a genuine parlor game. For two players."

"One of whom is the parlor maid?" she asked, her back arching, her body inviting more.

He paused, looking up seductively into her eyes. "Come to think, it's the Boscastle version of another game."

Her breasts ached from his arousing kisses. She knew she was playing right into his hands. "A game of trump with no cards?"

"It's more of a legerdemain." He sat back with an expression of utmost seriousness. "An illusion," he mused, shifting his position again to run his hand over her crossed ankles.

She stared down at his blunt-tipped fingers in fascination until they disappeared under her dress. "A very convincing illusion," she said, her eyes lowering in unwilling pleasure. "What must I do to win?"

His left shoulder lifted in a shrug. His hand,

meanwhile, slipped up over her stocking, then her garter. "Well, the quickest hand wins."

She reached down for his wrist before she completely lost her wits. He was too good at disarming her; the warmth pooling in the pit of her belly would soon flood her entire body if he continued to touch her. "The quickest hand wins? Is that all?"

He looked up at her again, desire kindling in his eyes. "There's a little more skill involved than that. Do you want me to teach you the game?"

Her body did. "I'm going to die if we are caught."

"I'll die if I can't have you." He lifted his knee between her legs, his hand gliding into the damp hollow above her thighs. She sank back against the tasseled bolster, releasing his wrist to touch the lower buttons of his waistcoat.

His eyes narrowed. "You're not undressing me, are you?"

"Goodness, no. It's all illusion."

Gabriel cast a smoky glance over her relaxed figure. The tips of her beautiful breasts peeked out darkly from the edge of her bodice. He felt his blood smolder, his heart pound, as he watched her sensual awakening. She had closed her eyes, but her body responded to his lightest caress. His fingers skimmed the silky hairs of her sex, deliberately not touching the pouting flesh below that so tempted him. Her belly muscles shivered.

"The rules of this game, Gabriel?" she murmured, moistening her lips with her tongue.

He lifted her dress all the way to her waist.

"I usually make them up as I go."

She vented a sigh. "I thought so."

"You may do the same. Open your eyes."

She obeyed.

He eased his thumb over her taut pearl, teasing it in lazy circles until her breathing grew ragged, her eyes glazed. When he sensed that her body could no longer bear the tension, he drove his fingers deep into her glistening sheath. Her low whimper of arousal sharpened his insatiable hunger for her. The sweet essence that seeped from her delicate sex tempted his appetite like ambrosia.

She caught the edge of her lip in her teeth. Her dusky nipples elongated. Her soft bottom lifted from the cushion, a sign that he knew meant she was near her peak. He leaned closer so he might savor the moment when she shattered. He pushed another finger inside her passage, leaned down, and licked her breasts. She took hold of his shirt and pulled it from his waistband. His shaft hardened in readiness for sex from the knobby head to the root. But if he had to wait until later for his release, he did not mind. Unraveling Alethea was the most potent aphrodisiac he could imagine.

And he played to win.

"Gabriel." She groaned, tugging on the tail of his shirt. "I think this—game—"

"Yes," he murmured, restraining a smile.

"I think you're cheating at it."

He laughed easily. "Does it matter, if we both win?"

She ran her hand down the fastenings of his fly. He clenched his jaw until his teeth hurt. A veil of lust blurred his vision. She was so close, so pulsing wet that he could have buried himself inside her and gratefully drawn his last breath. He quickened the movements of his fingers, drove inside her until her hips twisted.

She gave another groan, then convulsed, her gaze unfocused, her hand nestled against his rampant cock. He shuddered as he felt her body ripple in pleasure, the spasms ebbing away. Slowly he withdrew his fingers from her pulsing flesh.

He threw back his head, took several long breaths to bank the fire in his blood. "I win," he whispered, "although my heart is hammering so hard—"

She bolted upright. "That isn't your heart, Gabriel. It's the door."

He glanced around, unconcerned, "No it isn't. And it's locked—"

"It isn't coming from *that* door—it's coming from over there—the fireplace—"

Before she could point to indicate the narrow opening at the massive Gothic fireplace, Gabriel had pulled her bodice up, her dress down, and himself into his jacket and onto his feet. He had, however, forgotten to tuck the tail of his shirt back in, which he did at Alethea's frantic gesturing.

He had also forgotten that the marquess's house was riddled with secret passageways and hidden escape routes that had been used more by the Boscastle children for trickery than for emergency purposes.

It was trickery that he confronted now, in the figure of his dark-haired cousin Lord Drake Boscastle. "There you are, Gabriel," Drake said pleasantly, dusting off his shoulder as he emerged from the gloomy aperture. "And Lady Alethea. I don't believe I've ever had the pleasure. How good to meet you."

She smiled politely, although her hands shook until she clasped them in her lap. "It is an honor, my lord."

"Why didn't you knock?" Gabriel asked bluntly.

"Actually, I did. But no one answered. You were playing Boscastle Trump?" he guessed, his smile bland.

Alethea rose, not acknowledging the pleased grin that Gabriel sent her. "It was impolite of us to retire."

"I wouldn't say it was impolite," Drake said with a meaningful look at the bolster that had slipped off the chaise. "In fact, I rather detest these big affairs myself and always go off alone at the very first chance."

Gabriel cleared his throat. "Which is why you sneaked in here, because we are the better company?"

Drake's eyes glittered with good humor. "I came, actually, because *your* company is being sought by quite a few people at the party and I did not think either of you wished the inevitable conclusions to be drawn. I was running out of excuses for your sudden disappearance."

Alethea put her hand to her eyes. "*Oh*. I am mortified."

"It's quite all right," Drake said with a consoling smile. "The family is used to these . . . moments."

She lowered her hand. "My brother and aunt will be looking for me, too. I have to leave, Gabriel."

"Not by that door," Drake said, placing his hand on her shoulder to guide her to the fireplace. "This way leads out into a private hallway that gives onto any number of rooms. It is no lie to claim you took a wrong turn."

She glanced wryly at Gabriel. "Indeed."

"Don't worry," he said, smiling at her. "By tonight everything will be revealed."

He moved between her and Drake, staring into the darkened cavity. "She can't go through that tunnel alone. It's filthy and—"

Drake held up his hand. "It's all right. Weed is waiting to escort her."

Gabriel gave him a long, hard look. "You've thought of everything, haven't you?"

Drake smiled. "Well, it's not as if I've never played Boscastle Trump myself."

Chapter Twenty-eight

Alethea studied the medieval Italian tapestries on the hallway wall for several minutes before she deemed it safe to venture forth. When she at last rejoined the majority of the guests in the garden, she discovered that she had not been missed at all.

Her cousin had ventured off to greet old friends. Her brother and his sweetheart wove in and out alongside the other dancers on the sloping lawn. Gabriel had apparently rejoined the party.

As Alethea was more in a mood for contemplation, she wandered through the overgrown garden and its private pathways guarded by strategically positioned classical statues.

By tonight everything will be revealed.

Gabriel had meant that their engagement would be announced. But the time had come for her own confession. How? How would she tell him? Had she waited too long?

"Alethea?" a soft voice queried from behind a fountain statue of the Three Fates. "Are you alone? Do not turn around unless you are."

She halted on the gravel path and slowly pivoted to see an auburn-haired woman draped in white silk emerge from behind the fountain: Mrs. Audrey Watson, courtesan, celebrated hostess, and one of the most admired demimondaines in London. Alethea had not seen her since the night Audrey had sought to offer her a woman's understanding of her anguish. It was an encounter so edged in pain that she had thought of it as little as possible.

Indeed, Alethea cringed even now as flashes of memory from their conversation returned. Audrey had whisked her from the party in her carriage to a private room in her house on Bruton Street. She recalled how Audrey had given her a glass of wine and precious time to compose herself. In a burst of irrational emotion, Alethea had offered her services as a courtesan between salty tears and sips of Bordeaux.

Audrey had merely smiled and allowed her another few minutes to calm down.

"You are a lovely young woman, Alethea," she'd said at last. "I have no doubt you could make a fine living as a whore."

"A—"

"However," Audrey added, "I do not think you are suited to my establishment. You're simply too tragic. No man wishes to pay a fortune to romp with a miserable companion."

"I didn't realize it mattered."

"Darling, you have been despoiled and disillusioned. The ladies who work for me do not view their occupation as a punishment. It is a privilege to be a professional courtesan."

"A privilege?" she asked faintly.

"You'd have a certain freedom. If you end up marrying this cad of yours, you will share his bed and mistreatment for the rest of your life."

"Then what do I do?" she whispered. "What do I do now?"

"You wait."

"For what?"

"I have a feeling that this will resolve itself in time. How, I don't know."

She'd bowed her head, embarrassed, uncertain. She had taken Audrey's advice—and waited. Looking back, she realized how much it had helped to have a woman of experience listen to her.

"Forgive me," she said now, meeting Audrey's guarded smile. "I don't know—"

"—me at all," Audrey said with a warning shake of her head. "We are merely two ladies at a party who met by accident in the garden."

Alethea released her breath. "If the marquess has seen fit to invite you to his party, madam, I will not pretend to ignore you."

"Brave words," Audrey said wryly. "Sedgecroft, however, is above reproach and has no need to please anyone but himself." She examined Alethea with an expert glance. "It pleases me to see you looking far less tragic than the night we met. Is it true that you have captured the interest of Gabriel Boscastle?"

The threat of approaching footsteps diverted Alethea's immediate attention. She turned distractedly, continuing only when it appeared that the person had taken another of the garden's myriad paths. "Sir Gabriel and I are neighbors," she answered at length, suspecting that this reply would not deceive a woman of Mrs. Watson's experience.

Audrey laughed. "He's the last man on earth I would have pegged for a country farmer."

"The country does have its charms," Alethea said, her smile giving her away.

"You being one of them," Audrey said with a good-natured sigh. "I wish you both the very best. There was a time not long ago when I thought Gabriel would become a favorite visitor. I understand now what—who—has provoked his mysterious disappearance from our entertainments."

Alethea glanced around, lowering her voice. "You aren't going to tell him? I'm not even sure that when I spoke to you that night I was in full possession of my senses. I've no idea what he would do if he learned the truth."

"I promised I would keep your confidence," Audrey said softly. "I could hardly have built my reputation by divulging secrets."

"I hoped I could trust you."

Audrey looked at her in reproach. "There are precious few people in the world I trust. I am honored, however, to count the Boscastle family as my friends. I will not betray you."

"Thank you."

Audrey nodded graciously. "It might seem odd that a courtesan prides herself on discretion, but private affairs are my business."

"I understand," Alethea murmured, although the mention of Gabriel's past association with Mrs. Watson's house had not escaped her attention. She doubted he had gone there to seek advice or solace—well, not solace of the emotional nature that Alethea had needed on that unhappy night. As accommodating as Mrs. Watson had made herself, it would please Alethea to no end if neither she nor Gabriel ever availed themselves of her expertise again.

"I don't know how to tell him," she admitted.

"Do you think the truth would alter his feelings?" Audrey said.

"I am not—"

"Hush." Audrey turned abruptly to face the fountain. "Someone is coming. It would serve you well to ignore me until we are publicly introduced. Unless you choose not to make my acquaintance."

Alethea straightened. "I have learned, Mrs. Watson, that it is not the people Society most criticizes who deserve censure. I shall be honored to admit an acquaintance with you if we meet again."

Chapter Twenty-nine

❧ ⚘ ☙

Gabriel gazed down at the ground in a pose of amused reflection. He had gone straight to Alethea's brother to tell him of his intention to marry Alethea, but the earl had been engaged in a flirtation of his own. Gabriel had decided to wait a half hour or so, accepting Drake's offer to walk the garden. Naturally he had hoped to come upon Alethea. And he had. But not in a manner he expected.

He was aware that Drake had heard as much of that damning conversation between Alethea and Mrs. Watson as he had. No doubt his cousin had come to the same inevitable, indeed, the only conclusion that a man could draw.

The exchange, albeit brief, that had passed between Alethea and Mrs. Watson had cut him to the quick. It denoted a prior association, a furtive bond of more than casual acquaintance. He had studied enough skillfully masked facial expressions across countless card tables in his life to catch a marker.

And if there had been a feeble hope in Gabriel's

heart that he had misinterpreted this communication, it was dashed by his cousin's obvious attempt to ease the blow.

"Well, my brother's parties are an endless source of scandal and entertainment."

Gabriel shook his head. Beneath the sense of numbness, the pain intensified. "Don't say another word. There's no need for either of us to elaborate on what is obvious."

They began to stroll back toward the celebration in progress on the lawn. Neither man spoke for a while.

"I don't know that what we overheard necessarily implies any deception on Alethea's part," Drake said at length. "At least not of the depths you suspect."

"Do you hope to convince me she met Audrey Watson at a country dance?"

"The more I think of it," Drake continued, "there are a dozen possible explanations that do not denote any guilt on her part."

"I have the urge to hit someone, Drake. I would dearly love to commit homicide at this moment. Pray do not insult me further by asking me to deny what we both heard."

"I'm sorry."

"If you were in my place, would you believe she was entirely innocent?" Gabriel asked in scorn.

Drake shot him a guarded smile. "Probably not. But then again I've never been known to possess the most even temperament in the family."

Which was quite an understatement. Drake had been famous for the dark moods that his recent marriage appeared to have subdued if not conquered. He and Gabriel had, in fact, once quarreled often in a rivalry that had evolved into an unexpected camaraderie.

"And to which Boscastle," Gabriel mused aloud, "am I the most often compared?"

Drake laughed in sympathy. "If you insist on fighting, we shall have to go to Jackson's. Jane will have our heads if we ruin Grayson's day."

A young man with a shock of yellow hair emerged from behind a hedge. His face brightened as he recognized the Boscastle cousins. "There you are, Gabriel. I've been hunting all over for you."

Gabriel frowned as another man—the twin, actually, of the intruder—appeared on the path. The Mortlock brothers, Ernest and Erwin, a pair of Society's most visible embarrassments. Well-off, slender-boned, the innocent-looking duet ranked as steady participants in London's most disreputable pastimes. Gabriel was frankly surprised no one had killed them off by now.

"What do you want?" he asked coolly.

"Well, my ugly half and I have just caught wind of a plump pigeon roosting in Piccadilly tonight. Hazard is his game, and he's got cash to lose."

Drake sighed in disgust. "Did either of you get a proper invite here today?"

"Are you coming, Gabriel?" Erwin asked. "No one has seen you anywhere in almost a month."

Drake swore under his breath. "He's played out. Go to the hells alone."

"I beg your pardon." Gabriel sent him an insulting grin. "I haven't even *begun* to play yet."

Drake stared at him. "How am I supposed to explain your absence to a certain lady when she asks where you have gone?"

"She knows what I am." Gabriel shrugged, walking backward a few steps. "I doubt she'll be surprised when she discovers where I've chosen to spend the rest of the day."

He stared through the hedge that separated his path from the one that led to the fountain where Alethea stood. His chest grew tight as he looked at her.

She pivoted without warning and glanced in Gabriel's direction.

He couldn't imagine her in a brothel.

But then again, until these past few weeks, he would never have imagined her nude and passionate in his arms, either.

He closed his eyes. What an irony at his expense, to have worried that *he* would shame *her*.

He'd reconciled himself to the unpalatable fact that she had loved someone else before him. And now—well, whatever the truth was, he had to know. He had never played the fool over a woman.

It was probably too late to undo what he felt for her. But he'd damned well proceed with his eyes open.

Chapter Thirty

❦ ❧

Alethea was nibbling a lemon-cheese tart and gossiping with Gabriel's cousin Chloe, Viscountess Stratfield, and her sister-in-law Eloise, Lady Drake Boscastle, the former governess whose love had brought her wicked husband to heel. She was surprised at how warmly the Boscastle wives embraced her by sharing confidences. It made Alethea yearn for an understanding female besides Mrs. Watson to whom she could divulge her own burdensome secret. But it would make an ugly confession.

And yet this appeared to be a family one could entrust with private affairs and candid admissions. She had the reassuring sense that whatever was spoken among these women would not be betrayed.

It was Gabriel who deserved the truth, of course. But as the afternoon shadows lengthened, it occurred to Alethea that her dark knight seemed to have disappeared. Perhaps he did not want to intrude on feminine chitchat. Perhaps he was talking to her brother.

Her intuition whispered otherwise.

And when shortly afterward Lord Drake approached the ladies' circle, now enlivened by the presence of Jane, the Marchioness of Sedgecroft, and Alethea's own cousin, Lady Pontsby, she acknowledged the cold breath of foreboding. It chilled her bones.

Lord Drake's eyes bespoke unwelcome, but not unexpected, news. "Alethea," he began, giving his wife, Eloise, an intimate smile before he bent to kiss Alethea's hand, "I have been asked to deliver a message to you."

For several moments she did not hear for the disconcerting surge of blood to her temples. There was a touch of embarrassment in Drake's eyes that she could not misinterpret.

She knew.

Gabriel had abandoned her, and his own cousin, a reformed rakehell himself, had been sent to make excuses. How many times had he done this? To how many other heartsick young ladies?

"Where did he go?" she asked softly.

"He met up with some friends who reminded him of a prior obligation."

She felt a flush of unpleasant heat suffuse her face. Gambling, she decided. Or another woman. Perhaps both. She suddenly remembered why she had always preferred the quiet life to the masquerade of London society. At least her horses and country neighbors did not abandon her at the first temptation.

"I see," she said after an uncomfortable lapse of silence.

"Well, I don't," Lady Pontsby said, studying Alethea in concern. "I understood he wished to speak with our mutual families in private later this evening. This must have been a pressing obligation, indeed, that he did not make a proper farewell."

"Perhaps he plans to return before the party is over?" Jane asked, her gaze upon Drake's face.

He coughed. "I couldn't say. I didn't think to inquire. The reminder of this prior duty came upon him as rather a surprise."

Jane glanced up at Alethea with a comforting smile. She was the daughter of an earl herself, a woman who might have become notorious had she not married her scoundrel marquess. "Did it? Well, we shall enjoy ourselves without him. London has been deprived of Alethea's company for far too long to waste a minute missing Gabriel. Do you remember, Alethea, the dance you and I attended at which a certain countess dressed as a man and challenged her husband to a duel because he did not recognize her?"

Alethea dredged up a smile. "I couldn't forget."

It seemed difficult to believe that not long ago in actual years, Alethea had enjoyed a certain popularity in the ton. True, she had not visited London as often as a fashionable young lady should to make a decent show. But then, she'd had no need to hunt a husband or to parade up and down Rotten Row with her chaperone at a certain hour. She had been engaged to the perfect gentleman. She had cantered across the country hills of her home at her leisure and had taken sincere comfort in the fellowship of her neighbors. Her life had been planned by her parents.

It was at once disconcerting and interesting to fling herself back into London's social arena, un-armed and out of practice as she was. She expected the comments she received on the loss of not only her betrothed but of a stable place in Society. Her well-wishers would have gasped in shock to learn how inured she was to both these genuine and per-functory expressions of sympathy.

She did not expect, however, to be summarily abandoned by the man who had contrived to place her in this vulnerable position. Nor did the atten-tion his various family members paid her do any-thing but emphasize the fact that Gabriel had gone off to sins unknown without a word. They knew. What could they say?

"I have every confidence that Sir Gabriel will re-turn before we leave," Lady Pontsby murmured, sharing a tight smile with Gabriel's vivacious raven-haired cousin Chloe, who was less adept at hiding her annoyance than Jane.

Chloe lifted her half-empty lemonade glass to the attendant footman. "I don't care if he doesn't. I say we find another rogue to take his place. Come with me, Alethea. We shall not sit here and take root like wallflowers while there is fun to be had. It goes against the grain."

Lady Pontsby rose. "Lead the way, Lady Stratfield."

Alethea laughed reluctantly. Her heart physically
hurt. Why had he done this? An hour ago he had
been so playful—but then, he had won. Perhaps that
was all he had wanted from the start. "Sir Gabriel
does not owe me his attendance. We are merely old
friends and recent neighbors."

"Then let us make new friends," Chloe said in
contagious mischief. "You were a wonderful flirt
once, Alethea. I did envy how easily you flitted in
and out of Society without a misstep."

"Yes, but—"

"But now I am a married woman who is possibly
carrying a child. I shall live vicariously through my
friends. Not that I am complaining about Dominic."

Gasps arose from the other ladies present. Chloe
had miscarried her first child and had taken the loss
deeply. Always radiant, she did have an exceptional
glow and energy about her.

"I knew it," Jane said with a jubilant grin. "I told
Grayson only this morning."

"Does your husband know?" Alethea asked,
smiling despite her own disappointment. If Gabriel
had disappeared, had decided he was not a man
meant for marriage, there would not be a betrothal
announcement or joyful christenings of their children together. And if Alethea did bear a child, she
would raise it alone.

Chloe smiled. "He is in heaven at the thought of the baby."

"I'm happy for you," Alethea said, trying not to feel wistful.

"So, you will accompany me?" Chloe said, taking her by the hand. "I've told you my secret. Now tell me one of yours, and remember, it is bad luck to deny a lady in my condition."

In the end, as she had already learned to her detriment, there was really no denying a Boscastle at all. And even though Chloe meant only to atone for Gabriel's abandonment, Alethea felt the sting all the deeper. He had warned her he wasn't any good.

It was her own fault if she'd chosen not to believe him.

Chapter Thirty-one

❧ ❧

He was back on his familiar playground, plunged into the demimonde's pleasures, and yet he felt himself to be a stranger. How could that be? He had always been drawn to the darker dens, the danger of London's secret life, the uncertainty. If he could survive these streets, he could survive anything. He drank little as he and his companions visited a few old haunts. Once he had found the city night world emboldening, the edge he needed to stay alive.

None of it tempted him tonight. Not the assignations conducted in Vauxhall, the affairs in theatre boxes, plots hatched in West End lanes. When had he changed? At Waterloo? The night he'd crossed that bedamned bridge and fallen into something far deeper than a riverbed?

He wanted to go back and undo everything. Perhaps his entire life. He had nothing to show for it except a modest military pension and a country house as shabby as he felt. And what of the woman he had wanted for as long as he could remember?

And he still did, damn his obsession with her. He

wished he hadn't heard, wished her softly spoken words had not driven a knife through his heart. What if she had had a good reason for associating with Audrey Watson?

He walked past the two prize pugilists who guarded the door of the high-class hell. The heavily shuttered establishment catered to noblemen who preferred to gamble in a more dangerous atmosphere than the usual gentlemen's clubs.

He approached the hazard table and welcomed the rush of anticipation that raced through his veins. A game of dice with a good profit. His pigeon, a young gentleman who'd turned his silk-lined coat inside out for luck, was flushed with porter and false bravado.

Gabriel smiled bitterly over his shoulder at the Mortlock brothers. "I can't fleece that fool. He's an infant. His mama will flay me. I cannot believe I left my cousin's birthday celebration for this."

Not to mention the woman whose deceptive sweetness invaded his mind at every moment. Hell. He'd lived without her most of his life. How difficult would it be to pretend he did not need her now?

"Look, if you play, you'll have something to give him," Erwin Mortlock said from behind.

Gabriel looked up in irritation. "Who are you talking about?"

"Your cousin, the marquess. You can buy him a pretty birthday present now with what you'll win here. We'll all go back to the party later."

"You can buy me a gift, too," his brother added with a grin.

A waiter wearing a black apron approached the three men and bowed. "Sir Gabriel, I have been asked to invite you downstairs for a private game."

Gabriel straightened his cuffs. "By whom?"

"Baron Gosfield, sir."

Gabriel hesitated. The downstairs room of the hell was reserved for more intense wagers of chance. He knew Gosfield only casually, and disliked him.

"What is his request?" he asked.

"Ombre, sir."

"Go on, Boscastle," Erwin urged him. "It's your game."

Lucky at cards, unlucky at love. He'd never thought to prove or disprove the maxim. The concept of love had meant little. He had always gambled to lose at love affairs. Emotional intimacy had been a door upon which he had refused to knock.

He descended the winding stairs into the murky depths of the private hell. For the first time since he'd approached a green baize table and sized up an opponent, he knew a moment of uncertainty. It passed. Another chance to prove himself.

Lucky at cards, unlucky at love.

He sat in a chair pulled out for him, his posture relaxed. Gosfield glanced up and appraised him. Gabriel's blood quickened. He recognized the rivalry masked behind those pleasant features.

"It's your game," Erwin said again, sensing the

tension between the two players. "You always win."

He'd thought so too until he'd gambled on another game of chance. He had never bet on battles between dogs or gamecocks, believing that to risk a helpless animal's life was a coward's cheat. Concerning his own mortality and welfare, he had always been a bit more careless.

Tonight he didn't give a damn at all.

Alethea was packing her bags to go home only three hours later in the upstairs suite of her brother's town house. He and Lady Pontsby had stayed at Grayson's party and did not expect to leave until the small hours.

Pleading a headache, an excuse that was not an entire fabrication, she had returned to the Cavendish Square address so that she would not have to pretend to be enjoying herself. She saw no point in ruining her family's pleasure of London because of her private dilemma.

The Boscastle family had done everything to atone for Gabriel's behavior until she could not bear their kindness another moment. Nor was she particularly heartened by the promise of her gregarious host, Grayson, the Marquess of Sedgecroft, to take Gabriel to task when he got his hands on him.

Alethea would take care of Gabriel herself, if the blackguard ever had the courage to face her again. She was decent with a pistol. Perhaps she would shoot him in the arm or leg should he ever return to the country.

It did not seem likely, however, that she would be given this gratifying chance. If Gabriel could run out on both his own family's celebration and his promise to her, she doubted she would ever see him again.

Once before in London she had been disenchanted, wounded too deeply for words. But not like this. Gabriel had made her laugh, made her again believe in love. She was too numb to cry. She did not understand. Had everything been a game? She could not believe it.

At least now she would not have to reveal her secret to anyone. How grateful she was to have learned what Gabriel was before she had confessed what Jeremy had done to her.

Chapter Thirty-two

❦ ❧

The places to which his jaded imagination led were possibly far worse than the unrevealed truth. For all he knew Alethea had applied for a position as a maid at Mrs. Watson's seraglio.

But in the scenes his mind conjured up as he flung himself into his town carriage, and throughout the short ride to Grayson's house and hence to Cavendish Square, he was envisioning Alethea subjecting herself to every manner of degradation and depravity. When he finally reached his destination, he was all but expelling smoke from his nostrils and leaving a trail of brimstone and singed trust in his shadow. And when he instructed his stone-faced coachman to stay, vowing that he would not be long, the fellow merely cracked his whip in the air and urged the horses to the curb.

After he recovered from the initial blow at finding out that Alethea was truly acquainted with Audrey Watson, he had tried to reason with his anger. How much did it matter that Alethea had slept with other men? That she'd considered soliciting her charms to survive? He assumed that that had been her motive. Could he blame Audrey? No, unfortunately. In fact, he'd have to be a damned arsehole of a hypocrite to snub a woman like Audrey, who had befriended his family on more occasions then he could list. But that didn't mean he wanted her to befriend Alethea.

And while most gentlemen would prefer to bring a maiden home to meet the family's approval for marriage, Gabriel didn't have any parents living to impress. His brothers, who had never bothered to keep in touch with him anyway, and who might as well be dead, certainly couldn't complain of his choice of a bride when he had no bloody idea how to inform them that he was getting married.

He felt the shock she'd dealt him to the marrow of his bones as he ran up the steps of her brother's London residence. The servants of the household had not bothered to lock the door through which he fairly flew, his black cloak trailing in his wake.

He wagered that after tonight their mistress would stand better guard against the evils that nightfall brought. She would throw all her bolts from this evening on.

He stormed the stairs, his angry strides carrying him past the moonlit gallery to the drawing room without a single soul opening a door, or even an eyelid, in question.

He had no idea what he expected to find—his beloved entertaining seven lovers in seven lurid positions? He was prepared for anything. He doubted she could hurt him more.

* * *

The source of Alethea's misery was banging through the house like a marauder. She gritted her teeth and marched to the top of the stairs. The skeleton staff of household servants in charge of Robin's London lodgings had ventured from their quarters to stare up at her in bewilderment. She imagined they were terrified that she had brought her unrefined country friends to their door.

One of the footmen raised his voice in distress. "My lady, shall I go for the constable?"

She hurried down the stairs, her shoulders set for a confrontation. "No. I shall deal with this myself."

"But—"

"Go, please."

The six of them—two footmen, a butler, the young Scottish housekeeper, and a pair of house-maids—backed away in a collective silence that seemed to scream that Alethea would not survive an encounter with whoever had burst into the house like a beast unleashed.

But strangely, Gabriel's ill-mannered entry made her all the more determined to stay calm. She was furious at him, all right. And if he had truly lost his mind, it would explain why he'd run out on her to-day. Not that she would forgive him. She might, however, make an effort to visit him once a month in the asylum. Perhaps she would end up in a cell next to his.

She glanced around to make certain the servants had disappeared, strode down the hall to confront him, and said, "Get into the drawing room this minute, Gabriel, before the night watchman or my brother arrives."

Her bravado faltered as their gazes locked. He stared at her in bewildering defiance. His black jacket, coat, and cambric shirt, his buttoned waistcoat, appeared rumpled and smelled of brandy and smoke.

"What do you have to say for yourself?" she demanded, angry at how he'd treated her today, and even more so that he could still make her ache with desire afterward. It was unthinkable. How could she care for a man who had disappointed both her and his family? After what she had suffered at another man's hand? Was *she* the one who'd gone mad? Was love a poison that made logic impossible?

He walked right past her toward the drawing room without answering. His gait was languid, insolent perhaps, the graceful stroll of a cavalry officer. When he turned at last, she gasped in dismay. He had a black eye.

"What happened to you?" she whispered. "What have you been doing?"

"I broke up a fight between the Mortlock brothers," he said curtly. "I should have let them kill themselves. Or me."

She lifted her head at the clatter of coach wheels that came from the street. "Dear God. That sounds like Robin."

He put his hand on her shoulder and forced her

back to him. "I don't care if Ali Baba and the Forty Thieves arrive with the Archbishop of Canterbury."

"Do you care about anything?" she demanded, her eyes locked with his.

"I should think that was obvious."

"Your ill breeding is all that was obvious today."

"You've known that for years," he returned with a ruthless smile. "And yet you slept with me and agreed to be my wife."

She flinched. "I have cared about you for years, but don't ask me to explain why at this current moment."

"Yes. I don't deserve you. I want you anyway."

He wanted her. She wanted him. There was little solace in realizing these truths. Nor in admitting to herself that his mere presence comforted and threatened at once. She had given herself to Gabriel of her own free choice. The only other man in her life had stolen her love.

Gabriel was at least the devil of her own choosing, and if he had dragged her into his decadent world, she had followed willingly and could only blame herself for the descent.

But that did not mean she would descend any deeper.

Whatever Gabriel was, rogue or hero, their lives had been entangled even before she was aware of what entanglement could lead to.

What if his past has been troubled? Hers had been too, even though she had managed to keep the most humiliating part to herself. She had always won-

dered how different life would have been for her
and Gabriel had his father, Joshua Boscastle, lived.
She might have been betrothed to Gabriel from the
start.

Was it too late to amend history? Gabriel might
have been destined to break her heart, for all she
knew. And now that they had finally been granted
the chance to be together, what had they done to
prove that they belonged with each other?

"I'll tell you a secret, Gabriel," she said, suddenly
unwilling to tolerate his moody domination for another second. "I wish I'd never come to London."

He tore off his coat and sent it hurtling toward an
armchair. "Well, I wish I'd never left."

"You don't have to stay in the country," she said
indignantly. "You can sell that house. You have no
future as a country farmer. Everyone who has lived
in Helbourne Hall has left. Why should you attempt to aspire to better? Don't bother to answer.
You set upon a course of self-pity and punishment
when your father died."

"Is that right? Don't bother to answer. I agree.
Helbourne Hall is haunted and has an off-putting
reputation."

She refused to move as he advanced on her. "The
same might be said of its current owner."

He walked toward her until they stood only a
breath apart. "If I am haunted, it is by you."

Her heart fluttered. She had never seen such
naked pain on a man's face before. Her natural feminine instincts wished to coax him from his stormy

humor, even though he'd embarrassed them both today.

"You must be possessed by a devil," she said in distress. "I have never seen you in this mood."

"I have never before *been* in this mood, Alethea."

"Then do you mind telling me what has put you in such a temper? You were in good spirits when I left you with your cousin. You . . . were playful."

He smiled coldly. "Continue."

"Continue what?" she asked impatiently. "We parted with the agreement that we would announce our engagement. I took lemonade with your family."

His eyes raked her. "And between our last meeting and the lemonade?"

She shook her head in confusion. "I walked in the garden, Gabriel."

"The Garden of Earthly Delights?"

"The garden of the marquess, your cousin," she said as if he were simpleminded.

He glanced away. "Did you walk alone?"

"There were other people in the garden." She hesitated. "Other guests."

"You walked with Audrey Watson," he said, staring at her in accusation.

She stared back at him, her heart in her throat. "Yes."

"And your defense?" he asked quietly.

"Do I require one?"

He closed his eyes. "Am I in love with . . . an aspiring courtesan? If so, please tell me now."

She did not answer at first. She was too shocked to find the words. Had he spoken with Audrey? Could he have forced the woman, or charmed her into breaking Alethea's confidence? Who had told him she'd spoken with Audrey?

"Is that what Mrs. Watson told you?" she asked, dreading his answer.

"Mrs. Watson did not tell me a damned thing. In fact, I did not speak with her after I saw you together. I did, however, hear the conversation with my own ears. With Drake as a witness."

She felt her blood go cold. "You eavesdropped, Gabriel," she said in a low voice. "You skulked about in the bushes when you could have announced your presence and had your curiosity satisfied."

He laughed bitterly. "Perhaps I was not prepared to learn that the woman I love is a—"

"—courtesan," she said in a quiet voice. "You said it once. You may as well say it again."

"I did not accuse you," he said quickly. "I only asked—well, blast it, Alethea. What conclusions should I draw from your conversation with her? I think I deserve the truth."

"How much have you had to drink, Gabriel?"

"Not enough to keep me away from you."

"I think you should leave the house now," she said faintly.

"And never see you again?" he asked in bewilderment. "Am I not owed at least an explanation?"

She shook her head. What a tangle. "Yes. But not

when you are upset and have frightened the life out of my brother's servants."

"I lost my temper. You were not honest with me, were you?"

"Do you honestly want to know how I feel right now, Gabriel?"

"Yes. Honesty would be a pleasant change at this point."

She narrowed her eyes. "I want you to go," she said, her voice breaking. "Do not darken my—my life again."

He snorted. "You say that as if you have made mine better."

She looked insulted. "And haven't I?"

"No." His mouth curled into a hard smile. "You've made me miserable."

She caught her breath, refusing to cry. "If I were a man, I would call you out and kill you."

"Too late," he said mockingly. "I was dead the moment I saw you."

She gasped. "I despise the air you breathe."

"I curse the day you were conceived."

She pushed him away from her. "At least we know my parentage."

"Come to think of it," he said, "you don't look anything like your brother."

"Well, do you know what *you* look like?" she asked with a grim smile.

He lowered his face to hers. "Do tell."

"A—a damned blackguard, that's what. Now go away."

He snorted. "My escape cannot be accomplished fast enough."

"Are you still here?"

"Damnit, Alethea, I did not come here to quarrel."

"And yet you have done nothing else."

He looked bereft. She felt her anger crumbling, wanted him to hold her.

"May I come tomorrow morning?" he asked quietly.

"It will be chaos," she said. "I will not be alone."

"Then I will follow you back to the country." He stared at her. "Have you betrayed me with another?"

She laughed, tears filling her eyes. "What do you think?"

"Do you love me?"

She closed her eyes. His arms engulfed her. His mouth crushed hers, his kiss igniting little flames deep inside her. Still, she felt cold, afraid, ashamed that she had kept the truth from him, ashamed of that truth itself.

"Come with me now," he whispered in her ear. "Stay the night at my house and we shall talk. Prove your love."

"I have already proven my feelings to you," she said, softly. "It remains for you to wait until you know everything before you decide whether you still want me."

His breath warmed the hollow of her throat. "I'll always want you."

"As your wife?" she asked, refusing to react as he kissed the underside of her jaw.

"Is there a reason why you *cannot* marry me?" He bit her shoulder in gentle punishment. "Do you have another husband?" He clasped her hand and guided her to the sofa. "Do you have a secret avocation?"

She turned, but he still claimed her hand, drawing her down beside him. "You have a bruise coming out on your cheek," she said in despair. "And you— you've been somewhere dangerous tonight, I can tell."

"Perhaps."

"How uncouth."

"You knew what I was from the beginning." He smoothed his calloused fingers down her shoulder to the buttoned inseam of her sleeve. "Isn't that what you liked about me, Alethea? The true question, I believe, is what are *you*? What have you become?"

"You can be beastly, can't you?"

"You knew that, too."

"No. I knew I cared about you. Dirty, dark, hurtling down a road of self-destruction. I would have stood directly on that road to save you. But I never dreamt it was you I would battle."

"Are you giving up on me?"

She turned her head. "There is a coach outside. It is probably my brother and my cousin, both of whom were to be told tonight that we were getting married."

"Make love to me before they come then." He

stroked his black-gloved knuckles down her nape, her back, to the rise of her rump.

"Please go home now, Gabriel."

He buried his face in her hair. "No. I won't leave. As a matter of fact, I might encamp in this room until winter. Don't you want me anymore?"

A shadow of hurt darkened her eyes. She didn't want another man who claimed to care for her when he had only anger in his heart.

His mouth burned like a firebrand across her throat. "I want only you, and I want the truth. Be honest with me."

"And if you hate me afterward?" she whispered in anguish.

His chest tightened in forewarning. What truth could she be hiding? *Had* she offered herself as a courtesan? If so, he would have to accept this unpalatable surprise. He knew she'd loved another, but other *men*? What had she done the year everyone assumed she had been mourning? He did not know if he could tolerate the pain. Hypocrite he might be, but he had claimed her in his dreams a decade ago. He'd been afraid to assert his desire. Who had usurped him?

"Forgive me for insisting on honesty," he said with irony. "I do not always remember to be a gentleman."

Her eyes flashed. "They're in scarce demand these days."

"Am I not as decent as your dearly departed Hazlett?" he continued, unable to control himself. "Was it he who unleashed the desire we shared?"

She went still, and he knew he'd hurt her, wished he could take back the bitter words. "I did not mean that."

She angled her face away. "Didn't you?"

"Damnit, Alethea, I can't let you go, no matter what you are. Please come home with me tonight."

" 'No matter what I am'?" she asked softly.

"Whatever you are, I won't give you up."

She shook her head, her expression bruised. "I won't make love to you when you're in this mood."

Hoofbeats echoed in the street. A carriage door opened and slammed. Gabriel's cynical gaze searched her face. "Do you love me, Alethea?"

"Yes, but do not ask me why."

"Is there anyone else?"

She stared at him, tears threatening in earnest. "No, you stupid man."

"Then you will tell me everything?"

"Yes. It isn't what you're thinking. Audrey only gave me advice."

"Advice? On what?"

"I can't—I can't say it."

"My God, Alethea. What is it?"

She shook her head.

The door behind him opened. "I do love you," he said, his voice low. And now he had to face the truth that no matter what her explanation turned out to be, it would not change his feelings for her.

Chapter Thirty-three

❦ ❦

Lord Wrexham cursed aloud when he returned from the party and spotted Gabriel's town carriage parked outside. "Doesn't that man have any sense of decency at all?" he shouted to Lady Pontsby, who harbored an altogether different opinion of Gabriel's behavior.

"Do not charge into that house unannounced," she advised him as they descended from his larger vehicle and proceeded up the steps together.

"What do you mean?" he asked irately. "It's my house, and as far as I can tell that rakehell and Alethea are alone. "I have every right to interrupt whatever—"

Robin broke off as a footman opened the door to admit him. "What is Sir Gabriel doing here, Bastwick? And where the devil is my sister?"

The footman shook his head in confusion. "We were asked not to interfere, my lord."

"Interfere in what?" Lady Pontsby inquired, deliberately planting herself in the center of the hall to impede Robin's progress.

"You know perfectly well what," he retorted. "It is hardly a question one poses to a footman."

"I don't know. And neither do you. Control yourself."

"Stop trying to hinder me."

She raised her voice. "HINDER YOU FROM WHAT, ROBIN? SIR GABRIEL IS A TRUE GENTLEMAN. I DON'T IMAGINE HE IS ENGAGED IN ANY MISCHIEF IN THAT ROOM."

He threw her a scowl of utter disgust and marched up the stairs to the drawing room door. He knew bloody well she'd only been trying to trumpet Boscastle and his sister a warning. Truth be told, if Gabriel and Alethea were carrying on unbecomingly, he had no desire whatsoever to walk in and catch them unawares in a tryst. But it was time to put a stop to an association that seemed to have no decent boundaries.

"At least knock," Lady Pontsby urged behind him.

"I am not an intruder in my own house."

However, he knocked, but as compromise to his assertion he did not wait for an invitation before he entered. To his unspeakable relief Gabriel was standing at the window, and Alethea was sitting as stiff as a bayonet in an armchair.

"Pardon me," he said lamely. "I had no idea you had company, Alethea. I hope that your guest—"

Gabriel turned.

Lady Pontsby's eyes widened.

"—your guest—" Robin choked out, staring at

Gabriel's blackened eye. "Did Alethea do that to you?"

Alethea surged from the armchair to her feet. "What a ridiculous assumption."

Lady Pontsby edged around him. "Never mind, my dear. Your brother didn't mean to offend you. It's just that—how did you come by that nasty bruise, Sir Gabriel, if you don't mind telling us?"

Gabriel sighed. "I had the bad fortune to break up a fight only to find my face used as a buffer between the opposing parties."

Lord Wrexham studied his sister in concern. "And this fight—which you claim to have stopped— was the reason you so rudely abandoned Alethea at the party?"

"Not exactly."

"Then I don't understand what happened today," Lord Wrexham said.

Gabriel looked pointedly at Alethea. "Nor do I."

"Then perhaps you should leave, sir, so that my sister might render her version of the situation."

Gabriel hesitated, studying Alethea until she finally returned his gaze. "Perhaps I should," he said at length. "I shall call upon you as soon as you return to the country."

Lord Wrexham looked baffled at this pronouncement. "Have you further business with me, sir?" he asked bluntly, earning frowns from both his sister and Lady Pontsby.

Gabriel sighed again, retrieved his hat and jacket from the chair, and walked solemnly to the door.

"With your permission your sister and I are to be married at the earliest convenience. I believe she wishes a country wedding. The Boscastles, of course, will insist otherwise. It makes no difference to me where we are wed, but I would guess the marquess would prefer a private wedding in his house."

Lady Pontsby gasped in delight. Alethea might have reacted in any number of ways—Robin was too astonished to pay her any attention, despite her starring role in this unprecedented performance. He'd been of half a mind to throttle Gabriel for offenses assumed if unidentified. But now that Boscastle was to become his brother-in-law, he would have to swallow his criticism, and put on a good face.

"But—when did this happen?" he asked Gabriel's retreating figure.

"Seven years, four months, and thirteen days ago, to be precise." Gabriel paused at the door to smile darkly at Alethea. "Give or take a few hours."

Chapter Thirty-four

He had no idea what he was doing, only that he'd hurt her tonight and he was hurting even more. Now that he'd made a monumental fool of himself, in front of her and her family, he wondered whether her association with Audrey Watson even mattered.

Could he love her forever if she had been a courtesan in secret? It could not have been a long, successful career. And it wasn't as if he had not consorted with Cyprians and sought an open invitation to Audrey's. But, he was a man, and there was a difference.

Then again, he had debauched himself without compensation. At least a courtesan placed value upon her favors.

The very thought of her lying with another man, for love or money, made him feel ill.

How had he descended into this humiliating state of unmanly misery? He couldn't explain it. He did know, however, that he had never felt so at odds in his life. He couldn't imagine anything that could make him feel worse—until he climbed into his carriage and saw his three Boscastle cousins, Heath, Drake, and Devon, awaiting him, a trio of black-haired, blue-eyed devils.

He frowned and sat down opposite his cousin Devon. "I am in no temper to discuss my personal—"

"Did Alethea do that to your face?" Devon asked with a grimace of sympathy. "If so, I'd say she loved you very much."

Gabriel gazed upon his cousins in annoyance. It was disconcerting to realize how much, in both physical appearance and attitude, he and they resembled one another—proof, he feared, of the potent Boscastle bloodlines.

"Don't the three of you have wives waiting at home with your woolen dressing robes and bowls of gruel?"

Drake laughed. "I've a feeling you'll be joining that esteemed club yourself."

Sooner than anyone thought. At least Gabriel assumed—*hoped* it to be so, unless Alethea was at this moment informing Robin she had changed her mind. He resisted looking back at the town house as the carriage lurched into the street. It was bad enough to have the Boscastles aware of his hopeless attraction to Alethea without proving how besotted he was.

"Did it ever occur to the three of you that my private affairs are not your business?"

Devon hooted in derision. "You've been born into the wrong family. There is no privacy among us. Every sin and scandal is submitted to the cabal for scrutiny and discussion."

"My God," Gabriel muttered, glancing heavenward, as if he could ever remember help coming from that quarter.

No. That was unfair. He'd prayed twice in his life that he could recall. Once when his mother had a raging fever and the doctor said she would die. She hadn't. The second petition to the Almighty had been that day in the pillory when Alethea's carriage had entered the square. He'd prayed she wouldn't notice him. She had.

And as for being born into the wrong family? He wasn't about to show that the admission of inclusion pleased him and made him wonder what the hell had become of his own wilding brothers. No matter how many times he insisted to himself that he didn't care about his three vanished siblings, he felt the absence of them in his life all the same. Did he have nieces and nephews whom he'd never met? Some part of him lamented the loss. It was as if he had a limb or two missing.

Family. It could not heal all sorrows, but it made them bearable.

Heath leaned forward. "Cheer up, cousin. The story of your sins will not leave our lips under penalty of torture at my sister Emma's dainty hands. She despises low gossip."

"Which is no guarantee that others will not speak of your misconduct in public," Drake was hasty to add.

Devon stretched out his lanky arms and legs. "Actually it's a guarantee that any and all crimes you commit will be until your dying day subjected to the court of public opinion."

Gabriel stared, turn by turn, at each one of his blue-eyed cousins. "And you took it upon yourselves, from the goodness of your hearts, to gather in my carriage tonight to deliver this unhelpful advice?"

Heath stared back at him. "I would like to take you somewhere."

"What if I told you I don't wish to go along on one of your family jaunts?" Gabriel asked bluntly.

Heath smiled. "I think we should have to persuade you."

Chapter Thirty-five

❧ ❧

Alethea sat uncomfortably in the armchair, sipping a mug of skim milk while her brother and Lady Pontsby questioned her about Gabriel's startling announcement of their engagement.

"It's all rather sudden," Robin said for the fourth time in a row.

Lady Pontsby looked up from her fashion magazine. "They've known each other for seven years. I'd venture to say that if they waited any longer this would be a funeral, not a wedding, we were planning."

"When is the ceremony to be?" he asked Alethea. She frowned, gripping her mug, thinking idly that it should have contained sherry instead of skim milk. This was a night that called for sherry if ever she'd lived through one. "That's a good question."

Lady Pontsby put down her magazine. "The ceremony is to be in London? Is that what I understood?"

"You'll have to ask my—Gabriel," she said with a sigh.

Lady Pontsby regarded her curiously. "Well, this sheds a different light on his conduct today. Perhaps he had a good reason for leaving the party. Perhaps he went to the jewelers for your ring."

Her voice drifted over Alethea's thoughts, over the storm roiling inside her. She loved him desperately, but at this moment she almost wished she'd kept riding past him that day in the pillory. Her parents had been right.

She had been a girl who ventured where she ought not. All her papa's efforts at bending her to conform to her birthright had been futile. She had fallen in love with a pillory boy, then pretended to be content when she was betrothed to that immoral wretch Jeremy.

Her parents and Jeremy had died. She prayed their souls had found peace. For she had found a freedom unanticipated and more appreciated than was proper to admit. And with that freedom and impropriety she had also found the heartache that all the paragons of the world had predicted. Was it possible to have love without pain?

"Did you say something?" she asked her cousin with an air of embarrassment. "My mind was wandering."

Lady Pontsby gazed at her with an indulgent smile. "That you are *distraite* under the circumstances is understandable, my dear."

A quarter hour later, when their small party dispersed and Alethea excused herself for the night, her cousin crept into her bedchamber to continue their talk.

"I don't know what happened today, but I can see there was an upset. I hope you and Gabriel shall overcome it."

"I'm not sure that's possible, Miriam."

"If you love each other it is essential."

"But you *don't* know what happened," Alethea said.

"I know that he came back tonight and you wanted him to. The rest shall fall into place."

Gabriel groaned when he realized their destination was a very exclusive bordello on Bruton Street. The infamous Audrey Watson's heavily guarded house attracted and admitted only the most elite customers from high society and London's half-world.

The delights provided within her private rooms cost a pretty penny. For those gentlemen who did not seek sexual gratification the house also offered an excellent selection of wine and food, and the conversation and company of gifted guests. Artists, poets, and politicians often graced Audrey's salon. Gabriel had once craved the privilege of entry and the voluptuous pleasures of her house.

Now there was only one woman he desired, and she did not belong here. She belonged with him, and he had to believe that her association with Audrey did not have any dark significance.

"Is this a joke?" he demanded of his cousins.

Drake shot him a rueful grin. "You brought my wife here once to play a trick on me, as I recall."

Gabriel grinned reluctantly. God, he'd been a rotten devil. "It turned out well, didn't it?"

"No bloody thanks to you," Drake replied without rancor.

"Hurry up, Gabriel." Heath reached to open the door. "The rest of us are married, and this little excursion of ours will make the papers if we aren't discreet. Go around the gate to your left. A guard will escort you up a secret flight of stairs. Audrey is waiting. We'll collect you in an hour."

Within a few minutes he was escorted up the bordello's private stairs into Audrey's inner quarters—a suite of chambers cluttered with scented letters, books, two poodles, and a young man who was ushered out as furtively as Gabriel was granted an audience with the seraglio's proprietress.

"Oh, Gabriel," she murmured, languidly subjecting him to a head-to-knee inspection. "Love has given you a sultry look I really cannot resist. Did Alethea do that to your eye?"

He flung up his hands, not answering, then paced a spell before settling down on the only unoccupied space in the room—on the couch beside her. If she thought he'd be embarrassed or insist upon standing, he had another thing to tell her. He wasn't deliberately being rude, he was simply a man so at his wit's end that he didn't give a damn that he'd been summoned to the private chamber of one of London's most sought-after courtesans.

She frowned, almost as if she had read his mind. "For heaven's sake, Gabriel, could you at least pretend to pay me attention?"

His gaze traveled over her in slow perusal. "Forgive me," he said, sighing heavily.

"How is your mother?" she asked, taking his chin in her hand to turn his face into the light.

He pulled away. "What?"

"That bruise is darkening by the minute—your mother—*la duchesse*. I had so wanted to attend her wedding. After all, how many French *ducs* shall I meet in my lifetime? You did not go?"

"Not only did I not go, I did not know—my mother is married? To a French duke?" he asked, his shock genuine enough to supplant all his other woes. At least for the time being. He laid his head on the brocaded cushion. "Am I to understand that you brought me here to congratulate me on my mother's marriage?"

"Am I to understand that you were spying on me today at Grayson's party?"

"Well, what of it? It was a party. You were talking in the garden, not a confessional booth."

"It was a private conversation."

"And I, as Alethea's future husband, insist upon being privy to the nature of your association with my wife."

She pursed her lips, not quite hiding a smile. "Your future wife. And she loves you. That was the gist of what she and I discussed."

"It seems to me that there's a great part missing

from that simplified explanation . . . such as how you came to know each other, and why Alethea was seen visiting this house last year."

Her eyes narrowed. "Who told you such a thing?"

"So she did visit you."

"I admitted nothing of the kind," she said acerbically. "I have stated only that she loves you."

Gabriel nodded. "Yes. But I cannot help wondering how many other men she might have 'loved' before me."

Audrey's half-smile neither confirmed nor soothed his fears. "Does it matter? Would you desire her less for being the sort of woman that you not long ago found irresistible?"

His mouth tightened. "This is different. I want to marry her."

"How much?" she asked, her head cocked in curiosity.

"Enough that I will never return here, nor look at another woman again as long as I live."

A wistful laugh escaped her. "A Boscastle in love is a terrible force indeed. You are very forceful, Gabriel. I believe I shall dream of this conversation tonight. Why is it you Boscastle men have a way of warming a room?"

"Just tell me the truth."

"I did, Gabriel. She loves you. It's quite simple, isn't it?"

"Damnation, Audrey. You know what I'm asking—did she come here for work? Did she sleep with any of those men I passed downstairs? Or that I sit across from at a card table? I have to know."

"You must ask her then."

He stood, frustrated, afraid and yet—he needed the truth.

"I believe you have always loved her," she said quietly as he turned his back. "And now she returns your affection. It remains to prove yourself her hero."

"Her hero?" He glanced around, shook his head. "I am leaving your presence, madam, more confounded than I entered it."

"You do not have to leave at all, Gabriel," she said with an engaging smile.

But he was gone before she could elaborate.

Chapter Thirty-six

He hurried down the central staircase, propriety the last thing on his mind. Well, not *his* propriety, at least. Alethea's association with Audrey Watson remained a mystery to unravel. But as Audrey had pointed out, he had lived on the edge of polite society for as long as he could remember.

Gambler. Blackguard. In debt up to his eyeballs one day, his pockets bulging with cash the next. His stepfather had hit him across the head, shouted how worthless he was in his ear so many times that he was partially deaf on one side and suspected he'd sacrificed some brain function on the other.

Yet he'd survived. From his Boscastle father's strength of will and his mother's stubborn French blood, he'd managed to become a good cavalry officer, a damned unbeatable gambler, and part and parcel of the infamous London branch of the family.

And Alethea had not banished him from her life, a blessed miracle considering that she'd seen him at his worst, and had not given up on him, for reasons he would never fathom. He loved her. What man in his right mind would not? What did she see in him? He was suspicious, devious, impulsive, and scarred into the bargain.

He only knew that when he was knocked down, he got up, often reeling, too numb or dumb to do otherwise. The day he died would be the day he could not lift his battle-hardened body from the ground. Life assaulted him. He assaulted it, and himself, back. He'd never had any aspirations to be a hero, except perhaps where Alethea was concerned, and if she thought him brave, well, he'd done a damned good job of fooling her, that was all.

He descended the stairs to reach the ground-floor vestibule, staring upon a scenario that had appealed to him in what might be termed his previous life. The courtesans in attendance boasted a refined beauty; their skills were legendary in London. He recognized a prominent member of the War Office, a secretary in the East India Company, a viscount who had made his name known as a portrait painter. He heard his name called; he hung back in hesitation until a darkly clad figure detached itself from the sideboard, raising a glass of brandy in acknowledgment.

"It's past midnight, Cinderella. I have to return home a married man."

He and Drake walked together in companionable silence to the door, whereupon Mrs. Watson's stiff-rumped butler bowed and snapped his bony fingers in the air. Two footmen appeared bearing torches to light the men's way to the waiting carriage.

"Is there anything I might do to make your return journey home more comfortable, Lord Drake . . . Sir Gabriel?" he inquired, as tightly wound as a Continental clock.

Drake brushed past him. "We're fine for the night. If I may give—"

Gabriel looked down at a newly arrived guest, who loitered upon the lowest step to the house, and his gaze immediately hardened in contempt. He stopped as Drake continued toward the carriage.

The man in the leopard-lined evening cape glanced up at him with a wry smile of recognition. "Ah, Sir Gabriel, I see we meet again—at yet another whore's house."

Drake pivoted on the pavement, his handsome face darkening. "I beg your pardon, sir? Are you addressing my cousin?"

The subtle shift in Drake's posture must have conveyed a message. Within moments his brothers Heath and Devon Boscastle had joined him on the sidewalk, their coachman and two footmen a step behind. Gabriel glanced at the ominous-looking batons his cousins held, then firmly shook his head.

This was his fight.

"Lord Hazlett," he said in a cold voice, "I had actually hoped that you and I would find each other again. There is something unfinished between us."

Guy stared past him into the candlelit vestibule of the seraglio. He had the cruel face of a man of privilege, accustomed to using others, a man who truly believed he had the right to do as he pleased. Now,

as he stood before Sir Gabriel Boscastle and his
cousins, he seemed to assume that they would share
his demeaning views of women, and the world, in
general.

"Gabriel," he said with a patronizing smile, "we
are gentlemen who share the same weaknesses. I
would be remiss if I did not confide in you that
Alethea Claridge is no better than the girls within
Mrs. Watson's house."

Gabriel saw Devon step forward as if to guard
him. He gestured sharply, and his cousin fell back.
"What are you telling me, Hazlett?" he asked quietly.

Guy glanced around as if he'd just noticed that he
and Gabriel were not alone. "Are you bewitched,
my friend? Don't be. My brother was prepared to
marry her—he's already broken her in for you. I'm
sure that you will appreciate not having to initiate
another virgin. I understand she put up a fight at
first."

If Guy said anything else, Gabriel could not hear
it for the roaring of blood in his head. He stepped
down, his fists clenched. He felt someone, Drake or
Devon, putting a hand on his arm, trying to stop
him. But he wouldn't be stopped. He understood
that they only meant to stand up for him. But he
had spent his life fighting his own fights.

The truth was, he had never fought for anything
that mattered as much to him, except perhaps for
his mother. He hadn't felt this much passion even at
Waterloo.

He hit Guy right under the chin and heard the satisfying crunch of bone snapping. He might have broken his own knuckles, but he couldn't feel anything. Guy's groan of pain indicated that he'd suffered at least a fractured jaw joint, which ought to keep his mouth shut for a month or two.

"Come on, Gabriel," Drake said amiably over his shoulder. "It isn't nice to commit murder right before your own wedding. Wait a week or two."

Gabriel straightened with the intention of demanding that his cousin bugger off and mind his own business when Guy leapt up and punched him in the eye.

Gabriel saw lights explode behind his right eyelid as he staggered against Drake's hard frame, only to be shoved back toward Guy with a muttered incentive from Drake. "Give him a good one in the stones for me. That was a dirty blow, hitting a man when his head was turned. If I were in your place—"

Those words of encouragement took hold in the fertile earth of Gabriel's festering anger. Benumbed to the throbbing ache of his eye, ignoring the bloodied flesh that hung from his knuckles, he cuffed Guy again. And again. He attacked until when Hazlett finally staggered back and collapsed on the steps, he did not make any attempt to rise.

It had taken a moment for Gabriel to realize what Guy had said. Now a darker insinuation spread across his mind like a shadow. *He's already broken her in for you.* Men made crude jokes about sex all the time. Brothers shared secrets about their conquests, exaggerated their exploits to outdo the other. Half the time the remarks were only ballocks and inflated boasts to enhance one's idea of manliness.

But Guy's taunt had hinted of cruelty and violation. And now, all of a sudden, Gabriel understood, or thought he did, why Alethea hesitated to speak Jeremy's name. Why she had accused Gabriel of coming back too late.

Make me forget, Gabriel.

Forget what? Oh, God.

He had not been there to protect her. She had been degraded so profoundly she could not admit it to anyone. Idiot that he was, he hadn't made it easier for her to be honest about her humiliation. He had handled everything poorly, without consideration or honor.

It wasn't too late, though. He and Alethea might be broken in parts, but they belonged to each other, and always had. Together they would make a whole being.

He understood now that he had hurt her with his jealous accusations today instead of grasping what she and Audrey had not said. He swallowed the bitter taste at the back of his throat. He'd left her with an image of himself that was no better than that of the bastard who'd wounded her.

"Gabriel. Gabriel." A male voice, then a firm pair of hands upon his shoulders penetrated his bewildered fury. "Come on, into the carriage. You have made your point most eloquently. Look at me, cousin. How many fingers am I holding up?"

He swung around, not stopping to consider whom he assaulted, reacting from pure reflex.

A muscular forearm blocked the punch he meant to throw. He rocked back, caught his balance, and stared at his cousin Devon's forefinger waggling under his nose. "You've taken a good blow to the head, Gabriel. How many fingers am I holding up?"

Gabriel swatted his cousin's hand away with a snort of derision. "You can't fool me. That isn't a finger you're waving under my face. It's your rod, scrawny article that it is. I'd be ashamed to display it in public."

Devon laughed. "There's no need to stoop to personal insults. Let's go."

"But I'm not finished."

Devon stared past him to the cloaked figure sprawled out dazedly on Audrey's front steps. A pair of footmen were already on hand to whisk Guy out of the view of passersby. It would not please the upper-crust guests to have to walk around an offensive sight.

The under-butler emerged from the house, cast an approving look of recognition at the Boscastles, then said to the footmen, "Take this person to the rubbish heap. Mrs. Watson does not wish him to be admitted to her house nor to dirty her entrance. We have a reputation to maintain."

Gabriel turned to the three men gathered in a

semicircle around him. He grinned ruefully. No one had ever stood up so decisively for him before, with the exception of Alethea Claridge. He'd come to think he did not deserve such loyalty.

Hell, he'd worked hard enough to prove how bad he was, and now he had to make the ultimate choice—would the people who loved him be justified in their belief that he was a good man or would he prove he was as worthless as his stepfather had claimed?

Heath placed his hand on his shoulder. "We're going back to the party. Are you coming?"

"Party?"

"Grayson's birthday," Drake said, leaning against the carriage door. "You remember—the private to-do for the family and close friends after everyone else leaves?"

Gabriel smiled tiredly. "I appreciate the invitation, and at any other time I'd have been honored to celebrate Grayson's advanced age."

"But?" Devon said, grinning as if he hadn't a care in the world. "Another card game?"

Gabriel shook his head. "No. I have to go home."

Drake stepped away from the carriage door. "Home to an empty town house?" he asked wryly.

Gabriel didn't answer. There was no point in attempting to lie to his cousins, men who had sinned as he had, but had changed their ways. They could see right through him, and it felt good to not pretend for once that he didn't care. He was in love, about to embark on the biggest game of chance he'd ever played.

"I'm going home to Helbourne," he said.

Heath nodded. "Well, drop us off at Grayson's on the way. We shall raise a toast to you at the table."

Chapter Thirty-seven

It rained for three days in a row. The ancient yew that grew over the river had been struck by lightning and fallen across the bridge to Helbourne Hall. Several plucky village boys, and a girl or two, had already made a game of crossing to the other side.

The meadow had flooded and weeds sprouted up overnight, growing waist-high with a vengeance. In the moonlight the stone walls that divided Alethea's home from Helbourne Hall disappeared into drifts of damp mist. Autumn would indeed come soon, the farmers predicted. Their wives worried, but dared not say aloud, that some of the more defiant ghosts would risk eternal damnation by not returning to their places of rest after visiting their loved ones on Allhallows Eve. The devil always took his due. And love was no excuse.

Alethea took long walks in the rain, pretending not to gaze toward the road every few minutes for a certain dark knight to appear. Nor did she admit to staring from her window at night to count whether more lights than usual burned behind the mullioned windows of Gabriel's house. Her brother remarked that it would be foolhardy for a man to travel in this weather, and that Gabriel had asked for her hand and would keep his word.

But she knew that Gabriel wasn't the sort of man to let a storm stop him from doing what he wanted. Her monthly courses had come, and she told herself how fortunate it was that he hadn't left her carrying his child. There was nothing to say that even a rake would desire damaged property as a wife.

He had fallen in love with Lady Alethea, the pure and perfect. And if he'd been upset because he'd seen her talking to Audrey Watson, she could not imagine how he would feel when she admitted that he was not the first man to have knowledge of her body.

But she had promised him the truth. Would he return so that she could keep her word?

On a morning four days after she'd come home the sky dawned clear and a rainbow arced over the hills. She put on her old green-gray muslin frock and her battered half-boots, and helped muck out the soiled hay in the stables. The grooms gave her a wide berth as she wielded her pitchfork. If they guessed she was attacking an absent nobleman, they were wise enough to allow her; but Lady Alethea working in the stables was not an uncommon sight, so they pitched right alongside her.

Late that evening, after she had exhausted herself in paying calls that could have waited, she took a scalding hip bath and dressed for supper, then changed her mind and stretched across her bed with the windows open. She was surprised that she fell asleep, with so much weighing on her mind. But even then she could hear a horseman thundering through her dreams, the hoofbeats growing louder and louder until—

She sat up, shivering more from anticipation than cold, as the earth beneath her window thrummed, beating in synchrony with her pounding heart. Someone was riding in her garden.

She leapt out of bed and hastened to identify the mounted intruder prancing roughshod over the straggly geraniums and love-lies-bleeding that had barely survived the last storm. He was riding the most gorgeous gray Arab she had ever seen. The watery moonlight accentuated the animal's proud arched neck and sleek hindquarters, and its rider— he was a gorgeous animal himself.

She was dying for a closer look at both of them, and just as she found the breath to call to Gabriel, he set in his heels and took the south wall in an effortless jump that stopped her heart.

"You show-off," she shouted softly, and saw him half-turn to give her a cavalier wave.

He cantered off toward the hills, then wheeled with a grace she envied. "Don't you break either that magnificent animal's neck or your own," she whispered, turning from the window.

She flew downstairs in the dark and out into the garden, half-expecting both the rider and that fineblooded horse to have disappeared again. But Gabriel was waiting for her by the wall, still astride the well-muscled Arabian, its elegant head lifting at her ungainly approach.

"You're not dressed for riding," Gabriel remarked, his gaze traveling over her, so possessive and wistful that she almost forgot she'd vowed to live without him.

But she could not. What Jeremy had stolen from her was nothing compared to the pain she would have suffered had Gabriel not returned. For she had given herself willingly to him, with a woman's knowledge of what she stood to lose.

He had come back, not as a gentleman at all, which was a good thing since she considered herself more a gypsy than a lady, but as the dark unruly force he had always represented. The rebel boy who, as her parents had predicted, would lead her from the path of every virtue that Society cherished if she did not watch herself.

"Do you know what time it is?" she said.

He grinned. "No. Is it too late to go riding?"

Her heart ached with happiness at the sight of him, even though for two shillings she could have wiped that unholy smile from his face. "At this hour? You are insane. Only a madman—"

"—or one deeply in love—"

"—would be galloping about on that—that beautiful horse."

"You do like him. Good—he's your wedding gift.

My cousins advised me to buy you jewels. I assured them that you'd prefer a fine mount."

"Sure of yourself, are you?" she challenged, raising her face to his.

"Not at all. But I would like to be sure of you." He held out a gloved hand to grasp her wrist. Her bones felt fragile, but the spirit beneath was strong, unbroken. "Ride with me."

She laughed with uncertain delight. "If anyone sees us—"

"—then they shall know that the rumors of my abducting maidens are true." He leaned down and lifted her before him. Their bodies fit in perfect comfort upon the stallion's unsaddled back.

She turned to Gabriel, her laughter dying as he wrapped her in his arms. "I promised you I would tell you the truth the next time we were together."

"It's all right, Alethea."

"It *isn't*. You wanted the girl I was, who I was, a long time ago."

"I want you as you are now," he said quietly.

"Do you? I am *not* pure. I am despoiled, ruined— all that innocence that you found so beguiling is gone."

"Alethea."

"Once I was pure, then I was not. I wasn't a maiden when we made love."

He kissed her nape. "I know."

She pushed against his arm. "No, you *don't*. You can't—unless Audrey told you. *Oh*. She told you." Her voice shook.

He drew a breath. The air seared his lungs, clean with no taint of soot or soap boilers or sad endings. He wouldn't let her go, even though she was twisting to get away. "Audrey didn't tell me anything."

She angled her head to look at him. "Then you don't know. You don't understand what happened."

"I do. I saw Lord Guy Hazlett in London after I left your brother's house."

She went still, white. "Guy *told* what his brother did?"

He swallowed over the anger that tightened his throat. He wished Jeremy weren't dead so he could kill him. He wished he'd killed Guy when he'd had the chance. He wished he'd had the courage to stay in Helbourne so that nothing would have caused her this pain.

"Damnation," he said in a raw voice. "I did not desire you for your purity, whatever that is supposed to be."

"No?" She rested her head back against his shoulder. Her dark curls spilled into his lap. "You mentioned it more than once."

He cleared his throat. "Only because I believed you would be pleased that I—well, that I was not drawn to the impure, as my reputation would have it."

"Audrey was kind to me the night it happened."

He felt sick inside, ashamed of the conclusion he had drawn. "I wish I had known then."

"I wouldn't have told you," she said, breathing out a sigh.

"Why not?"

"You have seen me as if I were on a pedestal my entire life."

He tightened his arm around her midsection and dug in his heels. The Arab surged. "You saw me in the pillory once, and if I put you on a pedestal then, nothing that anyone has done to you will lessen what you are in my eyes."

Chapter Thirty-eight

🙚 ❦ 🙙

Alethea caught her breath as Gabriel half-dragged her up the creaky stairwell of Helbourne Hall. "What was that thing that just flew over my head?" she whispered.

"I didn't see it." He laughed. "It could have been a bat or a bullet. No, it wasn't a bullet. All the servants are drunk abed at this hour."

"Bats?" she said, her voice echoing. "I thought that was only a rumor. I realized that this house was a disgrace, but bats . . ."

"The owner is even worse, I've heard." He backed her into the balustrade, his hard body dominating hers. "I'd say he and this house are in dire need of a wife."

His thick erection prodded her belly through his buckskin trousers. An unexpected urge to explore the secrets of his male body seized her. She released her breath and hooked her arms around his neck as he lifted her into the air. "I'd say the wife will need a good supply of lye soap, a ladder, and several pairs of sturdy hands."

A slow smile spread across his face. "The husband has a pair of sturdy hands, but they're going to be pleasuring you tonight. We could move out to the stables if you're in the mood for a country tumble. It's as well-scrubbed now as the Cliffs of Dover."

"And as cold, I imagine," she said with a catch in her voice at the thought of his hands upon her.

He strode up the rest of the steps and carried her down the hall, kicking open the door to a bedchamber starkly furnished with a huge oaken bedstead, a scratched-up fall-front desk, and a corner washstand. The tall mullioned windows stood open to the night wind, as hers had been.

She shivered as he deposited her upon his unmade bed, then curled into a pillow that held his scent. His hard face excited her. She trembled at the thought of submitting to his most wicked desires. What had she become? She cared not. She belonged to him.

"I still watch you from the windows," he murmured, pulling off his gloves to undo her apple-green muslin supper gown, her embroidered petticoats, her silk chemise. He settled beside her naked body, his bare hand slipping down her back to the globes of her bottom. "Although I have to admit I prefer the view from here. Do you mind if I light a candle for a better look?"

She uncurled herself and grasped the lapels of his heavy woolen cloak. "Yes, I mind. Just take off your clothes and make me warm."

His eyes darkened. "I'll do better."

She arched her back, felt the damp heat between her thighs. "I want you so badly."

He leaned down closer and kissed her until she subsided beneath him with a sigh. "I'm yours." And when he slipped his hand along her thigh, she quivered in unabashed anticipation and lifted herself to invite his touch.

"Gabriel." She fell still as his fingers parted her wide and sank deep, then deeper, until she panted and surrendered any pretense of inhibition, her heels digging furrows in his mattress, her hips bucking to offer him more.

"Gabriel, I need you. I need to feel you inside me."

"I've waited my whole life to hear you say that."

He withdrew his hand. She groaned, her cleft throbbing, her arousal an ache only he could ease.

He slid back to pull off his shirt and trousers, stretching his muscles for a leisurely moment as if he knew how the sight of his sculptured body would tantalize her. He cupped his thick penis in his palms and stared down into her eyes. "I can't breathe when you look at me like that. I want you to touch me."

She laughed at that and opened herself willingly, allowing him to believe he'd claimed her when long ago, as a willful young woman, she had chosen him as her champion. "I won't wait another seven years for you, Gabriel."

"And a damned blessing that is," he muttered,

"because I don't think I'll last another seven minutes."

He kissed her as he knelt between her open thighs and guided himself into the intimate heat of her body. She moaned deep in her throat and strained upward to take more of him. Her nipples darkened, and her sex moistened, easing his penetration.

But he wanted to draw out her pleasure, refusing to fill her, teasing her with shallow little stabs of his shaft, rubbing the thick knob between her swollen labia until she moved in a slow, exciting rhythm.

She rose onto her elbows. "I'll do anything you ask."

"Anything?" he said, his brow lifting. "Lady Alethea, I do believe I've led you astray."

"Have you forgotten that I am not the paragon from your past? " she whispered as she stroked her fingertips down his impressive erection.

"And a good thing, too," he said, his breathing harsh. "What would a man like me do with a paragon?"

"What do you suggest?"

She bit her underlip, afraid she would lose her sanity. *Hot-blooded hero,* she thought. She wanted to thrust, her body not only answering his demands, but on a quest of its own. He smiled down at her as if he knew. Man. Woman. Gabriel and Alethea. Why had it taken so long?

"You're still tight," he said through his teeth. "I don't think you're ready for what I'd really like to do."

"I'm ready to play."

"Are you?" he muttered, thrusting slowly, his lean back arched. "I like to play." He withdrew from her, watched as she fought for breath. "And I always win."

"Not at whist."

"But this is my game."

She challenged his claim, and in that challenge broke the chains that had bound her. Upbringing, humiliation, acceptance of a lonely fate. It was all trickery unmasked by his hand. She could not believe she would have married another man, knowing deep inside that it would have been Gabriel whose face she saw in her dreams and hungered for every time she drove past the village square where he had been shamed—and stolen her heart.

And now she was in bed with Helbourne's most wicked boy. If nature took its course, she would be chasing a child across the village green by this time next year. She gasped for breath. She prayed for strength, and ran her hands greedily down his back, his supple flanks and buttocks. She could not take him deeply enough into her body; she could never be close enough to the man she had loved her entire life.

He went deeper. She invited every thrust, welcomed him, until she felt herself splintering, in two, into him.

Chapter Thirty-nine

❧ ⚘ ❧

Gabriel awakened an hour later, his legs entangled in the sheets that bore the monogram of Helbourne's previous owner. For long moments of incomparable bliss he did not move. He gazed in grave contemplation upon Alethea's back as she slept.

In his prior encounters this would have been the point at which he would surreptitiously dress and steal from the chamber. Now he felt no desire to escape but only a poignant gratitude that she had not left him. "And I won't let you go," he said quietly.

"Yes, you will," an angry voice said from the door.

He sat up, reaching slowly for the pistol on the bedstand. But when he recognized the figure that stepped across the threshold he drew his hand down and laid it across Alethea's shoulders. She did not stir. He eased himself up against the headboard, his body angled to shield her.

"I warned her about you," the intruder said. It was the conniving thief Gabriel had caught in the woods. And damned if the young reprobate had not only broken into Gabriel's bedroom but was brandishing the very sword he'd failed to steal before.

Gabriel pulled the coverlet up around Alethea's shoulders. "Everyone has warned her about me. What is your name?"

"Gabriel."

He laughed. "Who the hell named you that?"

"The people in the parish who took me in after I ran away from the orphanage. They said I reminded them of someone." The sword shook slightly in his grasp. "Did you hurt her?"

"No. Why would you think that?"

"I've seen her crying in the woods this past week, and you were gone. And now"—he didn't look down at the bed—"you're here."

"So is she. I'm going to marry her. That sword looks heavy. I think you should put it down. *Gabriel.*"

"Does she want to marry you?"

Gabriel glanced down at her profile. "Yes." He looked up with a wry smile. "Were you going to fight me if I'd hurt her?"

"Nah. I'd kill you."

"A brave ambition. Put down my sword."

"You're certain she's all right?"

"Yes," Gabriel replied. "And I'm also certain that if she wakes up and realizes you have seen her here, she will be very upset."

He backed away from the bed.

"Leave the sword at the door," Gabriel said, still not moving.

The boy shrugged but lowered his arm, his face registering a fleeting relief.

"Do you like horses?" Gabriel asked him curiously.

"God, I do."

"And you would fight to protect Lady Alethea? Why?"

He shrugged again. "She's been decent to me. I'm not moonstruck over her, though, if that's what you're getting at."

Gabriel smiled. "I wasn't. But I will need another groom for her and her horse."

"The Arab in your stable?"

"I thought I might breed thoroughbreds. If you're interested, come to my stables tomorrow."

He nodded eagerly.

"And Gabriel—"

"Yeah."

"You are never to lift a weapon to me again, but should anyone ever threaten Lady Alethea—"

"I know what to do."

Alethea sighed and turned her head. "Gabriel," she murmured with a smile. "Did you say something?"

He felt a rush of protective love and physical longing. "I have to take you home. It's almost daylight."

"Hold me. I don't want to go."

"I don't want you to, either, but I'm not going to anger your brother again. After breakfast tomorrow I shall go to him and make amends."

"He doesn't understand what happened between us," she said.

"I don't wonder why. But when we all travel back to London to rejoin my family and plan our wedding, I promise to be on my best behavior."

She touched his shoulder. She had always loved his dark, swarthy complexion, a combination of the sun and his Bourbon blood. "Do you think your mother will come?"

"I doubt it. She has apparently married a *duc*."

"A French duke?"

"So I've been told." He shook his head. "I hear from her only twice a year. She sends me money. I send it back."

She wriggled up against his chest. "And your brothers?"

"I've no idea." He stared out the windows. "They've pursued their own lives. If I'd been older I might have gone with them, but—well, I couldn't leave her with my stepfather."

"Would you have come back?"

"Yes, eventually, but I would never have stayed if not for you."

"Would you have loved me if I had become a Cyprian and worked in Mrs. Watson's house?"

He realized he would risk her ire no matter what answer he gave so he said the first thing that came to mind, never the wisest course when dealing with a lady.

"Yes. Every man desires a courtesan for his wife, assuming she's his courtesan only, and—" He rolled her beneath him, his heavily muscled body pinning her to the bed. "I've probably offended you. So I'm not letting you up until you forgive me."

Her mouth curved into a grin. "I'm not offended. Intrigued, perhaps."

He looked into her eyes. "I would marry you if you became a Prussian hussar."

She laughed at him. "It wouldn't be allowed."

"We'd find a way," he said, easing onto his side. "It's getting light." He gazed down broodingly at her bewitching body, flushed from a night in his bed. "Let's dress before you tempt me again."

"Gabriel?" Her voice was soft, thoughtful.

"Yes?" he asked, bending his head to draw one distended nipple into his mouth.

"Were you talking to someone when I was asleep?"

"Yes." He lifted his head. "To Gabriel."

His gaze wandered over her lush breasts and bottom as she rose from his bed. All that satin-peach skin and sensual beauty, his forever. His eyes followed her graceful movements as she reached down on the floor for her stockings. Her untamed hair spilled across the bed, across his thigh.

"You were talking to yourself?" she asked in amusement, glancing up, her petticoats in her hand.

He hesitated, glancing at the sword by the door.

He'd find a way to tell her later without admitting that her young defender had caught them in bed.

"In a manner of speaking." And there was truth in that, for he understood what she had perhaps seen in her foundling. The broken part of himself that had wanted to fight the world. "Were you only attracted to me because I was a wicked boy?" he asked casually, pulling on his buckskin trousers.

She brushed her hair back from her face, her brown eyes dancing. "As much as you were attracted to me only because I was the perfect lady."

It was arranged between Gabriel and Alethea's brother the following day that the wedding would be held on St. Michaelmas Day in London. When Robin divulged this information to Lady Pontsby, who had been waiting on pins and needles for the announcement, she heaved a sigh of relief that could be heard in the next room, where Alethea sat writing letters to the Boscastle ladies who had befriended her and would become her family.

"St. Michaelmas Feast?" Lady Pontsby murmured. "The day Lucifer was thrown out of heaven?"

"If there is a superstition against getting married on that date," Robin said, "please do not share it with my sister."

"The only superstition regarding St. Michaelmas of which I am aware is that one shouldn't eat blackberries after that day because the devil has spit upon them."

"Then let us hope that if there are blackberries served at the wedding breakfast, our devil will be on hand to feed them to his bride."

A week passed of gay correspondences sent back and forth among Sir Gabriel, his old friends, and the Boscastles; the earl, his sister Alethea, their friends, and the Boscastle family.

"Good heavens," Lady Pontsby said in pleasure at the assortment of letters and small gifts that arrived daily. "One would think she were marrying into an institution."

"The Boscastle family is," Robin said dryly. "And a most infamous one at that."

It was further agreed that the week before the wedding would be spent in London fulfilling social obligations and shopping for the bride, whom her older cousin lamented dressed like a country mouse. Alethea pointed out that there would not be time for a proper fitting anyway. But suddenly she did feel unfashionable, remembering the effortless elegance of the Boscastle women she had met.

She spent the first three days in town with her cousin and Chloe, Viscountess Stratfield, who dragged her from milliner to mantua maker to seamstress with unflagging energy. On the evening of the fourth day she was invited by Jane Boscastle, the Marchioness of Sedgecroft, to attend a private family affair.

Gabriel was invited by one of his former regiment officers to attend a supper party that same night, the purpose to lament the loss of one of London's rakehells to the parson's mousetrap.

Chapter Forty

❧ ❧

The supper party was given in Mayfair at the home of Lord Timothy Powell and his mistress Merry Raeburn, a popular young Drury Lane actress who had once pinned her hopes on claiming Gabriel as her protector. Even though other wealthier, older men had pursued her, she had been infatuated with him for almost a year, far too long for an aspiring courtesan. Allegedly the Duke of Wellington had counted himself as her suitor. Several pamphlets displayed in the windows of a London print ship hinted at a bona fide association. Merry denied these charges, as did the duke. Now she had settled for Timothy, who was neither as handsome nor as exciting as Gabriel Boscastle. Still, he had fought two duels in her honor and he moved in adventuresome circles.

Now that Gabriel, to everyone's disbelief, was marrying a lady who seemed to have little interest in the amorous games of Society, Merry's chances of seducing him seemed quite dim. She managed, however, to entrap him in the hall for a few moments on his way to the upstairs card room.

"Merry." He appeared uncomfortably amused to be alone with her. "I was just about to meet Timothy," he said, with no acknowledgment in his eyes that they had once been on the verge of a love affair. "This is a splendid party, probably my last as a bachelor. I—"

He was so polite, so formal in contrast to the rogue she had first met, that Merry knew she had lost him forever as a potential protector. Still, her pride would not entirely allow him off the hook. She consoled herself with the possibility that his manly instincts had been damaged at Waterloo. Why else would a rakehell suddenly adhere to standards he had previously flaunted? She believed herself to be at the height of her sexual desirability. She had turned down several offers before Timothy presented her with a generous contract to be her protector. She'd been told that Gabriel was unsurpassed in bed. She wanted him, if only once. He was delicious, a danger that women adored.

"Are you in love, Gabriel?" she asked softly, the possibility as intriguing to her as it was unlikely she would ever experience such an affliction. A successful courtesan dared not to think in such terms, even if she occasionally slipped into the mistake of caring for one of her admirers. If Gabriel had truly fallen in love with his country lady, Merry and her cohorts had to wonder how it had happened, and how they had missed the chance to capture his elusive heart. None of them had pegged him as a potential husband.

She positioned herself directly in his path. If he were in the slightest bit tempted to stray, Merry was offering him every incentive. She was slim, barely twenty-one, a well-read young ash-blond beauty who lived to please. "I never imagined we would lose your company," she added with a sulky sigh. "Do you *have* to marry her?" she asked, as if his having impregnated an earl's sister explained the sudden ceremony.

He laughed. "Yes, I'm in love, and I *have* to marry her, although for no other reason than that I cannot foresee my life without her. Does that satisfy your curiosity?"

She found it impossible to resent his honesty. "In truth, Gabriel, I confess that my curiosity is more piqued than satisfied. I never dreamt you were available for a permanent association."

He grinned down into her face. "I wasn't. In fact, I might have been locked in a pillory all my life, waiting for her to release me."

She wrinkled her nose. "What a ghastly sentiment. I hope you shan't turn poetic on us after marriage. You were a more provocative guest as a gambler."

"Speaking of which, I am on my way to the card room. Would you care to accompany me? I'm sure Timothy is missing you."

"Go yourself. I do not wish to reek of cigars for the rest of the night."

He turned. There were no footmen in the hall to guide the wandering guest. "It's on the left, isn't it?"

"Yes," she said distractedly as a voice called her name from the bottom of the stairs. "The third room from the end—across from my bedchamber, not that you're interested. The door is open. It's always open to you."

He laughed as she flounced off, glancing back once to give him a hopeful grin. "We could have had a beautiful affair, Gabriel. You'll never know what you've missed."

He shook his head and resumed walking down the hall, glancing in amusement into Merry's lavishly decorated bedchamber.

The amber satin coverlet had been laid down for the night. Wine and goblets sat upon a tray alongside a platter of crumbly white cheese, biscuits, and raspberry-cream cakes.

And it did not tempt him at all.

As he turned back to the hall, he heard the faint shattering of glass, followed by muffled footsteps. Did Merry have a secret admirer lying in wait? One who had lost his temper, or one who had not been invited at all? He counted off the number of guests with whom he had supped. Five had gone with Timothy to play cards. The others had remained belowstairs.

He walked through the door.

The window overlooking the alley stood open, a cool breeze ruffling the curtains. He felt a prickle of alertness on his nape. A small jar of some cosmetic lay broken on the wooden floor. Had a gust of wind knocked it from the dressing table? Unlikely, considering the distance.

He crossed the room and stared down into the alley below. There was another house on the corner being used as a gambling hell. He could see a few well-dressed men playing on the balcony, aristocrats who could afford to lose and who lost often.

He pivoted from the window and saw the masked figure of a man standing in the door of the dressing closet, watching him.

But tonight's entertainment had not been a masquerade.

"Are you lost, sir?" the man asked him with an air of authority.

Gabriel stepped around a chair. Something in that deeply resonant voice stirred a nebulous memory. Was this one of the Boscastles playing a trick on his final night of bachelor excesses?

He suppressed a grin. He deserved to be trumped after all the wicked gambits he'd pulled on his cousins, notably Drake and Devon, who had been invited to the party tonight but had never put in an appearance. If he didn't watch his back, he'd likely end up in a turnip cart rolled through Piccadilly or at another party attended by every woman and fellow gambler who held a grudge against him.

The thought of enduring another party made him impatient to see Alethea. His friends would laugh if they knew he'd rather play whist with her than faro with a foreign prince who didn't give a toss whether he won or surrendered a fortune.

But he would seem a bad sport if he did not at least pretend to go along with their prank, although he could not yet determine the identity of this masked gentleman-jokester. And that entire conversation with Merry—had it been part of an elaborate scheme to lure him into this room?

He could only imagine the humiliating consequences if he'd succumbed to her offer. It was the sort of dirty trick he'd play himself.

He relaxed, staring at the other man.

Was it his cousin Devon Boscastle, whose short-lived stint as a highwayman who demanded kisses from his female victims had brought him a brief but embarrassing celebrity? He narrowed his eyes.

Not Devon.

This man had slightly broader shoulders and a droll mystique about him—as if he were taunting Gabriel to identify him. Perhaps he needed to hear him speak again.

"Are *you* lost, sir?" Gabriel asked, coming closer.

"No," the stranger replied in amusement. "But as everyone believes I am, I would appreciate it if you did not enlighten them. I assume I can trust you."

Gabriel searched his brain to place that voice. "Are you part of a prank to be played on me?"

"I might have been at one time," the man answered with a wry smile.

"Then you are a Boscastle?"

"Yes. And you are to be married soon, I understand."

"Are you invited to the wedding?" Gabriel asked casually, trying to lower the man's guard so he'd continue talking. His mask and hooded cloak made it challenging to put a face to his vaguely familiar manner.

"Alas, I shall not be able to attend."

"You're coming to play cards now, though?" Gabriel asked in curiosity.

"Actually, no. I was about to leave."

"Through the bedchamber window of your host and hostess? That doesn't demonstrate very good manners."

"I'm not sure that Miss Raeburn has always observed good manners herself. Or so I've been told."

Gabriel nodded as if he were in on the conspiracy. "What am I in for tonight? You don't have to spill the whole bowl of soup. I'll do my best to act like the family nocky boy."

A soft footfall echoed outside the room. The man in masquerade looked up sharply. "You don't recognize me, do you?"

A suspicion rose in Gabriel's mind. Not one of his male cousins. "Dominic?" he guessed. "Chloe's husband?"

At the man's brief hesitation, that buried memory shifted in Gabriel's mind again. "Are you part of the joke?" he asked directly. "If so you may as well get it over with. I'll take my stripes like a man."

The sibilant whisper of silk behind the door might

have gone undetected by men less accustomed to stealing through shadows. As it was the pair of them turned to stare in unison at the disturbance. Gabriel's initial instinct was to escape. But then he reminded himself that for the first time in over a decade, he'd done nothing that would require him to flee or conceal his presence.

He was the guest of honor in this house tonight. The presence of the man beside him had not yet been clarified. Perhaps he wasn't a prankster at all. Perhaps Merry had a penchant for masked gentlemen sneaking about her bedroom. She had a lustful appetite, and suddenly he realized how awkward it would be to explain what *he* was doing in here.

He had absolutely no wish to be caught again by Merry, or even worse by another guest, who would understandably assume that Gabriel was up to no good. He was going to be married in a few days. Alethea would never believe he was innocent. And who would blame her?

"I think I ought to leave," he said hastily. "I assume that the lady is seeking you. Quite frankly, you're welcome to her." He glanced back at the masked guest, who had darted furtively into the dressing room. "Wait a minute," he muttered. "Don't you dare leave me alone with the woman who has gone to all this trouble to invite you to her bed."

The man's cloaked shoulders shook with laughter. "Her bed?" He locked the dressing room door and whirled about to open the casement window, which overlooked an alley crammed with small carriages, hackneys, and carts. "May I ask a favor of you?"

Gabriel came a few steps closer, snorting in amusement. How the hell had he ended up in this coil? "You aren't going to jump?"

"Yes, I am. I've enjoyed chatting with you, but I'm afraid we'll have to continue our conversation at another time."

The bolt creaked as it was manipulated by jimmy or skeleton key. Gabriel glanced around and noticed only then that two of the drawers in the veneered cabinet had not been pushed back properly into place.

"You're a burglar," he said in disgust. "You aren't anyone's lover and you aren't part of any Boscastle conspiracy."

The man laughed again, backing to the window frame. "Perhaps not the conspiracy you were thinking of. It *was* good to see you again. I regret I won't be able to attend your wedding. Your bride is very beautiful, as I recall. It occurs to me that you've done well for yourself."

Gabriel wrenched his dagger from his boot. "And it occurs to me that I shouldn't be so bloody cordial with a housebreaker."

"You, Gabriel—on the side of moral rectitude? I wish I could stay and discover how this happened to the rugged little brother I so fondly recall. I think I'm proud of you. One day you'll have to explain how this came about."

"Brother—you. *You!*"

The door opened and a brunette, also masked and dressed in an elaborate Elizabethan costume, crept in cautious degrees across the room. "Where are you, demon?" she whispered in a low voice. "I've been following you all night."

"She doesn't sound very friendly for a partner," Gabriel said wryly, leaning against the wall.

"Don't give me away."

"The hell I won't. Why should I help you? You never bloody did anything for me."

"I'll return the favor." The man's white teeth gleamed in a familiar grin, and Gabriel lowered his knife.

"You bastard. You're the Mayfair rogue I've been taking the blame for."

"Lovely to see you, too, Gabriel."

And the cloaked figure dropped from a rope that had been secured to the sill, dangled for two seconds in midair, then landed in a crouch on a cart filled with hay.

Another man emerged from the alley and jumped onto the cart to drive a pair of piebald ponies. Gabriel cursed and watched the night shadows enfold them until he felt the unmistakable muzzle of a pistol dig into his ribs.

"Turn around slowly with your hands lifted. I swear I'll shoot you if you leap from another window tonight. How did you change your clothes so fast?"

❧ ❧

Chapter Forty-one

At six o'clock on that same Thursday night, Alethea had been whisked from her brother's Cavendish Square town house into one of the most impressive carriages it had ever been her pleasure to behold. The younger sister of an earl, she was not as easily awed as one accustomed to trundling about in a post chaise. By the time two solicitous footmen had settled her inside the vehicle, its team of six white horses whinnying in aristocratic impatience, a crowd of curiosity-seekers had gathered at the pavement to observe.

Someone wondered aloud whether the Marquess of Sedgecroft had set himself up with a mistress.

She stuck her head out the window, and said, "Indeed he has not. He is faithful to the marchioness."

One of those gathered happened to be her cousin, Lady Pontsby, who had just returned from a lecture with her husband. She gave Alethea a nod of approval, raised her nose in the air, and curtly instructed the onlookers to allow her to pass. When this attempt failed, a tall, intimidating footman strode from the parked carriage, his heels clicking, and haughtily demanded that she and her husband be let through.

"Do you mind telling me where I am to be taken?" Alethea asked of this formidable person, recognizing him as the senior footman to the marquess, the very one who had guided her through the secret corridors of his master's house.

He was bewigged, long-nosed, and solicitous to this lovely young lady whom he had been informed was to become a desirable link in the Boscastle dynasty.

His name was Weed, he said, a fact she already knew. He revealed that he had a brother named Thistle, who was also in Boscastle service, and that there was no task too trivial for them, or for those beneath them, to undertake if it added to Alethea's ease.

Thereupon he made a thorough inspection of the spacious carriage's interior as if to certify her comfortable ensconcement. All apparently met his standards, until his shrewd gaze lit upon her worn blue satin slippers.

She thought she heard his breath gurgle as if he would choke. Her cheeks turned hot, even though there probably wasn't a single shoe in her entire wardrobe that did not bear some stain, scuff, or loose heel.

"Am I being taken to meet the marquess?" she asked, suddenly anxious at the prospect of a private meeting when a few moments ago she had been quite composed. There was no reason to be afraid of meeting Grayson again, but all this fuss bespoke an importance that unnerved her.

"No, my lady," he said gravely. "You have been invited to a light collation with the marchioness and the other ladies of the family."

"Oh, dear. I'm not sure I am properly dressed for the occasion." As Alethea remembered her, the marchioness could have posed for a fashion plate.

Weed rapped upon the roof, his smile reassuring. "We shall make one short detour, then all shall be well."

Alethea snuggled beneath the ermine-lined lap blanket offered for her comfort, recognizing herself in good hands. If Weed had any other relatives besides Thistle available for employment, such as Dandelion, Burdock, or Thorn, she would, with the family's approval, beg them to enter her husband's service. The prospect of returning to Helbourne Hall in its appalling condition and bringing up Gabriel's children there made her frown.

The carriage rolled through the streets and presently came to a darkened shop. She peered outside, not at all surprised when a light flickered in the shop's upper windows and a person soon after beckoned Weed inside from the door below. Scarcely did five minutes elapse before the senior footman returned with two boxes, which he gently deposited on the seat opposite her.

"Courtesy of Lady Sedgecroft."

The carriage set off once again. She stared out at the street and saw a young man, a stranger, sitting on the pavement. He stared at her in awe. From the day she had witnessed Gabriel's humiliation at the pillory, she had not taken a single carriage ride during which she failed to think of him. Even when she was happily engaged to another. Even when she knew Gabriel was far away, fighting alongside her brother, and his cousins.

Perhaps she would always have a tender haven in her heart for those lost, wicked boys and the girls who could not help loving them. And Gabriel seemed to share this empathy, for although he did not want to admit to any softness in his nature, she had found out before leaving Helbourne that he had taken his namesake under his wing.

At length, the carriage slowed. She glanced down, realizing that the boxes brought from Weed were meant to be opened.

"Are you ready to be escorted inside, my lady?" Weed asked from outside the carriage window.

She quickly opened the first box and found amidst a delightful extravagance of tissue paper a pair of gray silk pumps. The second box held a light silver cashmere shawl that sparkled with the subtle radiance of a cobweb on a midsummer eve.

She slipped on the shoes and then the shawl, a perfect complement to her storm-blue dress, and answered, "I am ready, but—this isn't the marquess's main residence."

Weed bowed and handed her down onto the sidewalk. "It is the home of his eldest brother, Lord Heath, my lady."

"Lord Heath," she exclaimed, her eyes widening. She had not made his acquaintance at Grayson's party, but in the country Alethea and the vicar's wife had enjoyed a good giggle over the infamous cartoon of Lord Heath's private pieces that his wife had drawn in jest only to lose and find circulated throughout England.

"Oh, dear," she murmured. "He's the intimidating one, isn't he? The one the family calls the Sphinx."

"Lord Heath is not at home," Weed informed her, his thin lips curling into what might have been meant to be a smile. "His wife and the other ladies of the family are waiting to receive you."

Indeed, it was Julia, Heath's wife, who held the floor in the drawing room for Alethea's welcome. Actually, the gathering seemed more like an initiation into a coven of becoming young witches. She did not know what it said for her character that she felt right at home in their gossipy circle, as she had the afternoon they had embraced her. The ladies paused in the middle of their conversation to greet Alethea and offer her a choice of beverages. The moment she was seated, their lively exchange resumed.

"The Boscastle men are devious," Julia announced with her wineglass raised in the air for emphasis.

"I take exception to that," Chloe Boscastle said from the sofa, where she lay with her head propped upon her sister-in-law Jane's shoulder. "Boscastle *women* are devious, too. We have a long-standing reputation for cunning developed as a means of self-defense."

"Jane and I were not born Boscastles," Julia said, pouring a glass of wine for Alethea. "But I do think we are devious."

"That proves my theory," Chloe said. "The Boscastle men have forced you to become guileful."

"I was guileful before I met Grayson," Jane admitted with a sly smile. "My reputation would have been ruined had I not married him."

"But it was a Boscastle male who forced you into deception in the first place," Julia said.

Jane shrugged. "True. Oh, I do like your shawl and slippers, Alethea."

"Thank you," Alethea said with a grateful smile. "They're ever so perfect."

"Alethea has a flawless reputation," Chloe said. "Or do you have a dark secret to confide?"

"She shouldn't confide anything until after the wedding," Jane said. "And I feel obliged to mention that our absent member, Emma, up to her dainty nose in ducal affairs, takes exception to the reputation of the entire family, male or female."

"The point that we were trying to make before you arrived," Chloe said, wagging her finger in Alethea's direction, "is that the Boscastle male—any male, really—must be trained from the very start. I trust you realize the task that awaits you. Gabriel has lived quite a hard life. But then so has my Dominic."

Alethea opened her mouth. "Well, I—"

"She has accomplished more than any of us here dared to hope," Julia interjected. "No one ever thought Gabriel would be tamed."

Chloe's blue eyes flashed in mischief. "Tell us about how you first met him, Alethea. We all of us thought Gabriel would never fall in love. You country girls are so quiet, but the country is where I got into the best trouble of my life."

Charlotte Boscastle waved her pencil in the air in a bid for attention. She was a willowy blonde who had recently been promoted to the position of headmistress in the young ladies' academy her cousin Emma had maintained in this very house until her marriage to the Duke of Scarfield, a title he had inherited two months ago. "Speak slowly if you don't mind. I am recording the family history for posterity."

Chapter Forty-two

Gabriel slipped his knife inside his sleeve, allowing the lady in the dressing closet to approach him before he turned in amusement and captured her hand in his. "That's close enough, love. More than a chat is by invitation only. And I don't believe we've had a proper meet."

She wrenched her wrist back hard, as if she expected him to fight to hold her. When he didn't, her eyes narrowed behind the mask she wore. Had she and his long-lost brother attended a masquerade together for the purpose of breaking into another Mayfair home? Were they partners in criminal ventures? He listened for the rumble of the cart in the street. All he heard was a soft burst of unladylike curses addressing the matter of his ancestry.

"You aren't him," she whispered in exasperation.

"Who would I not be?" he asked, waiting for her to enlighten him on the last decade or so of his brother Sebastien's life.

She moved to the window, ignoring his question.

Gabriel didn't follow her, instead studying the pistol he had confiscated from her grasp. He didn't need to identify the other man, of course, but he was curious what she knew of his brother. *He* could have told her that Sebastien had been a great one for mastering escapes since the day he could ride.

She looked around at him accusingly. "You let him go. Do you have any notion who he is?"

He had more than a notion. "I don't know who *you* are, or why you wanted to shoot him."

"I didn't, actually."

"Then why—"

"It's probably better that you never find out." She narrowed her eyes again behind her mask. Her hair was escaping the edges of her hood. "You look uncannily like him."

"Do I? Well, I can't argue or disagree, having only seen him in disguise." He paused. "You don't mind telling me why you're both dressed like that, do you?"

"We went to a masquerade party," she said slowly. "Our host sent us on a treasure hunt."

"Ah. And you broke into this house instead of simply knocking at the door and requesting help from the owner?"

"Not exactly. We're not stealing anything. The rules of the game are that we keep our identities secret."

"Why did your companion run from you then?"

"We're in competition, of course. I'm afraid I cannot give you any more answers."

"You're going to have to answer to the authorities."

Gabriel glanced at the tall cabinet against the wall of the dressing closet, and suddenly noticed that a folded letter had been caught in the uneven seams of the two partially open drawers.

He shifted his weight to shield her view of the cabinet. When her gaze shot right to it, he knew she and Sebastien were on no ordinary treasure hunt. And that theirs was no innocent masquerade.

He sensed her tension. Perhaps he could have used it to extract more information from her, but suddenly they were not alone.

Another person had entered the outer room, a woman calling playfully, "Gabriel, is that you waiting for me? In my bedchamber? Why, you wicked darling, what changed your mind?"

Merry, good God above. He glimpsed her through the crack in the closet door and grimaced. Nobody in the world would believe that he hadn't come here for an assignation. No one would believe that he'd caught two strangers in the act of what he didn't know, and that one of them had been his brother.

And the other—

He turned his head. His brother's companion had vanished, just like that, stealthy as a cat. He swore under his breath and stepped to the window, watched her shimmy down the rope and land agilely on her feet, her cumbersome skirts billowing.

"What's going on in here?" a man demanded in the background.

He backed away from the window. Merry was now standing behind him, talking excitedly to his host, Timothy. Gabriel looked at her, relieved that she had not done anything stupid such as starting to undress while he was distracted.

He motioned Timothy into the closet. "I heard something break in the bedroom and saw a man skulking about in here on my way to the card room. I thought he looked suspicious so I followed him to investigate. He just escaped. Look."

Timothy and Merry crowded beside him, the three of them staring down at the rope that fell to the street.

Timothy glanced up at Gabriel in gratitude. "We might have all been murdered over brandy had it not been for you, Boscastle."

"Gabriel," Merry said in a crafty voice. "There *are* rumors that you have been pilfering gentlewomen's drawers in Mayfair the past few months."

Gabriel smiled. "A charming fabrication. I am engaged, heart and soul, to a beautiful lady. I have no interest in pilfering any other woman's drawers."

"Not those sort of drawers," Timothy said wryly. "The villain in question has been rifling through—"

The three of them turned simultaneously and stared at the letter protruding from Merry's chest of drawers. "My private correspondences," she exclaimed in horror. "If anyone publishes those—"

"—your price shall rise on the market, and I shall not be able to afford you," Timothy said over her shoulder.

"Are you truly the man the authorities are searching for, Gabriel?" she asked, surreptitiously tucking the letter back into the drawer.

Timothy snorted. "Of course he isn't. I do wonder though, Gabriel, whether you had a good enough look at this intruder to help the runners identify him. Do watch Merry for me while I call a footman to summon help."

Chapter Forty-three

❧ ❧

Sir Gabriel answered every question the runners put to him as honestly as he could.

Did he know the intruder?

No. Gabriel did not know his brother at all. He was a stranger to him, and that was exactly what he said.

Could he recognize him in a crowd?

Unlikely. And if he did, he would not stop to renew their relationship. Nor did he bother to mention the mysterious woman who had appeared to be following Sebastien.

He still had her gun, however, but since the runners who questioned him did not ask, he did not offer this information. It was empty, anyway.

"Gentlemen," Gabriel said at length to his inquisitors, "I have given you all the information I can, and—did I mention that I am to be married the day after tomorrow? I had hoped to spend my two last nights as a bachelor in more stimulating pursuits."

The two runners offered profuse apologies. They explained that they were merely thief-takers, and that the regular constable of this division had been called to a murder on Old Bond Street.

An hour later the excitement of the Mayfair Masquer's current adventure had spread across London. He hadn't stolen anything. He was probably a prankster. And the most reliable witness so far, the only person who had actually spoken to the man, Sir Gabriel Boscastle, could not provide any useful information to identify him.

Unfortunately there were a few suspicious souls who questioned the coincidence of Sir Gabriel's claiming to confront a person to whom he was said to bear a great resemblance. Was this a clever plot hatched to throw the authorities off his trail? Some would have been convinced of this possibility had an old hackney driver not given a statement that same night that he had almost hit a cart carrying a man who also appeared to be wearing a disguise.

It was as the interrogation ended that Lords Drake and Devon Boscastle finally arrived to take Gabriel out on the town. He explained what had happened, declining to go into detail.

It was his last night as a bachelor. Tomorrow evening he was taking Alethea to a play. His cousins couldn't decide whether to drag him to Covent Garden, to the most disreputable gaming hells, or to drop him off at Mrs. Watson's for some high-quality conversation.

In the end gambling won out. Alethea would merely be angry if he came home with another mortgage. She'd never speak to him again if he set foot in Audrey's, their mutual fondness for the woman notwithstanding.

So they set off in three separate carriages, Gabriel and his cousins in one, another set of friends from Timothy's party in a second, and the third conveying a set of hangers-on who would follow the Boscastles anywhere for the privilege of being able to claim they'd been invited to accompany the infamous brood.

The clubs welcomed the Boscastles. Old friends lingered to share a joke, a drink, a memory of days before wives. But for most of them life had changed in London. The war was over, and world expansion consumed every politician's mind. Those wise enough to realize that effort would be required to heal problems at home had no interest in pushing territorial boundaries in far-flung kingdoms. Others sought riches and new lands to plunder.

The rest seemed content to return to their lives at home. Gabriel had too much on his mind to enjoy himself. He was already bored with the game of faro he'd been winning. His cousins Drake and Devon weren't playing at all, talking politics with a cabinet member. The dedicated players had emerged as the night deepened. This was the time Gabriel would typically make his appearance.

But now he merely played out the game and split the three thousand quid he won among his friends.

The cardsharper he'd beaten took his loss in silence, regarding Gabriel without expression from beneath his broad-rimmed straw hat. Gabriel had never played him before, but a friend said the man had been winning steadily and was a cheat. He was a former Yorkshire army surgeon who ran with a rough group of disgruntled soldiers.

"I'm going to Brooks for a coffee," Gabriel called over his shoulder to Drake. "I'm done here."

"Wait," Drake said. "We'll all go."

"Meet me there," Gabriel said, stretching his arms over his head. "I need the walk."

In truth, he needed the time alone to think about what had happened tonight.

This was probably the last night he'd walk the streets of London, at least on his way to some entertainment. The urge to seek some distraction had died such a natural death he hadn't realized it was gone. In the past he'd have gambled half the night, had a meal of steak and fish at Covent Garden, then spent an hour at Ranelagh or Vauxhall. There had been clubs and horse-betting and gourmet suppers and pretty women willing to share their boudoirs with a Boscastle rogue. He'd enjoyed taking risks.

But none of his former haunts tempted. Even when he crossed the street and an old group of officer friends recognized him and shouted out an invite from their carriage to join them on Bond Street for lobster, he merely laughed and waved them off.

He would not be good company in his mood.

He had convinced himself he didn't give a damn

that his brothers had deserted him. He'd been angry when he was younger—when his stepfather broke his hand for bringing a stray dog into the house, when the man bruised his mother's face for defending him. He had grown up, fought in a war, become a gamester who lived off the losses of other men. He'd never harmed anyone who wasn't asking for trouble. There were rules to play by even in his world.

Because Alethea had chosen him, he could choose to walk away from the life that would sooner or later have killed him. He and his lady would raise children and thoroughbreds together and bring stray dogs and even lost boys into their home whenever they could. And if he died young, as his father had, he would know that his Boscastle relatives would protect his wife and family after he was gone.

He was a man, his days of rage and irresponsibility behind him. He had been given a chance to fulfill the dreams his parents had once held for him. Any thoughts of revenge that had fueled him no longer seemed worth the effort.

This was what he had believed until a few hours ago, when his brother had reappeared in his life.

Suddenly he was angry again, his demons awakened, and the memories he'd thought were buried rose from their graves to torment him. His stepfather's throwing a bucket of filthy wash water in his face whenever he overslept, or taking a knife to Gabriel's mother's lustrous black hair because a village man had complimented her at market. The books Gabriel brought home from school to read, smoldering on the hearth. The cruel taunts about his father's death and Gabriel's attempts to hold back tears.

Alone. Three brothers gone. The eldest had taken himself off before their father died, but Sebastien and Colin could have chosen to stay. Why should he protect Sebastien? Why didn't he turn the rotten bastard over to the authorities? He owed him nothing.

And wanted nothing from him.

He turned a corner, realizing that he wasn't on St. James's Street but on a side wynd to Piccadilly.

And that he wasn't alone.

Three darkly clothed men stood in front of a pair of parked curricles, too well-dressed to be pickpockets, pretending too hard not to notice that he was approaching.

He cut a glance across the street. The cocoa shop was long closed; there was a drunk ambling down the street in the other direction.

He took a breath, kept walking. One of the men looked up. And Gabriel recognized the angle of his shoulders. The Yorkshire surgeon he had beaten in the hell. With him were two tall youths, pacing in agitation. His gaze dropped to the baton one held tucked in the fall of his cloak.

He muttered a curse, slid his knife from his boot without missing a step. There were no other vehicles on the street. Only a battered donkey cart piled with rags and newspapers—bloody hell, could that be the same cart as . . .

He stared at the drunk slumped against the wagon wheel, a bottle dangling from his hand. Had he imagined that their eyes met?

It wasn't . . . it was. Sebastien.

Was this a setup? An ambush?

Could that last game have been a trap from the start? Some political intrigue? A personal debt that involved a woman?

He would have to figure out the particulars later.

For now he had to react. He gripped his knife.

And he could perhaps thank his brother later for involving Gabriel in a street-gang attack when he had to appear at the wedding altar in one piece the day after tomorrow.

Yet he knew he could run. He could still turn around. His instincts told him they'd give chase, but he was damned fast on his feet.

He hadn't passed the street watchman with his sign warning to "Beware of Bad Houses." The Yorkshire bone-scraper and his two ghouls were most likely foreigners to London. Gabriel could make a dash across Half-Moon Street and lose them in Piccadilly. Then again it was starting to drizzle. He'd rather fight than run like a coward in the rain.

He was curious about what his brother had to do with this unsavory bit of business.

He searched the street; his footsteps echoed in the lowering mist. The figure slumped against the cart-wheel did not move, apparently dead to the world, his hair snarled, his face shadowed in filth.

Good disguise, Gabriel thought in amusement.

The three men rushed him as a small carriage rattled around the corner and vanished into the foggy mizzle. The first man to attack him fell in the gutter at Gabriel's hand before the other two pinned him around the neck and shoulders to drag him into an alley behind a tavern. A cat darted past. A shutter lowered in the candlelit window above.

"Where's my money?" the surgeon asked with a smile, holding a scalpel at Gabriel's throat while his companion struggled to restrain him.

Gabriel went still for a few moments, leaning with deceptive submission against the second man's chest for leverage. With a humorless smile, he drew his legs inward, then snapped a one-two kick that sent the taller man crashing back against a low flight of steps.

"I gave it to charity," he said, brushing off his cuffs. "If you want to collect more, there's a church on the next corner that allows beggars."

The surgeon jumped back onto his feet. "I don't want mere money." Spittle punctuated his words and a large curved blade glinted in the misty rain. "I want your blood to flow in the gutters. I want to disembowel you and feed you to the city rats."

Gabriel sighed. God knew he enjoyed a good fight

as well as the next unemployed cavalry officer, but he already had one black eye, and he'd be damned if he'd pledge his troth to his bride with a toothless grin.

"You're a bloody bad gambler," he said. "I've no reason to believe you're any better at fighting. And for the sake of all the poor bastards who probably died under your knife in the name of medicine, I'm going to even the score."

Gabriel's knife flashed, and in the next breath, he was holding the damned fool against the wall with the tip of his blade pressed delicately into the jugular. "I really ought to kill you, but the sight of fresh blood—"

He broke off as he heard footsteps running up behind him, then felt a baton crack against his shoulder. The first bastard he'd fought had recovered enough to take revenge. And he took it hard, swinging the baton at the back of Gabriel's head this time.

He ducked, swiveled, and butted his head into the man's stomach.

"Hold him still," the surgeon said, and Gabriel thrust back his elbow as the scalpel sliced through the sleeve of his coat. His skin stung. Nothing fatal. Just another scar.

"Gabriel!"

He saw movement to his right, angled his head only long enough to recognize the street wretch who had been slumped against the cart. His two assailants noticed also, their momentary inattention giving him the opportunity to break free as his brother advanced.

"Who asked for your help?" he said, catching the sword Sebastien threw his way.

"Our mother." Sebastien's dirt-stained face broke into a handsome grin. "It appears I have neglected my brotherly duties toward you and need to make amends."

Gabriel tested the sword's weight in his arm, grunting. "I haven't needed my family for—I don't even think I have a family, save for a few London cousins."

Sebastien backed into Gabriel until they stood shoulder to shoulder, swords raised, their bodies slowly circling in unison to defend against attack from any quarter.

"Do you still want to disown me?" Sebastien asked casually.

Gabriel laughed. "You disowned me a long time ago. I don't want anything to do with you. What do you want with me, anyway, aside from stealing my identity to rob women?"

"Do you think I would fail to give my youngest brother my best wishes on the advent of his wedding?"

Gabriel narrowed his eyes. The surgeon had drawn a pistol from his belt. "You failed to say farewell when you left. Why bother now—he's got a gun, you know."

"Aren't you the hero who confiscated four enemy

cannons and played cards on a fifth? You managed quite well without me."

He thrust Gabriel behind him as a pistol flashed in the drizzle. "The gun works, too."

Gabriel started to curse. A burn that spread across his lower left ribs smothered the words in his throat. He looked down, expecting to see a dark stain of blood. And so he did—blood that flowed from both his own flesh and from the arm his brother had thrown around him to absorb the blow.

Blood brothers. Hell, he wasn't going to be swayed by sentiment.

"I am not about to forgive you that easily, Sebastien, you bastard," he muttered, positioning himself into a protective crouch to hurl his knife, sword held aloft in his other hand.

Sebastien dropped alongside him, grinning darkly. "I don't give a damn whether you forgive me. It's our mother I'm worried about."

The three other men closed in around the two brothers who had once taken on every boy in their village for sport. "She isn't coming back to England, is she?" Gabriel asked worriedly.

"That depends on her new husband. If she does, we'll all have a lot to explain to her."

Gabriel sprang upward, fending off one attacker with his sword, the other with a sharp kick in the groin. Sebastien's saber flashed. The surgeon dropped with a groan into a puddle of filth.

"I've written to her regularly," Gabriel said distractedly. "While I may not be proud of everything I've done in my life, I don't have anything to hide."

"It probably won't come as a surprise"—Sebastien launched into a flawless riposte—"but I do."

"The last I heard"—Gabriel paused to advance—"you had left the infantry and were missing."

"Well, I still am," Sebastien answered. "Officially speaking, that is. Don't let *Maman* mourn me if she comes to England. I'll make it all up to you later."

Gabriel backed his opponent into the wall, the saber pointed at his neck, then had a change of heart and motioned him to escape, which he did without a backward glance of regret at his cohorts. "Should I even ask about my brothers?"

Gabriel whirled around, lowering his sword. Dragging the surgeon with him, the other attacker disappeared. And so apparently had Sebastien. Not counting the damage done to Gabriel's body, only the thin French sword he held in his hand offered proof the assault had even occurred.

By the time he reemerged from the alley onto the street even the mizzling rain had lifted. The cart on the corner was also gone, as if it had never been there, and a procession of carriages from a party letting out on Curzon Street lit up the road with their lanterns.

His arm ached. His head throbbed. He looked like a disreputable tomcat on the prowl for trouble.

In two days, God willing, he would have a wife, unless she took one look at him now and called off the wedding. He would have his own family, which did not include the three brothers who'd abandoned him.

"Oh, my God," a deep male voice said from the corner to which he'd walked. "We leave you for an hour and look at the mischief you make."

"I don't suppose you have a bottle of brandy and a clean handkerchief on you, Drake?"

Drake straightened in concern. "Get in the carriage. Where are you hurt?"

Devon and Heath Boscastle jumped down onto the sidewalk, holding back at Gabriel's wave of annoyance. "How many men were there?" Heath demanded. "Are they gone?"

"Where did you get that fine sword?" Devon asked, staring at the saber Gabriel had almost forgotten he still held. "You didn't have it when you left the hell."

"I . . . I found it."

"You found it?" Heath said in that quiet voice that had disarmed and deceived untold numbers of enemies into believing that he was exactly what he appeared to be: a gentle-spoken English aristocrat who was more interested in academics than anything else.

Gabriel knew better.

Heath had survived unspeakable tortures and had not broken.

And Gabriel was not about to break himself. "One of the men who attacked me must have dropped it," he said with a shrug. "Or maybe it belonged to that rough-looking character with a cart parked outside a dolly shop when I walked by. Perhaps he stole it. All I know is that I picked it up, and it came in handy."

"Do you mind if I take it home with me?" Heath asked.

Gabriel hesitated. "Now that you mention it, I might like to keep it as a talisman. I'll look it over later tonight. If I notice anything suspicious or any clue that indicates its owner's identity I shall come to you posthaste."

"So, you didn't ask his name?" Heath asked, pulling open the carriage door.

Gabriel shook his head. "No. And I didn't ask for a certificate of character, either."

"I find it all a bit puzzling."

"You know how London is. Most of the people out this late at night are either seeking danger or are insane."

"Well, I trust you rewarded this mysterious Galahad."

"I might have if the Boscastle guard hadn't arrived to scare him off." He pushed his hand against the door. "I don't mean to be rude, but it is late for a tête-à-tête, and I'm becoming a reformed man."

Heath grimaced. "Your shirt is torn, one eye is blackened, and you've the start of a swollen lip. Alethea is with Julia and the ladies. You're going to give them a good scare."

Gabriel rubbed his face. "She'll never believe that I did not cause the fight."

Heath flashed him an ironic smile. "That makes two of us, then."

Gabriel lowered his hand. "I confess, Heath, I'm too tired to make sense of anything tonight."

"I hope you know that you can trust me. If you or any member of our family was ever in trouble—"

So he knew, or at least suspected, that the stranger who had come to Gabriel's aid tonight had been Sebastien. What else did he know? Or was this a bluff?

He slung himself down inside the carriage. "The only trouble I foresee is explaining to my fiancée why I am returning home battered and bleeding when I promised I would behave."

Chapter Forty-four

❧ ❧

Alethea luxuriated in the company of the Boscastle ladies. She had been served watercress soup, sausages, stuffed figs, and French pastry, as well as savory tidbits of town gossip. How she had missed the company of other women, though this was no ordinary group of females. She had never heard such frank conversation from members of her own sex.

Jane, the honey-haired marchioness who had charmed the ton with her inimitable aplomb, had ordered her best champagne to celebrate the addition of an ally against the dearly beloved men of the family. Chloe Boscastle, or rather Lady Stratfield, had generously offered her wedding gown to Alethea, warning that it might be a bit short in the hem.

"I don't mind," Alethea said a little too quickly, although fortunately, no one seemed to notice.

She had no desire to explain her reluctance to stand at the altar beside Gabriel wearing the wedding dress that Jeremy had chosen for her from a French fashion magazine. It would have felt more like a shroud than the beautiful baroque pearl-seeded creation it was. She had been tempted to burn it. Now she supposed that donating it to a charity would be a less wasteful gesture, and certainly not as dramatic.

"I don't expect that any of Gabriel's brothers will attend the wedding," Charlotte Boscastle said, glancing up from her notebook.

Jane turned her head. "Gabriel has brothers?"

"Three of them," Alethea murmured, nibbling another fig.

"Why did no one mention this to me?" Jane frowned in irritation. "How am I to invite them to family affairs and include them in holiday festivities if I am not made aware of their existence? This really is unforgivable of him. Grayson ought to have told me if Gabriel could not be bothered."

Alethea wriggled in her chair. As Gabriel's future wife she supposed it came to her to defend—well, she couldn't defend his brothers.

"They set out into the world at an early age and I do not believe Gabriel has maintained contact with them since then. I understand he does write—if infrequently—to his mother."

"Heavens above," Jane said, her eyes flashing with a fire that eclipsed that of the brilliant diamonds upon her neck. "Gabriel has a *mother*, and she is not to be a guest at his wedding?"

Alethea smiled. She remembered Gabriel's mother as a vital, half-French young lady whose very essence seemed to enliven village functions. Until she had lost her husband, Joshua Boscastle, she had kept her handsome sons under control. "I believe she lives in France these days."

"I've heard she is to become the wife of a wealthy French *duc*," Charlotte said unthinkingly. "All I know of her paramour is that he lost his family in the Terror."

"I think it's true," Alethea said, "although Gabriel has not revealed this in as many words. He never speaks of his family. One can assume from his silence that to him they no longer exist."

"Well, I do wish someone in *my* family had thought to inform me," Jane said in a miffed tone. "Still, I expect that as a mother she will be relieved her son has made such a fortuitous match in Alethea— Where is Gabriel, by the way, Alethea? I have some instructions for the ceremony from the minister."

Alethea set down her champagne glass with a sharp *clink*. "That is a question devoutly to be answered. I can only assure you that if he is up to any mischief at this moment, it will be one of his last nights in this pursuit. Helbourne Hall is literally falling down as we speak. His duties as landowner should keep him well occupied for many nights to come." As would his marital duties. Alethea had a good idea of what would occupy her time with Gabriel during their chilly autumn evenings together.

Jane pursed her lips. "I understand."

"Let us hope that he does also," Alethea added,

dimly aware that three glasses of champagne and an absent bridegroom did not a good temper make, although it did loosen one's tongue to an alarming degree. If she did not take herself in hand, she would be confessing more than anyone wished to hear.

"I should not worry about Gabriel tonight," Charlotte said in a knowing voice. "Drake and Devon promised they would keep him company until the wedding. By which, I assume, they meant to steer him away from any roguery."

"He has one black eye already," Alethea said before she could stop herself. "If he has gotten into some mischief simply to prove he is still capable one final time, then, well, it *shall* be the final time. That is all I have to say on the subject."

"You can say more if you wish," Chloe prompted. "I love scandal."

Alethea paused. "There are bats in Helbourne Hall."

Chloe gasped. "Bats? Truly?"

"Yes." Alethea sighed. "Bats and bad servants."

Chloe sat up on the sofa. "I married a ghost. Boscastle challenge—you next, Julia."

Julia's gray eyes brightened. "I shot Heath before we were married because I thought he was a rabid fox."

"That's nothing compared to that cartoon you drew of him," Chloe murmured in mischief. "You go next, Jane."

Jane smiled ruefully. "I fell in love with Grayson in the middle of my wedding to another man."

Chloe gestured to Alethea. "Your turn."

Alethea hesitated. "I fell in love with Gabriel when he was in the pillory."

"My goodness," Jane exclaimed. "I hope you let him out."

"What about you, Charlotte?" Chloe asked with a teasing grin.

"I've never been in love," Charlotte said, glancing up. "And I'll probably never get married."

"Not if you keep your nose in a book all the time and remain the headmistress of a girls' school," Chloe said bluntly.

"Her turn will come one day," Jane said with a forceful nod that even the Fates would not have challenged.

Chloe rose from the sofa. "There's someone coming in the door now. Probably my devil brothers."

Alethea turned her head. "And have they my devil bridegroom with them?"

Chloe backed away from the windows with a soft gasp. "Yes, but he's with—"

Alethea and the other ladies came to their feet. "Another woman?"

Chloe shook her head. "No. He's with our doctor and I'm afraid he's been hurt."

Chapter Forty-five

❧ ❧

Alethea was too exhausted to do anything but sit on the edge of her bed when she returned two hours later to her brother's town house. She had felt ill when she'd seen the blood on Gabriel's shirt, then angry, and at last relieved when she realized he would survive this latest misfortune.

Yet even after the physician tended him, he'd seemed distracted and not himself. She thought that perhaps he had been in more pain than he would admit.

"I am not in pain," he insisted. "I am, however, embarrassed by all this bother."

She fell backward onto the bed, closing her eyes. Confessions. Watercress soup and champagne. An impending marriage. What had happened to Gabriel tonight? Even his cousins could not explain why he'd chosen to walk the streets by himself. Or that saber he'd refused to relinquish for even a moment.

"What happened to you tonight, Gabriel?" she whispered. "I told you *my* secret."

His voice startled her. "I'm not sure I understand myself what happened. Perhaps it will make sense in the morning."

She opened her eyes in disbelief, gazing up into his hard, angular face. "You won't be alive in the morning if my brother catches you in my room. How did you get in? The servants have locked the doors every night since you burst in like a barbarian."

"Your brother invited me into the house." He stepped back and dropped into the chair beside the bed. "I suspect he thought I would get into less trouble under his scrutiny than left alone."

"In that case—" She got up from the bed and walked behind his chair, sliding her hands down his shoulders. "You ought to make yourself feel at— you've brought that awful sword into my bedroom. I hope there's not any blood on it."

"Please. May I leave it here? It doesn't belong to me."

"Did you really find it?"

"I was given it by a man who does not wish his identity known."

She came around the chair to kneel in front of him, her eyes grave. "Espionage?"

"I don't know. I doubt it."

"But you're not involved in something dangerous?"

"No."

Her gaze searched his face. "Is he the one who hurt you?"

"No." He stroked her cheek, then said abruptly, "I'm going to leave."

"Why?" she said. "*Are* you in pain? Are you meeting this man?"

"The only pain I feel is that of wanting you while honoring your brother's trust in me."

"Then trust me now as I have had to trust you," she said, staring at him in challenge. "Who did you meet tonight?"

He shook his head. "A ghost."

"For heaven's sake, Gabriel!"

He looked down at her and laughed. "It was my brother Sebastien. He was at Timothy's party tonight."

"Sebastien?" She could only conjure the vaguest image of a taller, slightly older Gabriel. "You had three brothers."

"He was the third son."

"And you were reunited by coincidence at the party?"

He raised his brow. "We did not exactly meet across the supper table. And I cannot say whether it was coincidence or not. I believe I caught him in the act of breaking into the house."

"Your *brother*? Did he confess to you?"

He smiled tiredly. "Under strained circumstances. I had no idea *what* he was doing or even that he was still alive. So when I referred to him as a ghost, it is how I have come to think of him. Of them all. They have never tried to contact me."

"Did you try to contact them?" she asked, smoothing a wrinkle from his jacket sleeve.

"Why should I?"

"Honestly, Gabriel. One cannot maintain affection without a modicum of effort. You never came to visit me, despite what you claimed about your dreams."

He leaned his head toward hers. "Do you know why?"

"No. Tell me."

"Because even in my dreams I never thought you'd have me."

She rose higher onto her knees and slipped her arm around his neck. "Are you in too much pain for a shameless seduction—your last as an unmarried man?"

He inhaled deeply. "No."

She walked her hand down his shoulder to the buttons of his shirt. "Then allow me."

He caught her hand, his blue eyes kindling. "Not tonight, sweetheart."

"Are you refusing me?"

"I am showing your brother that I am a man of my word."

"And what of your lust for me?" she whispered.

His low-pitched voice made her breath quicken. "The longer it smolders, the hotter it burns." He glanced meaningfully at the door, clearing his throat. "I forgot to mention that Robin is sitting right outside reading a book."

She surged to her feet. "He isn't?"

"Yes, he is," her brother said from the other side of the door. "Let me know, either of you, if you'd care for a cup of chocolate before Gabriel takes his leave."

Chapter Forty-six

❧ ❧

Gabriel and Alethea were married on Michaelmas Day, the Feast of St. Michael, in the private Mayfair Chapel of the Marquess of Sedgecroft. Only the family and their trusted friends attended. Still, the pews were packed to overflowing with the passionate Boscastle clan and a tiny cluster of Alethea's closest friends from Helbourne. Her brother stood waiting to give her away—and lifted his brow when Lady Pontsby began to sniffle.

Alethea restrained an inappropriate urge to giggle, a condition not helped by the guffaws and jests Gabriel's cousins made in an attempt to ruffle his demeanor. Wisely, he kept his back to the audience, except once when he glanced around. His gaze searched the chapel—for his brother, or someone else? Was there a person he had invited or hoped would bear witness to this wedding? And if any of his brothers had bothered to show, would they represent themselves as friends or enemies?

She sighed at the realization that he cared more than he would show. For all his claim to have forgotten about his brothers, he hadn't been quite himself since the night he saw Sebastien. When she caught his gaze wandering a second time, she sent him an understanding smile. He smiled back with a promise in his eyes that left her feeling pleasantly weak.

"The ghost?" she whispered.

He blinked as if he were surprised she had noticed his brief inattention. His reply, however, was more surprising. "I doubt he'll come."

"Do you want him to?" she asked in an undertone.

He leaned his face close to her. The spicy fragrance of his shaving soap fair made her swoon. "I'm not sure."

She stared down at her bouquet of late red roses, white chrysanthemums, and ivy. "I have to admit I hope he doesn't come. Not if he's going to dress in a silly costume and swing a saber."

Gabriel's face relaxed in a grin. "They say that when the Boscastle family gathers together, scandal is inevitable."

"Not at a wedding?" she whispered.

"Especially at a wedding," he retorted. "Well, perhaps not at *this* wedding. My cousin Emma has warned everyone in the family to behave, under penalty of death."

The minister looked up from his psalter. All of a sudden Alethea felt a niggling sensation of being stared at. Turning her head to the right, she found herself under the scrutiny of Gabriel's cousin

Emma, the Duchess of Scarfield. She smiled. The duchess smiled back. Silence fell over the chapel, but to Alethea's disconcertment, her mind was not content to remain obedient to the moment.

In the village where she and Gabriel had grown up, in the public square where he had been punished, a celebration would be in progress. A strong village lad, usually a lord's son, would be dressed up like St. Michael in order to slay the dragon—a chain of other boys wearing a costume of pieces of billowing green cloth stitched together.

The best celebration in Helbourne history, it was generally agreed, had been the autumn when the high-spirited Boscastle boys had first played the role of dragon and made St. Michael—in this case Lord Jeremy Hazlett—chase them across the common and into the hills until he gave up the pursuit in embarrassed anger.

Until that year St. Michael had always won. He might have lost the following year, too, had tragedy not struck the Boscastle family when Joshua Boscastle died and the lives of his widow and sons disintegrated.

It seemed strange, therefore, to Alethea to be marrying the village dragon when she was supposed to belong to his saintly, if unsuccessful, slayer, the hero of her parents' dreams for her.

Only now she understood that a false hero could hide a cruel heart behind his valiant deeds.

And that a man who had sinned as second nature

could be the strongest hero of all when given the chance to prove himself.

His voice was so self-assured when he exchanged his vows that his cousins Drake and Devon made a few catcalls. Chloe's husband, Dominic, grinned openly. A pair of cavalry officers who knew Gabriel stomped their feet, and just as general anarchy threatened to ensue, the Dainty Dictator, the Duchess of Scarfield, rose from her pew and swept the congregants a quelling scowl. After that, throughout the breakfast of prawns, roast turkey, and crab croquettes, during the first dance, the champagne toasts, and the cutting of the cake, everyone behaved.

Put on guard by the persuasive glint in her husband's eyes as they traveled the bumpy roads back to Helbourne Hall, Alethea decided it had been wise of her to insist upon returning Chloe's wedding dress to her before leaving London. Gabriel had refused to stop at the two respectable inns along the way. He stated in a convincing tone that having been away from home this long, they might as well make the sacrifice to journey into the night.

Alethea knew his true motive to hasten home. It was also hers. He could not wait until they were together in their bridal bed.

"Home," she said, smiling wistfully. "I do hope the servants remember we are to arrive."

"I hope they've gone."

When the carriage reached the old Norman church that faced the village square, he asked to stop for a few moments so that the two of them could walk among the ghosts.

"It still looks the same," he said. "I don't know why I thought it would be different."

Nothing had changed since he'd been punished years ago. The ancient cage swung in the breeze behind the pillory and the parish whipping post.

There hadn't been any miscreants disciplined here since Gabriel had come back. No rebel boys who looked so forlorn that a highborn lady would insist her father halt his carriage.

"I don't know what lesson I was meant to learn from it," he said, his tall, black-cloaked figure overshadowing the place of his humiliation.

"Do you remember what you were punished for?"

"Yes."

And he remembered the soft brush of a girl's gloved hand on his cheek, the rustle of her dress as she knelt to regard him, and that when she'd risen, she'd had a stain on her gloves.

"Incorrigible," his wife said, wrapping her arms around him.

He gathered her into the heat of his body, his heart. "Are you speaking of me or yourself?"

"Both of us, I suppose. But . . . I wouldn't have it any other way."

As distracted as Gabriel was by his desire for his incorrigible bride, he managed to restrain himself until they reached Helbourne Hall. He was relieved that the servants had made an effort to set the house in order for their new mistress, having sent a message ahead days ago that there would be hell to pay otherwise. Young Gabriel, his namesake groom, was waiting up in the stable to attend his master, eager to prove his worth.

He carried Alethea toward the stairs, the indecent smile on his face announcing his intentions. The mullioned windows of the house might require glazing, but moonlight still managed to pierce the unpolished panes, and, well, if there were any bats in residence, they had gone into temporary hiding.

He unfastened her cloak with one hand, then the sleeves of her gown even before he'd borne her to the landing.

"Gabriel," she said with a soft moan, inflamed by the sinful heat in his eyes. "I want you."

"Don't say that again until you're in my bed," he warned her. "Or I'll be taking you right here on the stairs, bats and servants be damned."

"What a way to talk to your wife," she said in a breathless voice. "Anyway, it's almost morning. I prefer a little privacy myself."

Her cloak slipped off her shoulder. She should have protested, but instead she kissed his strong brown neck and unknotted his neckcloth with her free hand. His iron-muscled body felt warm and inviting. He shifted her weight. The hard bulge of his erection pressed against her rump.

"Now look what you've done," he said with a grin.

She closed her eyes. "Hurry, or I shall faint."

He gripped her firmly. "You won't faint until I give you good cause." His eyes devoured her. "Which I will."

A fever raged in his blood as he entered their chamber and laid her upon a bed made with a freshly washed counterpane and crisp sheets redolent of rosemary sprigs and lavender soap. Her smile invited his seduction. She had become uninhibited in his bed, but he had other lessons in sensuality to reveal.

Apparently, she did, too.

She lifted her hand and sketched her fingers down his chest, unfastening both linen buttons and links as she went. Her descent continued past his waistband, whereupon she made quick work of unbuttoning the leather that bound him.

"Doesn't that feel better?" she asked, tracing the length of him through his loosened trousers.

"It feels . . . I can't . . ."

For a moment his throat closed so that he had to struggle to breathe in a normal fashion. Or perhaps he would quit breathing altogether and survive on sheer joy. Angel. Gypsy. Lady. Of all the images he had held of her over the years, none brought him the rush of raw pleasure that thinking of her as his wife did.

He rendered her naked between slow breath-stealing kisses, studying her soft, rosy body as if he were unwrapping a long-awaited gift.

"May I finish undressing you?" she whispered.

And she pushed his shirt from his shoulders without waiting for his permission.

"In a minute," he muttered, trapping her hand in his. His tongue circled hers with such erotic skill that her hands dropped to her sides in surrender. "I mean to erase every memory that made you sad."

"But I *want* to touch you," she whispered stubbornly.

"Scars and all?" he asked, already at her mercy before she raised her hands again, this time tugging over his hips.

"I mean to make you forget how you came by those scars."

He pulled off his coat and shirt and threw them in the direction of the Jacobean wardrobe against the wall. Swinging around briefly to remove his boots and trousers, he shuddered as he felt her hands wander down his spine.

"I have scars everywhere," he said, rising briefly, the moonlight accentuating the hard angles of his body, his erection.

Her breathing became shallow, uneven as he stretched out between her legs, one hand slipping under her hip. "To think I fell in love with Helbourne's most wicked son."

He traced her delicate nipples with his tongue until she bowed her spine in shivering pleasure. "A good thing for me you weren't really an obedient girl." He worked his other hand between her thighs, his fingers deft, subjecting her to a sensual agony that enslaved her every sense.

"Perhaps," she whispered, her dark eyes taunting him, "I won't be an obedient wife."

"Only a well-pleasured one. Obedience is secondary."

"I love you, Gabriel."

"I love you more than you love me."

"I've loved you longer."

He laughed. "Then I shall have to love you stronger."

"Love me right now," she whispered, running her heel lightly down his hard-muscled leg to his foot.

But he was in no particular hurry on this night, his time of homecoming, of honeymoon. He treasured every moment, relished each detail, the cold wind that howled but did not penetrate this strange house, the warm-blooded woman who had waited seven years for him. Let her wait a little longer. He'd make it worth her while. A gambler, he had known the first time she kissed him that the odds were in his favor.

Read on for a taste
of Jillian Hunter's next irresistible romance,

Wicked at the Wedding

Coming soon to bookstores everwhere

All the talk at the costume ball marking the final fortnight of London's Little Season was of a notorious personage known as the Mayfair Masquer. His escapades had invigorated a year remarkable only for debts and hailstorms.

The ladies who braved the masquerade that foggy October night professed alarm that sightings of him had become more frequent. Their escorts vowed to protect these cherished gentlewomen in the event that the blackguard dared to appear in one of their bedchambers.

Which meant, as a consequence, that these gallant young men must first be ensconced behind closed doors to catch him in the act.

The act of *what* exactly was not understood.

No one knew what the cheeky scoundrel wanted. . . .